The Homecoming

A NOVEL

DAN WALSH

Revell

a division of Baker Publishing Group
Grand Rapids, Michigan

© 2010 by Dan Walsh

Published by Revell
a division of Baker Publishing Group
P.O. Box 6287, Grand Rapids, MI 49516-6287
www.revellbooks.com

Paperback edition published 2010
ISBN 978-0-8007-1959-3

Printed in the United States of America

The Library of Congress has cataloged the hardcover edition as follows:
Walsh, Dan, 1957–
    The homecoming : a novel / Dan Walsh.
      p. cm.
    ISBN 978-0-8007-3389-6 (pbk.)
    I. Title.
  PS3623.A446H66 2010
  813'.6—dc22   2010003584

10 11 12 13 14 15 16   7 6 5 4 3 2

To my wife, Cindi, my one and only love and the inspiration behind any and every romantic thought I've ever had.

One

January 4, 1944

Shawn looked down at the empty seat beside him, trying to imagine Elizabeth there. He tried to remember the smell of her hair, the sound of her voice, one of her smiles. It all seemed just out of reach.

She wasn't there. She would never be there again.

He came here, in part, thinking some time alone might help. He was tired of pretending to be fine. It was exhausting. Pretending to see scenes out the window, pretending to read a book, pretending to listen. Elizabeth preoccupied his every waking moment. Shawn had known a depth of love with her he'd never imagined possible, a love he was sure most men would never see, not in a lifetime.

"Care for another cup?"

Shawn looked up toward the sound. "Excuse me?"

"A refill on the coffee? It's on the house." The waitress, all smiles.

"No, thanks. I've got to be going."

He stood up to pay the bill. The Corner Room Restaurant hadn't changed a bit. If he closed his eyes, he could almost see their old college friends, all sitting in their proper spots. He'd gotten a room at the hotel upstairs but wasn't ready to turn in for the night. Too much left to do. The main reason he came back was to remember her, to reclaim moments of time, conversations they'd shared, places they'd visited. He wanted to see and feel all these things again. To do anything that helped him see and feel all these things again.

Before it got too late, he decided to call Patrick. He walked toward the back by the restrooms to use the pay phone.

"Hello?"

"Dad?"

"That you, Shawn?"

"It's me."

"You get in all right? Everything okay?"

"I'm fine, Dad."

"I suppose you want to talk to Patrick. I'll get him."

His father never did like to talk on the telephone. He heard him yell Patrick's name, heard Patrick shout some loud, happy thing in the background. Shawn smiled. At least he still had Patrick.

"Daddy!"

"Hey, little man, how ya doing?"

"I'm fine. You at your college?"

"I sure am."

"When you coming home?"

Shawn must have told him three or four times he would only be gone a night. But after all Patrick had been through, Shawn didn't mind telling him again. "I'll be home tomorrow, before dinner. You be good for Grandpa till I get there."

"I will. Wish I could be with you."

"Is everything all right? Is Grandpa treating you okay?"

"Yeah. I just miss you. You were gone so long before."

"I know. But I'll be home before you know it."

"You still going to do what you promised?"

"Uh . . . yes . . ." Shawn tried to remember what he apparently had promised.

"You know, you said when you got home you'd tell us about how you escaped from those Germans after your plane crashed."

"That's right, I did. Yep, I'll tell you all about it tomorrow."

"Mrs. Fortini wants to hear it too. Is that okay?"

"Sure."

"Also, Miss Townsend wants to hear it. Okay if I invite her? You know the lady who ate Christmas dinner with us? The one who took care of me?"

"I remember her. But I don't think she'd really want to drive across town to hear some war story. She sounds like a pretty busy lady."

"I know she would. Don't you remember she asked you about it Christmas night? Can I just call her and see?"

Shawn didn't want to say yes. He sighed. "Okay, I guess you can call her."

Two

Katherine Townsend stared down at her typewriter, reading the last paragraph over and over again. There was just no good way to say it. If she said what she wanted, she could forget about putting this job down on any future resume. If she kept it professional, she'd hate herself for letting her creep of a boss, Bernie Krebb, get away with forcing her out of this job. Not to mention treating every woman around this place like they were part of his personal harem.

"You don't see him anywhere, do you?" she whispered loudly to Shirley O'Donnell, a redheaded co-worker in the cubicle next door.

Shirley stood up and scanned the perimeter offices, all glass and mahogany and all occupied by men. She took another quick glance at the small sea of cubicles in the center, all occupied by women. "Uh-oh," said Shirley. "Here comes Krebb. Quick—"

"What?" Katherine looked up. "Where?"

Shirley peeked over the cubicle wall. "Gotcha."

"Don't do that."

"Relax. Krebb ain't back from lunch yet. It's only 1:15. You got a half hour easy. Why do you care, anyway, aren't you writing your two weeks? What's he going to do, fire you?"

"I wouldn't put it past him," Katherine said. "I'm going to need every day of those two weeks. I don't have any savings or anything else lined up yet."

"You really got on his bad side over that last case. You know the one I mean, just before Christmas."

"I know the one."

"Really, Kath. You need to lighten up. I get nervous just looking at you."

Katherine had been tense lately. Her only breaks from the tension were the moments she lapsed into total depression. But these dips weren't about Bernie Krebb or even about losing this lousy job.

"Know what you need?" Shirley asked.

"Let me guess . . . a man?"

"That's right, you need to start saying yes to all those good-looking guys keep asking you out."

"All of them?" Katherine asked. It seemed like Shirley's custom.

"All right, then some of them, one of them. I haven't seen you date anybody the whole time you been here. What are you waiting for?"

"I don't know . . . I'm just not like you," Katherine said.

"What's that supposed to mean?"

"I mean I don't like dating just for the fun of it. It's not fun for me. I wind up getting hurt too easy."

"Well," Shirley said. "The way I handle that is . . . you gotta be the one that does the hurtin'. Dump them before they dump you."

"See, that's what I mean. That's so easy for you. I could never do that."

Shirley sat down again. "Then you better take up knitting or something, start putting that pretty hair of yours in a bun."

Shirley's telephone rang. She sat down to answer it. "Hello, Child Services, Shirley speaking. We deal in family tragedies, one right after the other."

Katherine laughed. That about sized up this job, and her love life too. She was twenty-six years old, had never been married, and, after two years at this job, had pretty much decided she could live without the joys of wedded bliss. Her previous experiences with men only reinforced this view. First there was Charlie, a guy she'd dated out of high school. They'd even gotten engaged. Then she found he'd been cheating on her with one of her girlfriends. A year later she began seeing a sailor named Gregg, and dated him for almost a year before the attack on Pearl Harbor. Out of the blue he got his orders, and without even saying good-bye, shipped out, leaving her a note saying not to wait for him. It had been fun.

Fun . . . was that what they had been having?

But her pathetic love life wasn't the source of her gloom. It was the case Shirley had mentioned a moment ago. The one that had put Katherine on Bernie Krebb's bad side. The case of little Patrick Collins. Krebb said she'd gotten way too personal on this case and spent way too much company time.

But Katherine couldn't help it. Just thinking about him brought an involuntary smile.

Patrick had lost his mother in a car accident. Katherine was assigned to help him get situated with a grandfather he'd never met, while the army tried to locate his father in England. The grandfather had been perfectly horrible about the whole thing and treated Patrick terribly. But Patrick never whined or complained. He endured the tragedy of the loss of his mother better than any adult she'd ever known.

She didn't heed Krebb's warning for one reason: she was entirely smitten.

But too soon, it was all over. Once Patrick's situation had mended, she had no reason to stay connected to the Collins family. But being with them, especially Patrick, was the only thing she thought about now. What had he been doing since then? Was his grandfather still treating him well? Did the old man and Patrick's father ever reconcile? Did Patrick ever think about her anymore? How do you just turn off thoughts like these, shut down the emotions that followed? She couldn't find the switch.

The phone rang, breaking through her thoughts. "Hello, Child Services, Katherine Townsend speaking. How may I help you?"

"Miss Townsend?"

That voice . . . it couldn't be. "Patrick? Is that you?"

"It's me, Miss Townsend. How are you?"

"I'm . . . I'm fine, Patrick. I've missed you so much." She realized she was talking loudly; she could barely contain her joy.

"I've missed you too. A whole bunch. How come I don't see you anymore?"

He still wants to see me, Katherine thought. "I wish I could, Patrick. You don't know how much." How could she explain? "See, now that your daddy is home and your grandfather is treating you better—is he still treating you nice?"

"Yeah, he's been pretty nice since my daddy came home."

"Well, now that you're safe and sound, the way my job works, I have to—" She couldn't say the words "let you go." "I have to work with other kids who need help. Do you understand?"

"Does that mean you can't come over anymore?"

"Well, kind of. At least not as part of my job."

"Could you come for dinner? Like tomorrow night?"

Katherine smiled. "Patrick, I'd love to, but you can't just invite me over to dinner. Your dad or your grandfather would have to do something like that."

"My dad is inviting you, well, sort of. He said it was okay if I called you to come over."

"He did?"

"Yeah."

"Why isn't he calling me himself?"

"He's not here. He went away for one day and one night to the college he went to before I was born. But I just talked with him on the phone, and he said you can come to dinner tomorrow night. Mrs. Fortini's gonna be there and my grandfather. He's going to tell us the whole story about how he escaped the Germans after his plane crashed. Can't you please come? Please?"

"Are you sure your dad said it was okay?"

"Honest."

"Is there anything I can bring?"

"You'll come?"

There is nothing in this world that could stop me, she thought. "Yes, I would love to."

"Yippee!"

Katherine laughed. "Do you know what time? No, don't worry about that. I'll call Mrs. Fortini and get the details."

"I'm so glad you're coming," said Patrick. "Remember how to get here?"

"Of course I do."

"I can't wait."

"Me neither. I'll see you tomorrow then?"

"Okay, bye." And he hung up.

Just like that.

And just like that, Katherine felt alive again.

Three

As a rule, snow improves the scenery of most settings.

But not graveyards, Shawn thought.

Graveyards were cold, hard places on the best of days. The snow just made the entire scene colder and bleaker. The white erased all color from view. Headstones and monuments peppered the landscape, condensing entire lives down to a few words or a phrase. Even the trees didn't help in their wintry, skeletal stage. They looked more like dead sticks stuck oddly about the perimeter. No wonder children were afraid of cemeteries. Shawn certainly didn't want to be here.

It was mid-afternoon. He had just arrived after making the five-hour drive back from Penn State. His last stop had been the theater along West College Avenue. So many dates with Elizabeth had begun there. Dinner and a movie. She loved the movies. He'd thought about stopping in to catch the afternoon matinee, but *Gung Ho* was playing, starring Randolph Scott. The last thing Shawn needed was some Hollywood rendition of a war movie. He just sat across the street for a while, reliving some pleasant memories.

But Shawn knew this stop—his last stop before heading home to see Patrick—would be anything but pleasant. He hadn't visited Elizabeth's grave since he'd come back into town on Christmas Day. It was an appointment he knew he must keep, but one he'd been dreading, even the thought of it, every time it crossed his mind.

He walked through the main iron gate and looked for the cemetery caretaker. The woman in the office said he shouldn't be too far away, maybe just up the first hill. Shawn noticed a man wearing a gray overcoat and carrying a shovel, coming down the nearest walkway. He walked toward him, but before Shawn could say a word, the man saluted. Instinctively, Shawn returned the salute.

"Sergeant in the last war," the man said, smiling. "Couldn't be prouder of you fellas and what you're doing over there."

"Thank you," Shawn said. He mentioned why he had come and whose grave he'd come to see.

"I remember that day very clearly," the caretaker said. "Just a few weeks before Christmas. Personally dug the grave myself, a week later set the headstone."

"I appreciate that, sir. Could you take me to it?"

"Be happy to." He started walking back the way he came. "I remember reading about the car accident a few days before in the paper. Read about the little boy being left behind. Your boy, I guess. Talked about you being in England, a bomber pilot, if I recall."

"Yeah," Shawn said. "I flew a B-17."

"Great plane. Call it the Flying Fortress, right?"

"They do."

"Tell you one thing," he said as they climbed a small stone stairway. "I'll never forget your boy, the way he handled himself at that funeral. Would have made you proud."

Shawn tried not to let the images form. He needed to keep his composure intact, at least a few minutes longer.

"At first I thought it must be a military funeral, when I

saw the little boy standing next to that brunette. Usually is these days, you see a woman that age with a child. Then I saw there weren't any soldiers around, no flags or anybody playing 'Taps.' Just that woman, your boy, and a few friends. A very impressive young man, your boy."

"Thank you," Shawn said.

"I'll take real good care of things for you. This place will be a lot nicer to visit in the spring."

"Thanks."

"It's right over there," he said, pointing. He turned to go then reached out his hand. "I'm honored to do anything I can for you fellas. And . . . very sorry for your loss. Glad you're home to look after your boy. They gonna give you any time off?"

"Not sure how much. We're working on that now," Shawn said.

"Well, you have a nice day, take all the time you need."

"Thanks."

He had escorted Shawn to within fifty feet of Elizabeth's grave then headed back down the hill.

∽

Twenty minutes later, Shawn was still standing there, fifty feet from Elizabeth's grave, still staring at the headstone.

"Elizabeth, I don't think I can do this." Tears began to roll down his face.

In his hand, he held the last letter she had written him, written on the day she died. He hadn't read it yet but knew its basic message. His dad had actually cried explaining it. From Shawn's childhood until that moment, he couldn't recall ever seeing his father cry. Knowing the hostility his father had previously felt for Elizabeth, Shawn knew this must be a powerful letter indeed.

He wanted to pray for the strength to close these last fifty steps, but he found it hard to pray about anything lately. Really from the first moment he'd gotten the news of her death back in England. Shawn knew he needed God's help, probably more now than at any other time in his life. His struggle was ironic in a way, because he had been surrounded by death, almost nonstop, for well over a year. Even the death of close friends. Then he prayed constantly. Many times he'd felt the power of God's sustaining grace and would have told anyone who asked that it was only the comfort he'd received through prayer that had kept his sanity intact.

But this was different. This was Elizabeth.

Elizabeth was supposed to be off-limits to harm or danger. Shawn was the one they had both worried about making it through this war alive. They'd talked about it many times. What Elizabeth should do if Shawn didn't come back, what she should do with Patrick, what she should do financially, and so on.

There was no plan for this.

Shawn vividly remembered the last conversation they'd had on the subject, sitting in a Horn and Hardart's Automat in downtown Philly, an unusual restaurant that functioned more like a huge vending machine. It was all he could afford at the time. She was eating macaroni and cheese, he a chicken potpie. At least the food was fresh.

"You most certainly are going to remarry," Shawn had said.

"Don't even say it," Elizabeth had replied. He could still see her beautiful face, lit up by the sun pouring in the big glass window. And that adorable pout she'd make with her lips. "I'm not going to remarry, because you're coming back."

"Liz, we have to talk about this. We don't know what's up ahead. It's a war, things could happen."

"But we've already talked about this. Why are we going over it again?"

"Because you've never promised me you will remarry—after a respectable amount of time," he said, smiling. "Maybe a year or so. I need to know you aren't going to live alone the rest of your life. It's not just for your sake but Patrick's too."

Elizabeth looked away. He could tell she was trying not to cry. He put his hand over hers on the table. "I'm hoping and we're both praying I make it back okay. If it means anything, I believe in my heart I really will make it back. But you're much too young and far too beautiful to live your life alone. And if the worst did happen, I'd want Patrick to grow up with someone he could learn to love like a dad while he's still young. So promise me you'll think about it, at least pray about it."

"All right," she said. "I can promise that. So we can stop talking about this now?"

And now standing there in this cold dark cemetery, Shawn realized that the feeling he had about making it home alive was real. God had remarkably preserved his life through the horrors of war. But why had he abandoned Elizabeth here at home?

He took a deep breath and walked straight to her grave. He forced himself to read the words on the headstone aloud. First her name, then the date. That's all there was, apparently all they could afford. But Shawn would fix that. This was a woman who deserved so much more said about her.

He tried to remember . . . what was he doing that day, the day inscribed on this stone? Was he flying his plane? Filling out reports? Sitting around playing checkers to pass the time? He couldn't remember. All that really mattered was . . . he wasn't here and couldn't be here to do anything about it.

He lifted the letter up and began to read, hands trembling, but not with cold. Barely through the first few words, he dropped to his knees, still clutching the letter. Her hands had touched this paper. When she was alive. The words written here were her words, written down with her own hand. And as she wrote, she had been thinking about him. With every word, every paragraph. He had thoughts similar to these when he'd get letters from her, when the gap between them was a mere ocean away. He looked down at the headstone, then up at the gray sky. The gap infinitely wider now.

"Where are you, Liz?" he cried. "I know you're not here, not in this cold ground." He looked around to see if anyone was watching. "I know I will see you again, but I want to see you now. It was supposed to be me coming home from the war, to you . . . and Patrick. The three of us starting our lives over. Maybe getting a house, having some more kids. Growing old together. Not me coming home to this. I don't want this. Not without you."

He just knelt there awhile and cried. He didn't know for how long. When he finished, he stood back up and read the letter.

The letter she had written to him on the day she died.

Dec. 18, 1943

My dearest Shawn,

Your last letter was so wonderful. You can't imagine what it does to my day when the mail includes something from you. Every day I quickly rummage through whatever comes in, looking for only one thing. And when it comes . . . to know I'm holding something you wrote just for me. Something your fingers have touched.

Well, today is the big day. With your blessing

now, I'm going to ride across town and pop in on your father for a visit. I don't mind saying, I couldn't be more nervous about this. I know you've told me not to get my hopes up, but I can't help it. Something has got to give on this thing, and I know it grieves God that our family is so torn apart. I'm willing to do whatever it takes to make an end to all this strife.

Perhaps today will just be a beginning. I'm not expecting your father to throw his arms around me and give me a big kiss on the cheek. In fact, I'm bringing Patrick with me but not telling him where we're going, just in case it doesn't go well. I'll leave him in the car until I see how your father responds. Hopefully, he'll at least invite us in, and I can begin to chip away at the dividing wall between us. But I don't think I'm going to be the primary instrument of peace.

I don't know how, but when I pray, I get the sense that Patrick is going to factor in on this somehow. He looks so much like you and yet he is so innocent (not that you are so guilty . . . you know what I mean).

Wouldn't it be an amazing thing, though, if by this Christmas this long-standing feud would finally be over? That for the first time in Patrick's young life he'd actually get a present from his grandfather? It doesn't have to be a big one, just <u>anything</u>. And then 1944 would usher in a new beginning. The war would end, and you'd come home, and we'd all be together again.

I can just see your face as you read this, scrunching up in disbelief at my naïveté and optimism. Then you'd break into a smile as a glimmer of hope broke through that what I said could possibly come true (and then that smile would quickly return to a frown as you thought of the right words to say that would balance me out).

Well, don't balance me out this time, my love. Hope with me. I don't know what God is going to do, but I'm confident his wisdom and power will make a way. He is famous for "making roadways in the wilderness, and rivers in the desert."

I know we're called to overcome evil with good. So, I'm going armed with a mincemeat pie (which I abhor), because you said it was his favorite (I'm trusting you on this). And I'm wearing my green dress and hat, even though I'm not Irish. I know this is what your mom wanted too, so that gives me strength. She told me herself just before she died. I promised her, if it took the rest of my life, I wouldn't stop trying to bring us all back together again.

I'm holding on to this letter until tomorrow, so I can include with it another letter after the visit, to let you know how things went. So there should be two letters in this envelope.

And there will be something else in the envelope, not so easily seen but always present . . .

That is, my unending love,
Liz

Four

Ian Collins stood in his living room, giving everything a good once-over, getting ready for the crowd coming over for dinner. It was still hard for Collins to get used to his new life, one that included other people.

But he wasn't about to complain. He'd learned that lesson this past Christmas, when he'd almost lost his son and grandson in the span of one week. Some of the darkest moments of his life. He wasn't about to let anything come between them again. And Collins had to admit, having a big meal every week or so wasn't too bad, either. He'd never say it, but he'd come to believe Mrs. Fortini's cooking—albeit an Italian version— was every bit as good as his wife Ida's had been.

Collins glanced up at the mantel clock. Almost 4:30. Shawn had called a short time ago, saying he'd be home about 6:00. His grandson, Patrick, was next door helping Mrs. Fortini make some rolls. He wished he could've found a way to get her to prepare the meal over here, just to have the smells filling up the house. But every idea he'd come up with sounded too much like a compliment.

Before heading next door, Patrick had mentioned they'd invited Miss Townsend, the government lady, to join them tonight. It was the only sticky point in the evening for him. It was still his house, after all, and it might have been nice if they'd included him in the decision. She and Collins had some pretty harsh words in the weeks before Christmas, back when Patrick had first arrived.

Since his big wake-up call, Collins had to admit that most of what she'd said about him was true. But you just don't say things like that to a man in his own house. She might have at least apologized for her tone after relations between them had improved. What are you gonna do, Collins thought. She was coming over just the same.

He inspected the dining room table, everything set according to Mrs. Fortini's instructions. All the special occasion stuff from the hutch. The boy from the package store delivered a nice bottle of Chianti. Got the coffeepot set to brew for dessert, supposed to be a homemade cheesecake. Took some doing on Collins's part to get all the ingredients for Mrs. Fortini. His ration coupons came up a bit short. But cash still made small miracles happen down at Hodgins's Grocery.

And Collins had plenty of that, as it turned out. Shortly after Shawn came home and settled in, he'd spent some time helping him get a handle on just how much money he had. It was a shock to Shawn, since Collins had come into all this money during their feud. Shawn said he wasn't that far from being a millionaire. It sounded absurd to hear it, but he figured it could be true. He'd stopped counting. His 5 percent from Carlyle Manufacturing, the company he'd sold his business to, had apparently mushroomed since the war began.

Collins took one more look around but couldn't think of another thing to do. Plenty of time to light up a nice Cuban and read the paper in his favorite chair. He'd still have time to open the windows, clear the smell out a bit before everyone arrived. He picked up the *Philadelphia Inquirer*, sat down, and began to read the headlines.

Soviet Troops Recapture Kiev. "Who cares what the Reds are doing?" he said aloud.

32nd Division Kills 1,275 Japs in New Guinea. "That's what I wanna hear, more dead Japs."

Top Marine Ace Pappy Boyington Captured. "Pappy . . . they got old men flying now?"

Allies Attack the Gustav Line. "Where the heck is that?"

He took a long smooth draw on his cigar, gently flicked the ash in a brass tray beside his chair, then turned to the sports page. The first story he came to was about Red Ruffing, a pitcher with the Yankees who just got drafted by the army. It said Ruffing was thirty-eight years old and missing four toes. "We really that bad off?" Collins didn't care for the Yankees, being from Philadelphia. He found it hard to get excited about any of the teams anymore. The best ball players were either off fighting the war or being drafted.

Like poor old Red here with the four missing toes. As he turned the page, the telephone rang. "What now?"

He set the cigar in the ashtray and let out a moan as he rose to answer it. He felt a sudden wave of dizziness as he crossed the wooden floor and had to hold on to the mantel a moment till it passed. Probably the cigar, he thought. Hadn't been able to smoke hardly at all the last month. "Hello? Collins residence."

"Is this Mr. Collins, the father of Captain Shawn Collins?"

"It is."

"An honor to speak with you, sir. This is Colonel James Simmons. I'm calling from Washington DC. Is your son at home?"

"Not at the moment. But I expect him in an hour or two. You say you're from Washington?"

"Yes, sir . . . could you have him give me a call when he gets in? It's very important that I speak to him."

"He know your number?"

"I don't think so. Can you give it to him?"

"Let me get a pencil here, hold on." Collins put the mouth-piece part of the phone down. "Okay, go ahead." The officer gave him the number, repeated it two or three times to make sure he had it right. I'm old, Collins thought, not stupid. "Can I ask what this is about? Shawn told me he's supposed to have at least a thirty-day leave. Seeing he just got home Christmas Day, I figure he's still got two weeks left. You heard about the reason he came home, about him losing his wife?"

"We know all about that, Mr. Collins. I'm not calling to cut his time with the family short. We do have to talk with him about his future plans, however. As you know, he had to leave England in quite a hurry, and we really didn't get much time to talk everything through."

"I wouldn't know about that. All I know is . . . he's got a little boy here who just lost his mom and just now got his father back from the war. I don't know what all you folks do in a situation like that, but I'm thinking my grandson needs his father a good deal more than the army needs a pilot."

"I understand, sir, but I can't really discuss these things with you."

"Seems like Shawn's done more than his fair share, you ask me. Got shot down, you know. Then he escaped."

"I know, Mr. Collins. You should be very proud of him."

"I am."

"Well, if you could give Captain Collins the message, I'd be very grateful."

"So you can't tell me anything about this?"

"I'm sorry, under orders. I can only discuss the nature of the call with your son."

"All right, then."

"But, Mr. Collins, I can tell you this much . . . what I have to tell him is good news, very good news. In fact, I think it will dramatically change your son's life . . . for the better."

Five

Katherine looked at her watch as she drove along Baltimore Pike. She was headed toward the Collins home, hoping she hadn't misjudged the time. The last thing she wanted was to walk in on everyone sitting around the table. She'd hoped the drive over would blot out her troubles. Starting with Bernie Krebb. He'd read her two-week notice that morning and had already begun to treat her as though she were halfway out the door.

When her job ended, so would the paychecks and the use of this car. She had no job prospects and soon would be forced to use the noisy trolleys and smelly buses like everyone else. The only jobs in plentiful supply were at the defense factories. Driving along, she'd been constantly reminded of this through the billboards and signs all over town. You'd think the entire country worked in a defense plant.

One billboard she'd seen twice already declared boldly: "We Can Do It!" depicting "Rosie the Riveter" in blue overalls, face all fierce and determined, showing off her muscles.

Another showed an entire assembly line of airplanes. "This Is America, the Arsenal of Democracy! Keep It Free!"

Just now she drove past another one, mounted on the side

of the Carlyle tank plant—a menacing hand ripping through an American flag, thrusting a pointy finger right at her: "Are You Doing Everything You Can?"

"I don't think I am," she said aloud. One thing she did know . . . she didn't want to work in some dirty defense factory: dressing in overalls, hair tied up in a scarf, growing her muscles. But outside of defense work, her choices were slim. A secretary, maybe a waitress. Perhaps she'd find work at a bakery. She shook her head. "I can't get up at 4:00 a.m." And she knew she'd put on twenty pounds the first month.

This drive wasn't washing her troubles away; it was adding new ones.

Up ahead she saw the sign for Springfield Road. Just a few more minutes. A right turn at Clifton Avenue. In the neighborhood now. She hadn't been back here since Christmas, but it was all becoming familiar.

A picture of Mrs. Fortini's warm, plump face popped into her mind, prompting a smile. She could just imagine her now, all dressed in black, hair in a bun, rushing between kitchen and table, getting everything just right, but doing it all with kindness and a little humor. She especially loved the way Mrs. Fortini put old Mr. Collins in his place. She thought of Patrick, and it widened her smile. He made it all worthwhile. What would she do in two weeks when they yanked her car and gas coupons away? How would she see him again?

She pulled into the driveway and was surprised to see Captain Collins, Patrick's father, just stepping up to the vestibule, carrying a small suitcase. She hadn't seen him since Christmas Day. He turned toward her and stared a moment as if trying to see through the glare of the windshield. He smiled slightly and nodded, then headed into the house.

He looked so sad. But of course he would.

He'd been through so much hardship in such a short span

of time. Katherine had only played a small role getting him an extended leave and knew very little of what actually happened after his plane was shot down. She really wanted to hear the story. But no matter how exciting it was, she couldn't imagine anything that would offset the magnitude of such a loss.

She took a deep breath, put on her gloves, and stepped out into the cold.

⌒

Shawn opened the front door. "Daddy! You're home!" Patrick ran from behind the dining room table across the living room floor and jumped into his arms.

"Hey, my little man. How ya doing?" Shawn dropped his suitcase on the throw rug and spun him around. "Told you I'd be home soon."

"That wasn't soon."

"C'mon, it was just one night." He set Patrick down, but Patrick clung to his leg as they walked into the room. "Patrick, someone else is coming in right behind me."

"Who?"

"Go see." Patrick let go and headed for the door. Shawn smiled. *Thank God, I still have you.* He heard the door swing open behind him.

"Miss Townsend . . . you came!"

"Patrick."

Shawn looked down at the hand-carved wooden soldier standing watch on the coffee table, Patrick's Christmas present from Shawn's father. He thought about what Elizabeth had said in her letter, hoping Patrick might finally get a present from his grandpa this Christmas, however small. Well . . . this one was huge. He was sure Patrick would remember this soldier for the rest of his life. He looked up. The dining room table was all set for dinner. He felt the warmth of the furnace on his face. The stress of the cemetery started to fade. "Hey, Mrs. Fortini, let me help you with that." She had just stepped in from the kitchen carrying a big basket of something.

"These aren't heavy, just some rolls." She walked over and gave him a big hug. "Come, sit down. If you want to do something, you could open the bottle of wine."

"Sure. Where's my father?"

"Should be coming downstairs any minute. Miss Townsend," she said, talking past him. "How good to see you again."

Shawn turned and followed her back into the living room. Patrick was just releasing Miss Townsend from a hug, and they now walked hand in hand toward the dining room. The scene felt a little off for Shawn. He knew the whole evening was going to feel odd, and he knew why. It was Patrick and this strong affection he had for Miss Townsend. Shawn realized she'd been by his side almost since the moment Elizabeth died, right up until she'd brought him here. Then she'd gone far out of her way to care for him after that, treating Patrick with almost motherly tenderness.

And that was the problem. Elizabeth was his mother. It seemed as though Patrick had almost forgotten his mom and replaced her with Miss Townsend.

"Daddy, you remember Miss Townsend." Patrick's face was beaming.

"I certainly do. How are you, Miss Townsend? Nice of you to come." They shook hands. "As you can see, you've made Patrick very happy. Can I get your coat?"

"Thank you. I was so surprised when he called. Are you sure it's all right? I don't want to intrude."

"You're not intruding at all."

"Well, come on, everyone, sit down," said Mrs. Fortini. "Let's eat while everything is hot. Patrick, will you go call your grandfather upstairs, tell him dinner is ready?"

Shawn stood until Miss Townsend took a seat then sat across the table from her. "I've never gotten the opportunity to properly thank you for all you've done for Patrick while I was away." Mrs. Fortini sat down at the far end of the table, where Shawn's mother used to sit, strengthening his odd feeling.

"It didn't feel like work at all, caring for Patrick," Miss Townsend said. "I've worked with dozens of kids over the last two years. I've never met anyone like him."

"Patrick's a very special boy," Mrs. Fortini added.

"I don't know how I'd make it through all this without him," Shawn said.

"Without who?" asked Patrick, walking in.

"You, you little squirt." Shawn poked him in the ribs. "Here, you sit right here next to me." Shawn heard heavy thumps coming down the stairs. He looked up to see his father rounding the stairway.

"Sorry, everyone, moving a little slower these days."

"Just these days?" Mrs. Fortini asked.

The elder Collins made a face at her and took his seat at the head of the table. "Everything looks . . . well, it looks fit to eat," the elder Collins said.

"Fit to eat," Shawn repeated. "It looks incredible."

"Miss Townsend," said Patrick. "Isn't it so great, my daddy being home from the war?"

"It most certainly is," she said. "Do you know how much time off they're giving you?"

"He's home for good, right, Daddy?"

Shawn looked down at Patrick and smiled but didn't answer. He didn't have the heart to tell him yet that he was only home on leave. He rubbed his head and changed the subject. "So you've worked with Child Services for two years?" he asked Miss Townsend.

"Just about," she said. "But my days there are numbered, I'm afraid."

"Oh no," said Mrs. Fortini. "I hope they didn't fire you because of us . . . they didn't, did they?"

"Well, not really, it was a mutual decision. I don't think I'm cut out for social work. And I think getting involved with Patrick just made it very clear." She was looking right at him, and he back at her . . . big smiles all around.

"So what are you going to do now?" Shawn asked.

"Now?" She thought a moment. "I have absolutely no idea."

"I'm sure you will find something worthwhile," said Mrs. Fortini. "You are obviously a very competent young woman."

"Thank you," Katherine said.

"Maybe you could work at Mr. Hodgins's Grocery," said Patrick. "That boy Harold had a birthday and now he's join-ing the navy. It's right down the street, remember? And it's so close."

"That's an idea," Katherine said. "The problem is . . . it's not close to where I live, and this car belongs to the agency."

"So you won't have a car in a few weeks," Mrs. Fortini repeated.

Katherine shook her head no.

"But you can still come to visit, right?" asked Patrick.

"I don't know," she said. "I guess we'll just have to wait and see."

At that, Shawn's father cleared his throat in a message-sending manner and said, "Okay if we say the blessing? I'm hungry."

∽

After everyone had eaten dinner and downed a delicious slice of cheesecake, Mrs. Fortini ushered them into the living room for coffee and to hear all about "Shawn's wonderful story of when he escaped from the Germans." She even made Patrick a cup of hot chocolate and warned the elder Collins not to even think about lighting a cigar. Then she insisted Shawn sit in a dining room chair in front of the radio, so everyone could see him clearly as he talked.

Shawn's insides were doing somersaults. He wasn't sure what they expected to hear. He had barely thought about his "escape story" since it happened. How could he begin to explain what he'd been through? How much should he share, could he share? Their ideas about war, he was sure, were fueled by all the stupid Hollywood war movies they kept turning out. What he experienced was nothing like the movies; it was the difference between real life and comic strips. Shawn looked at their faces, all smiles and bright eyes. The only thing missing was the popcorn.

God, don't let me say too much. He knew he'd have to hold back most of the details. Some of the images were already drifting through his mind. There were some things that happened on that last mission that Shawn never wanted any of them to know.

"Okay," Shawn said, "where should I begin?"

Six

Three Weeks Earlier

The savage battle raged on, high above the German skies, just beyond the outskirts of Bremen. On their way in to the target, eighteen bombers had been shot down. Dozens of young men in the prime of life had already died. Everyone knew these missions must be flown. There was no other way to take the fight to the Germans. For the first time in military history, all the battles in a war were being waged in the air instead of the ground.

Tucked deep inside this aerial battlefield, Shawn wrestled the controls of his B-17, nicknamed *Mama's Kitchen*. The entire formation had already dropped their bombs and were heading back to England by way of the North Sea. Before reaching safety, Shawn knew what lay ahead. They must fly through a hundred more miles of Nazi-occupied territory, at a speed that felt as slow as a flock of geese.

For a few moments, the sky was quiet. The formation had flown beyond the flak gunners' range. But Shawn knew the enemy fighters would soon return. There was no hiding the presence of several hundred planes flying overhead. The sound on the ground was deafening, and, high above, majestic contrails of water vapor peeled off the planes' wingtips for miles, like big white arrows.

"Nick, how's Anderson?" Shawn yelled into the intercom. "Is he conscious?" Nick Manzini was their starboard waist gunner.

"Let me check, sir."

Shawn's eyes shifted through a half dozen checkpoints, including the plane's airspeed, the bombers all around him, and a picture of Elizabeth and Patrick.

"Anderson's awake now, sir. Looks like the bleeding stopped. He ain't gonna be any good on his gun though. Maybe he can still work the radio." Hank Anderson had taken some flak in the leg on the way in and had almost bled out before Manzini patched him up. But Hank wasn't their first casualty. Tommy Hastings, the other waist gunner, had been hit by an even bigger piece of flak and was killed instantly.

Shawn turned to his co-pilot, Jim MacReady. "You're gonna have to get back on Anderson's gun, Jim. I can fly without you, but we're gonna need guys on every gun. We're gonna get pounded by those fighters any minute."

"Here they come," said Manzini. "Kraut fighters, three o'clock high. You guys see 'em?"

"More coming in at ten o'clock," shouted Bill Davis, the bombardier.

Man, that was fast, thought Shawn. "All right, you guys know what to do. Don't waste your ammo." Suddenly a black shadow flashed by above them, an enemy fighter. It was so close, Shawn ducked. He looked up to see a stricken B-17 with one engine on fire, banking to the right. The bombers around it moved to one side or the other to avoid colliding.

Shawn's eyes followed the bomber as it drifted below them. Suddenly it began to spin. It looked unreal, like a child's toy.

Two chutes opened. The plane exploded in a fireball. Shawn's head snapped back. He looked for more chutes but didn't see any. The two survivors floated down through the cloud of smoke and debris. Shawn followed the scene, mesmerized, until they faded out of sight. It had all happened in a matter of seconds.

Just then, he heard a loud explosion inside their plane. Then screams throughout the intercom. His flight controls began to shudder. The plane veered to the left. Shawn kicked hard on the rudder, trying to get it back in line. They were starting to lose altitude. He fought hard to hold it steady.

"Jim, you better get back here. Pronto. I'm losing her. What happened back there? Damage report . . . somebody."

"Took some cannon shots from a 190, sir. Looks bad." It was Rick Adams, the flight engineer. "Came up from below us. Bosco, you all right?"

No response. "Bosco," said Shawn. "Check in, Bosco, you okay?"

Still no response.

"Captain, Bosco is gone," said Manzini.

"What?"

"That 190 took out our ball turret on that last pass," Manzini said. "Bosco is gone, the whole ball turret got blown away, sir. It's just . . . gone."

For a few moments, no one made a sound. Shawn knew what they were thinking. Could have been me. Might be me the next time. Then . . . poor Bosco.

"Anyone see a chute?" Shawn asked. "Jim, where are you? I need you up here now."

"Almost there. Climbing through the bomb bay now."

"No chute, sir. I'm looking down, but I don't see anything." It was Tim Hatcher, the tail gunner. "Can't believe Bosco's gone."

It took all of Shawn's strength to keep the plane flying level. They were definitely losing airspeed. He looked out his window. Both engines on his side seemed fine. But he could see the bombers beside him slowly pulling away.

"Three bogies coming in from the rear," said Hatcher. "Six o'clock. Anyone see 'em? Rick, you see 'em?"

"I see 'em, Tim," said Adams. Gunfire erupted.

As he fought to hold the controls steady, Shawn felt helpless; there was nothing he could do. He heard a loud boom and looked up at one of the higher squadrons. Another B-17 had just been dealt a death blow by a German fighter. It had lost two engines and was on fire, smoke pouring off both wings. Shawn saw something like a package fall out of the waist-gunner's window. He shuddered as it smacked into the tail section and dropped out of sight.

Was that a body?

Something else broke loose from the other side of the plane, a piece of flaming debris. Something shot up from it. Shawn realized it was a parachute, the owner engulfed in flames. The flames consumed the chute as soon as it unfolded. Shawn cringed and looked away. Moments later, the entire plane exploded. Huge chunks of smoking metal sailed off in different directions; some pieces hit the planes beside and below it.

Shawn could barely contain his terror. His arms were just about to give out from the strain when MacReady sat down and grabbed his set of controls.

"Sorry it took so long, Shawn."

"Let's see what we can do here, Jim. How your engines looking?"

MacReady looked out his side window. "Oh, man. Engine number four is dead. It's just feathering, no power at all. Big holes all through it."

For the next several minutes, both men fought together,

trying to maneuver *Mama's Kitchen* back to her place in the formation.

"She's not keeping up, Cap," MacReady finally said.

Shawn knew what this meant. If he and MacReady couldn't keep *Mama's Kitchen* in formation, if they had to pull away . . . the German fighters would go after them like a pack of hyenas. It was common knowledge back at the base—you drop out of formation, your chances of survival drop from slim to none. He'd seen it himself, many times. Planes sustaining serious damage who radioed in their position as they faded out of sight.

No one ever heard from them again.

But Shawn had a plan, something he'd worked on many hours back at the base. A plan for a scenario just like this. Oddly enough, it came to him after reading a passage in the book of Proverbs. He didn't have it memorized, but it went something like "A prudent man sees the danger ahead and protects himself; the naïve go on and suffer for it."

Shawn knew the "danger ahead" for them occurred every time they took off on a mission. He couldn't stomach the thought of their plane being the one that slowly faded out of sight, only to get shot to pieces by German fighters. If that happened, the best he could hope for was everyone bailing out before the plane blew up, and they sat out the rest of the war as POWs. Or worse—maybe even more likely—the plane could just fall from the sky, spinning like a top, trapping them all inside. Shawn had thought of a way to protect himself and his crew from either fate.

But would it work?

Seven

Shawn looked at his co-pilot. "Jim, we're losing airspeed and altitude every second that ticks by."

"I know," MacReady said with the weight of a judge banging a gavel. In the background, they heard guns firing off every few seconds, the crew trying to pick off enemy fighters that flew by.

"I have an idea," said Shawn. "If it works, we might still have a chance of getting out of this thing alive."

"I'm all ears," MacReady said.

"You're gonna have to get back on Anderson's gun again. You know what'll happen when we start to pull away."

"They'll be on us like flies. You don't need me up here?"

"Not anymore. I did when I thought we had a chance of keeping up, but it's too late for that. Head on back. I'll inform the men."

MacReady nodded. He hooked up a portable oxygen bottle and headed back.

Shawn turned the interphone on so everyone could hear him. "Men, listen up. I'm not going to fool with you. We're in bad shape. One engine's gone, the controls are all shot up, and we've got a slow fuel leak on the starboard wing. No way

Mama's Kitchen's getting us back to England tonight." He paused to let the words sink in. "But I've been working on a plan back at the base for this very thing, and we might have a fighting chance of staying alive. Hopefully, not ending up in a POW camp by nightfall."

"We're with you, Cap."

"Whatever you say, sir."

"Just tell us what to do." One by one, the men checked in.

"Okay, in a minute we're gonna radio in that we're pulling out. Then we're on our own. Kraut fighters will come after us like easy pickings. We've got six working guns and seven healthy men left. I'll fly the plane, but I need every one of you guys on the guns. But fellas, hear me on this—do not waste that ammo. The goal here is to chase planes away, not shoot them down. Get greedy and we'll run out in no time. Keep just enough fire on 'em so they don't get too close."

"But Captain, what about Bosco's spot? We got no guns on our belly." It was Adams, the flight engineer. "Any Krauts come up from below, we'll be sitting ducks."

Shawn had thought about that. "That's where my plan gets a little sticky. I figure we got about ninety more miles before we reach the sea, but we'll be going a different direction from our group. The only way this works is if I fly low enough to avoid enemy radar. The upside is, flying that low will keep enemy fighters from getting below us for a shot."

"That'll work," said Hatcher.

"But there's a big downside," said Shawn. "Once I go down on the deck, we'll be flying too low for anyone to bail out. You follow me?"

"So it's all or nothing," said Manzini. "We bail out now, before we get too low, and we end up as POWs . . . maybe. We do it your way, and there's no chance of bailing out anymore."

"That's right," Shawn said. "But if we can keep this thing together, keep from getting too shot up, I can navigate us to a place I picked out near the coast of Holland. As best I can tell, it's far away from any German bases. We might just have a chance of avoiding capture, steal a boat and get across the English Channel. But I'm not going to order anyone to do this. You guys have to decide. Anyone wants to play it safe, no hard feelings. You can bail out now, and the rest of us will just take our chances."

For several moments, Shawn heard nothing but static and the drone of the three remaining engines.

"I'm in," said Manzini.

"Me too," said Adams.

"Not going anywhere," said Hatcher from the tail spot.

"We're with you," said MacReady, his co-pilot. Davis and Ted O'Reilly, the navigator, weighed in the same.

"Okay, guys, then let's do this," Shawn said. "I'm calling it in. We're officially pulling out. Look sharp. Things could get pretty rough here in a few minutes."

✎

As soon as Shawn pulled *Mama's Kitchen* out of formation, as expected, the fighters came pouring in like hornets. They came in groups of three, it seemed from every angle. After their attacks, they'd peel off then come back around one at a time. All the while, their guns blazing. His crew called them out over the intercom—"Two o'clock high, see 'em? . . . Six o'clock, coming in straight and level . . . Nine o'clock, look out, comin' out of the sun." Each time, the guns from *Mama's Kitchen* fired back. The noise was deafening. Shawn sat alone in the cockpit, trying hard to keep the plane on a steady dive away from the formation, shouting out reminders to his crew to conserve their ammo.

It was the scariest twenty minutes of his life.

He looked up and saw dozens of B-17s growing smaller and smaller, fading in the distance. Would he ever see any of them again?

As he banked, he glanced at the ground below. At least a dozen large bonfires burned across the countryside, heaving thick black clouds into the sky. Shawn realized the fuel for these fires were other B-17s, shot down on the way in to Bremen. The sight soured his stomach. After a few moments, the radios and guns of *Mama's Kitchen* went silent. "How's it looking, guys?" Shawn asked. "Somebody talk to me. Everyone okay?"

"Seems like we're in the clear, Cap. For a little while, anyway." It was Hatcher, back in the tail section.

"I can see the fighters ripping through the formation, though, to the north of us," said Adams. He manned the top gun turret and had an unobstructed view.

"So guys," Shawn said, "nobody got hurt since we pulled away? No serious damage?"

One by one, the rest of the crewmen checked in. Not a single injury to report.

"It's a lot brighter back here," said Manzini. "Got several new rows of holes above my head, about six inches apart."

"You guys did great back there," said Shawn.

"You think they're gone for good, Captain?" said O'Reilly.

"No way to know. Most of the fighters will stay with the bombers till they run low on fuel. A lot more targets up there. What we gotta worry about are the ones heading back to refuel. That last bunch that attacked us will radio their buddies about us. Somebody's gonna want to make us their last kill for the day. I'm going to change course every few minutes to throw 'em off, zigzag till we get closer to the sea. We're below ten thousand, guys, you can come off oxygen."

"How low we gonna fly, Captain?"

"Gotta get below a hundred feet to avoid the radar," said Shawn.

From this point, survival depended on not being seen. He was taking them far off course, to a place on the map Shawn had never been. As best he could tell, it was an area of mostly small fishing villages, very close to the sea. He had read the people of Holland hated their Nazi occupiers. If they ran into anyone, he prayed they'd be sympathetic.

"Okay, guys, we should be seeing the sea in about twenty minutes. I'm hoping to put us down in a farm or a field nearby, but I've got no idea how shot up our landing gear is. We need to prepare for a crash landing. Start throwing anything out the window that could either explode or fly around and smack someone when we touch down. And O'Reilly?"

"Sir?"

"You got the map in front of you?"

"I been tracking where you're taking us since we broke away."

"Good man. Where do you put us right now?"

"Right about where you said. We should be seeing that sea north of Amsterdam in about nineteen minutes. The Zuider Zee, they used to call it."

"Keep me on course then. Flying this low, I gotta stay focused. Say, Rick and Nick. We only got a few more minutes till I give the order to brace for the landing. Nick, do what you can to make sure Hank's leg is ready to travel. We need to be able to move pretty fast once we hit the ground."

"You don't mean 'hit the ground,' right, Cap?"

"Figure of speech, Nick." Shawn laughed. He looked down for just a second at the picture of Elizabeth and Patrick.

Please, Lord, keep us invisible a little while longer. Please let me get home to them.

∞

The memory of seeing Elizabeth and Patrick's picture jarred Shawn out of storytelling mode to the present. He looked around the living room, first at his father, then Mrs. Fortini, then Miss Townsend, and finally Patrick, who had fallen asleep leaning on Miss Townsend's shoulder.

Gone were the popcorn smiles.

Shawn hoped he hadn't gone too far. He'd purposely held back the scenes of death and dying, the bodies falling from the sky in flames, the terror that gripped every one of those final minutes in battle.

"I'm sorry, folks. This is too much. Maybe I should stop."

"Are you kidding?" Miss Townsend said in a loud whisper. "This is the most exciting thing I've ever heard."

"It's better than any of the newsreels down at the theater," said Mrs. Fortini. "I can't believe what you went through over there, Shawn. And I'm over here making Christmas cookies."

The look on his father's face was hard to interpret. "Shawn, I had no idea" was all he said.

"Do you want to call it a night?"

"I don't," said his father, "unless it's bothering you to talk about it."

"You can't stop now, Shawn," said Mrs. Fortini.

"I'd really love to hear how you made it all the way back," Katherine said. "If you're okay sharing it. Should I wake up Patrick?"

"No, let him sleep. It's probably a good thing. This last part gets even more intense. Someday when he's older I may tell him the rest."

Eight

Three weeks earlier
Somewhere in North Holland

Mama's Kitchen had made it safely across the Zuider Zee and was now over land once more. They had flown over a few German patrol boats but were flying too fast to attract enemy fire. It was late in the afternoon, the sky wintry and overcast. As Shawn expected, the German fighter that had taken out the ball turret gun, ending Bosco's life, had also destroyed the landing gear on one side. He'd just ordered everyone, except MacReady, his co-pilot, into the radio room to prepare for a crash landing.

Since there were no German airbases nearby, there were no radar concerns. Shawn pulled up on the stick to gain a few hundred feet in altitude, hoping to find a decent spot to land. "Very close now, guys," he said. "I see water up ahead, should be the North Sea. I'll give the word when I start my descent."

Most of Holland actually dipped below sea level, the water held back by a network of levees and dikes. But not around here. Shawn was glad to see the familiar patchwork quilt of farmland and pastures. Everything looked flat and level. He could just make out the details of local farmhouses and outbuildings.

"I'm not seeing any people," Shawn said to MacReady. "How about you?"

"Not a soul," MacReady said. "I'm glad."

"Me too."

Out the left window, a large dark area caught Shawn's eye. It ran along the coast for several miles. "You see that, Jim? I'm no expert on shorelines, but that looks like sand dunes to me." The area was heavily shrubbed.

"That's odd," said MacReady. "The dunes back home hug the shoreline. Look how far inland they go, couple of miles at that one spot."

Shawn pointed up ahead. "See there, running along the inside edge of the dunes. Looks like a village." It gave Shawn an idea. "If we could bring her down on the beach, between the sea and these dunes, we might be able to hide the plane from prying eyes, at least for a day or two."

"I follow you," said MacReady. "Beach looks wide enough from here."

Hiding the plane had been one of Shawn's great concerns. It was not like you could throw a bunch of branches over a four-engine bomber lying in a pasture. He banked the plane until it ran parallel with the shore. He'd have to do this on the first pass; circling would attract too much attention. "Okay, guys, this is it. I'm putting her down on the beach."

"The beach?" someone asked. "How's the tide?"

"I don't think Hatcher can swim," someone else added. "Don't worry, Hatch. I'll save you."

"Shut up," said Hatcher.

"The tide's nice and low," Shawn said. "It's plenty wide and flat up ahead. Nobody's gonna do any swimming."

After lowering the flaps and easing up on the throttle, he glanced out the side window. Just off the shoreline, north of where the sand dunes began, he noticed a small cottage. Along a dirt road in front, an old man and a young boy rode a horse-drawn cart. "See that?" Shawn asked MacReady.

The old man stopped as *Mama's Kitchen* passed by. He looked up, and both of them waved.

They had finally been seen. But the two men were Dutch, Shawn reminded himself, and they had waved. Shawn couldn't wave back, but he realized just then that God had answered his prayers. He hadn't seen a single German the whole way in. He had picked this general area on the map, but it seemed God had sovereignly directed him to the one spot along the Dutch coast hidden by miles of sand dunes. It was the first time since they'd left the formation that Shawn began to believe they might actually make it. He shifted his attention ahead, eased up on the throttle some more, and lifted the nose of the plane to slow it down. He kept resisting the urge to lower his landing gear.

"Below a hundred feet, guys. Gonna try to keep her in the air till the last minute. Soon as we stop, I want everyone out. I've burned off most of the fuel, but I don't want to take any chances of an explosion." No one answered.

The plane continued its steady descent. They were flying at their slowest possible speed, but the lower they got, the faster it seemed they flew, waves flashing by to the right, dunes to the left. "Steady, steady . . ." Shawn muttered. Both he and MacReady looked at each other at the same moment, the moment they would normally feel the wheels touching down. Very strange to still be in the air. "Hold on, guys."

BOOM!

The plane bounced. They were airborne again, a precious few feet off the ground.

Then BOOM again.

This time she stayed down, the bottom scraping along the beach, a roaring sound filling the cockpit. Both men were thrown forward; their bodies slammed into the controls as the sand instantly cut the speed in half. Shawn heard screams and loud bangs behind him. He looked over his right shoulder, about to call out to his men, but the plane started sliding to the right. He looked up just as it began to swerve toward the water. He and MacReady jammed their feet into the rudder pedals, trying to shift her back to the left. It didn't work.

"We're going in," said MacReady.

Shawn looked over at him; the bottom half of his face was covered in blood pouring down from his nose. Shawn was about to say something, but the plane jerked even harder to the right. He gripped the controls. Huge plumes of water rose up as the right wing made contact with the water. The plane went into a spin as the front end slowed and the rear end came around. Shawn feared it was just about to flip over. More screams from the back.

Then suddenly another jolt, and they stopped.

And all was silent.

A moment later, the sound of small waves broke on the fuselage.

"Okay, everybody out," Shawn screamed into the intercom. "Let's go, let's go!" he yelled toward the back. MacReady was already making his way out.

"You guys need help?" Shawn asked. "Anyone hurt?"

"Little banged up, but we're okay," said O'Reilly.

"Don't forget your weapons," Shawn said. "And your big coats. Everybody get across the beach, meet up at the first set of dunes." Shawn followed MacReady out of the plane, dropping down into three feet of water. It instantly began seeping into his boots, cold as ice. Three of the men were already running across the beach. He looked toward the rear and saw Manzini and O'Reilly all but carrying Hank Anderson through the surf, his legs dragging uselessly behind him. "You guys need a hand?"

"We're okay, Cap," said Manzini. "Freezing my butt off over here." Besides the freezing water, an icy wind blew offshore. It seemed as cold here as thirty thousand feet up.

"I always hated the beach," said Anderson. "Now I really hate it."

In a few minutes they were all sitting around the base of a large dune, soaked from the waist down, pistols out and ready. MacReady had his head back, trying to stop his nosebleed. "Anyone get the first aid kit on the way out?" Shawn asked.

Silence and blank stares. No, they hadn't. "Hatcher, head back and get it."

"Yes, sir."

Shawn's eyes followed Hatcher toward the plane. It looked so odd just now, the back end of the plane sticking up out of the water, the nose pointing down like a head bowed in surrender. He noticed a large crease just before the waist gunner's window. Another fifty yards and *Mama's Kitchen* would have cracked in half. She had served them well. It saddened him to think of leaving her here, drowning in the surf.

"Captain, what's the plan?"

Shawn turned toward the voice. The men were crouched close together, shivering in the cold. He imagined the sun—if he could see it through the hazy gray sky—was close to setting. "Guys, I think we should move a few dunes inland, get out of this wind. Start gathering wood for a fire, but don't start it till it gets dark. We can't take a chance of the smoke giving our position away."

"Sounds like you're going somewhere," said Hatcher, arriving back with the medical kit.

"I'm going back to where the dunes began," Shawn said. "Lieutenant MacReady and I saw an old man with a young boy as we came in. He might be willing to help us. Hatch, do what you can to clean up Lieutenant MacReady's face."

"It's just a nosebleed," MacReady said. "Smacked it on that first bounce."

"Still," Shawn said, "you've got blood all over your face. Anyone else need any help?"

"I could use a few aspirin," said Bill Davis. "My head is killing me."

"We've got some in there, right, Hatch?"

"A whole bottle."

"Seriously, anybody need aspirin, don't be shy. That was some serious banging around on the way in."

"You're telling me," Davis said. "Not one of your better landings, Cap."

Shawn laughed; so did several of the others.

"But seriously, you did an incredible job, sir, bringing us in like that," said Adams. "I thought we were goners."

"That why you screamed like a woman?" Manzini asked. Everyone laughed, except Adams.

"I did not."

"I'm sorry, but you did. I had my eyes closed, thought I was back in the Bronx with my kid sister."

"Okay, guys, let's get going," Shawn said, standing up. "Our light is about gone."

"Hey, Captain, look," said Hatcher.

Everyone turned and looked down the beach where Hatcher pointed. Shawn heard guns clicking all around. Walking from the same direction they had just landed were two figures, one slightly larger than the other, staying close to the line of dunes.

"Hold on, guys," Shawn said. "They're not in uniform, and I don't see any guns."

"I think it's that old man and the boy we saw coming in," said MacReady.

"I think you're right," said Shawn. "Nick, you come with me. The rest of you stay here."

Shawn started to walk toward them, Manzini right behind him. In a few moments, he could see it was the old man and the boy. They both waved again as they saw Shawn and Manzini coming. Shawn waved back. A few more moments, they could see each other's faces. The boy wasn't so young; a teenager, maybe fourteen or fifteen. And the old man wasn't so old, though his hair was mostly gray. He had the face of a man aged by long years of sun and harsh weather. Both wore dark wool overcoats that had seen better days.

"Americans, we are friends," the man shouted. "We see you come in. We are Dutch."

"I know," Shawn answered, the gap between them closing. He wished they would stop yelling. "We saw you too."

"That is B-17, yes?" the teenage boy shouted, pointing toward their plane. Just then a gust of wind whipped the wool cap off his head. He caught it before it hit the ground. "I know my planes; they fly over us all the time. B-17s, B-24s. The British bombers, Lancasters, and Halifaxes. But B-17 is my favorite."

"Quiet, Johan," the older man said. "You talk planes later. My son wants to be a pilot, I think, not a fisherman. Are any of your men hurt?"

"Not too badly," said Shawn. "Just a little banged up. We do have one who can't walk, took some shrapnel on our last mission. But he's doing okay now."

They shook hands; the father and son's faces were full of excitement, as if Shawn and his men were liberators, not downed airmen. "We are so glad to see you," the father said. "We never see Americans here, never hear how the war is going. The Germans keep us in the dark always. Make our lives terrible."

"Speaking of Germans . . ." Manzini whispered to Shawn.

"Sir, my name is Captain Collins, and this is Sergeant Nick Manzini."

"I am Wouter Beekman, this is my son, Johan."

"Mr. Beekman, are we safe here? How far away are the Germans? I didn't see any as we flew in."

"They are not many up this way. Our village is small, all we do is fish. At the start of the war, there were over a hundred soldiers running a work camp nearby. Inside there they treated people terribly. Thank God, it closed down two years ago. Now is just a small garrison of soldiers stationed at the south end of our village, maybe four or five men. I don't think they are good soldiers, though. They talk like they resent being here, as if the war is passing them by. But they rule us like each is a king, and we are their subjects. No one in the village helps them."

This was encouraging news. "Will they come here?" Shawn asked.

"Not easy to get back here through the dunes," Mr. Beekman said. "It's to our advantage. But I think they will send someone to my home soon, which is why I come. My house is the last and closest one before the dunes begin. Everyone in the village would hear your plane coming in, so low and so loud. I think the Germans will send someone to see what happened."

"Then you better get back," Shawn said. "We'll come with you in case there's trouble."

A pained expression came over Beekman's face. "Maybe not," he said. "I don't want trouble, for you or for me."

"What do you suggest?"

"You and your man follow us but stay back by the dunes.

We will wait in our home until the Germans come to check. Act as if nothing happened. I will tell them, yes, I hear your plane fly over my house, look up, and see you fly past us, out to sea. You were wise to land where you did. They don't ever come this far back on the beach; their vehicles get stuck in the sand. They may just believe me and go away. Then we bring you food and water for the night to take back to your men."

"What if they don't believe you?" Shawn asked.

"Then, I think . . . trouble comes."

Nine

Shawn and Manzini followed the Beekmans back toward their cottage, all the while young Johan kept looking over his shoulder at them, smiling. Just up ahead Shawn could see the dunes coming to an end. Mr. Beekman turned and motioned for them to stop at a certain spot, just inside the shadow of the last dune.

"We go alone from here. I have some food for you, but I think not enough for all your men. You are hungry, I am sure."

"We haven't eaten since early this morning," Shawn said.

"I will send Johan to our friends nearby. All will help us." Beekman looked at his son. "Johan, you must tell everyone do not come to the beach, or we will all be in danger. First, you come into the house, and we will see what we have and what we still need."

"Yes, Father."

"Thank you so much for your kindness, Mr. Beekman," Shawn said. "We are in your debt."

Mr. Beekman turned and put his hand on Shawn's shoulder, then looked deeply into his eyes. As he spoke, tears began to form. "You don't understand," he said. "You are an answer to my most fervent prayers." He turned. "Now we go, before the Germans come." He and Johan hurried off around the corner and were gone.

"What do you make of that?" asked Manzini.

"I don't know," said Shawn. "But I'm glad God connected us with someone willing to help."

"You sure got some connection to the man upstairs," said Manzini. "All the guys see it. Not just me."

Shawn didn't know what to say. For the next ten minutes, they sat crouched behind some tall dune grass, trying to stay warm, but it was hard. The dampness in his pants seemed to freeze right through to his bones. His legs ached. They both watched the cottage for any activity, their eyes adjusting to the oncoming darkness. A few moments later they saw Johan leave and head south down the road out front. Fifteen minutes passed and they heard the sound of a loud car engine coming from the same direction. They looked toward the cottage and saw a Kubelwagen, Germany's uglier version of a jeep, drive by between the dunes and the side of the cottage, stopping abruptly out front.

"Uh-oh," Manzini whispered. "Not good."

"Just stay put," Shawn said.

They couldn't see the front door but quickly heard a loud banging then a man yelling in German. They heard Beekman's voice answering back. The German shouted something else.

"C'mon," Shawn said, "let's move to that back wall, but stay behind me."

Shawn and Manzini hustled toward the back of the cottage, ducking behind a stack of wooden crates near the back window. Shawn heard the German barking out demands and making a racket inside. He heard Beekman's voice respond quietly. Shawn didn't understand them, but it was clear Beekman was afraid. Shawn peeked through a pair of weathered, wooden shutters partially closed over the window. A young German officer in a long gray overcoat was holding Mr. Beekman up against a wall and screaming into his face.

"Nick, sneak around the other side there and see if this guy's by himself."

"Right," said Nick and hurried off.

Shawn looked back through the window. The German was slamming Beekman back and forth against a wall. Beekman said something, pleading. The German slapped him hard across the face. As he did, he let Beekman go, and he fell back toward a table. He cowered and put his hands up to protect himself. The German then started hitting him with a stick he picked up by the fireplace, over and over again. Shawn couldn't just sit there. As he stood up, the front door swung open. Young Johan rushed in and jumped on the back of the German, yelling and pounding him with his fists. The German threw him off, then turned on Johan, hitting him across the face with the stick.

"No, please!" Mr. Beekman yelled.

Shawn rushed around the other side and came in the front door just as the German removed his pistol from its holster. His back faced away from Shawn toward Beekman, now backing up against the table. Shawn pulled out his knife and ran at the officer; their bodies slammed together with a crash. The German fell face forward and Shawn landed on top of him. In a moment, Shawn's knife was sticking through the German's heart from the back. The German let out one loud, painful cry then went silent, his face lying sideways on the wooden floor, eyes staring ahead, seeing nothing.

Sitting on the young officer's back, Shawn couldn't believe

what he had just done. He shook his head and took in a deep breath. He had just killed a man.

He had probably killed hundreds of people flying *Mama's Kitchen*, but that thought had never really found a home. They were just dropping bombs on factories and buildings, not on real people. But here was his knife sticking out of a man's back, a man he had just killed.

"Thank you," said Beekman, bending down toward Shawn. "You saved my life. He was about to shoot me." Shawn looked up into his gentle eyes; the left side of Beekman's face was all red and chapped from where the German had slapped him.

Shawn got up as Mr. Beekman went over to Johan still lying on the floor. Just then Manzini came through the door, his rifle leveled, ready to shoot someone. "You okay, Cap?" He looked down at the dead German, then at the knife sticking out of his back. "Way to go, sir. Bagged a Kraut, close up."

"He was beating Johan with a stick," Shawn said. "When Mr. Beekman tried to stop him, he pulled out his gun."

"Hey, don't need to explain anything to me. Only good Nazi's a dead Nazi, you ask me. On the upside, this Kraut was by himself. That jeep thing is empty."

"More will come in an hour or so," said Beekman, "when he doesn't come back to report." He helped his son to his feet. Johan's face was bleeding and starting to swell.

"Are you all right, Johan?" Shawn asked.

"I am now," he said, wincing as he smiled, looking down at the dead German officer. Then he looked at Shawn. "Thank you for saving us."

"What were you arguing about?" Shawn asked the father.

"He asked me if I saw your plane. I told him what we discussed, that I saw it fly out to sea. He called me a liar, yelling, trying to intimidate me. I said I wasn't lying, where would I hide a plane, but then he saw the food I was gathering on the table. He said it was too much food for me and Johan and insisted I was getting food to help you. He started to beat me, and then Johan came in." Beekman paused a moment. "It was good you used your knife. If he shot me, or you shot him, the rest of the garrison would be here in moments."

Shawn nodded. "Well, if they're all going to be here in an hour or so anyway, we better get moving. I've got an idea. We'll drag this German back to our plane and leave his body there in the sand where they can easily see it. When they come here, you can tell them the truth . . . you saw our plane trying to land on the beach as we flew by the cottage. Just say you told this German that, and that he headed down the beach looking for our plane. It'll be dark then. I'll have my men hiding around the dunes, waiting to ambush them. You said there were only four or five, right? We can easily take them out. They'll stop at his body, figure we killed him, and before they can react, we'll attack."

Mr. Beekman smiled and pulled his son to his side. "It's a good idea, but not a good plan."

"Why?" asked Shawn.

"If you kill them all, it will only bring the wrath of the Germans down on our whole village. Everyone pays then. You remember I said you are answer to my prayers?"

Shawn nodded. Mr. Beekman looked at Johan and said, "It's time for you to be brave, Johan."

"Why, Father? What do you mean?"

"Remember what we have talked about, our plan to leave here and go to England, if God ever made it clear that we could?"

"We're going to England? Tonight?"

Mr. Beekman shook his head. "No son, not *we* . . . tonight *you* go in our boat, and help these men to escape."

Johan pulled away. "No, Father. I can't leave without you. We can all escape. There is plenty of room on the boat."

"No, Johan. Someone must be here when the Germans come, to buy you all time to get far away. If they come and find this man here dead, then find the plane, and that we both are missing, they will know that we have helped them. They will come after us in their patrol boats with vengeance, to destroy us. It has to be this way."

Johan burst into tears and flung himself into his father's arms. Mr. Beekman turned to Shawn and Manzini, tears streaming down his face. "I think I have a plan that will get you and your men safely to England by morning. With my Johan. But you must act quickly. There is very little time."

"What do you want me to do?" Shawn asked.

"First, Johan, get your things together," he said, smiling through his tears. "Tonight . . . you will be free . . . in England."

"But Father—"

"Johan, there is no time to argue. Get your things. We will be together, after the war. You are getting older. I can't take the chance that they will come and take you away, off to fight for them or to work in one of their camps . . . or worse. I will be fine here. What do they care about an old man?"

"But if I take the boat, how will you fish? You will have no work."

"Our friends will care for me. You know this. I will find work. But you must go. I will stay here, and when the war is over, you will come find me. Here, take this." He reached up and lifted a framed picture off the wall.

Shawn saw it was Mr. Beekman and a woman, probably his wife, and Johan when he was much younger.

"When you see this, pray for me," he said to his son. "And I will pray for you every day." He turned to Shawn. "Captain, you must send for your men right away. Bring them all here. My boat is in the other direction from where they are, tied at a jetty a few blocks down the beach. Johan knows where, and he knows how to get from here across the North Sea to England. I've charted the course and we've talked about it many times. Johan, you know where I've hidden the maps on the boat."

Johan nodded.

"How long will it take?" asked Shawn.

Beekman looked at the clock on the wall. "If you leave now, you will be well out to sea before the Germans figure out what has happened. Darkness is on our side. You will probably not get across the sea before daylight, but with God's help, you could make it to English waters. My prayer is that you will find an English ship, and they will help you make it the rest of the way. The Germans have few ships patrolling these waters, mostly submarines. They will not bother a boat so small. And no one will even see you until dawn."

"Manzini, go get the guys."

"Got it." And he was gone.

"Captain, you must change into some of my clothes, and your sergeant when he returns. Johan knows what to do on the boat, but he will need some help. The rest of your men can stay in the cabin below until you reach safety. Johan, did you get any more food?"

"It's outside in the wagon."

"Very well. Now go, son. Get your things together."

Johan did as he was told.

"There is one more thing you must do, Captain," Beekman said quietly. "I need you to tie me up in this chair, and I need you to hit me, hard, in the face."

"What?"

"I must convince the Germans that you forced me to help you, and that you took my son."

"Will they believe that?"

"I will make them believe. They have threatened us many times that if we ever helped any downed Allied pilots, we would be tortured and killed. I must convince them that I refused to help you, and so did Johan. Then I will say we fought, and you took my food, and then Johan to guide you, promising me that you will let him go once you escape. I will say I don't know where you went. They will think this is true if I am tied up. It will be dark. They will probably search the village tonight, maybe even the beach. I am hoping they don't find your plane and this dead man until morning. Please . . . you must tie me up—now. And you must hit me in the face." With that, Beekman picked up a coil of rope, handed it to Shawn, and sat in the chair.

How could Shawn hit this man? Every impulse inside him was to protect him and help him. He was risking everything to help them, even giving up his only son. Shawn began to tie him.

In a few minutes Manzini returned with the crew.

"A couple of you guys drag this dead German back to the plane, except you, Nick," said Shawn. "You stay here with me. Then get right back here. Leave him somewhere easy to find but far enough from the water so he doesn't wash out to sea."

Johan came out with a sack tied at the ends with rope. He saw his father all tied up. His father quickly explained why. They hugged and kissed, but Johan wouldn't let go. "Johan, you must go, son. I love you. We will be together again, and between now and then I will have the peace of knowing you are safe. God has made this night possible. He will be faithful to bring us back together again."

Johan stood up and backed toward the front door. "I love you," he said.

"I love you too," said Beekman.

Johan turned and hurried out the door.

Shawn's eyes welled up with tears, but he shook them off. "Okay, guys, you leave now. Follow Johan to the boat. He's the captain on this trip. He's going to take us across the North Sea tonight. Nick, you and I will change our clothes and catch up in a few minutes."

Everyone left, except Shawn and Manzini.

"Now you must hit me, Captain. Please."

Shawn walked over and stood by him. "You are one of the finest men I have ever met. I can't hit you."

"But you must. If the Germans are not convinced, they will do much worse to me."

"I promise you, I will get your son safely to England."

"I trust you, Captain, as I trust the Lord."

Shawn couldn't believe what he was about to do. "Forgive me, Lord." He closed his eyes and hit Mr. Beekman hard across the face.

He opened his eyes and saw Beekman grimacing from the blow. "Thank you," he said. "You must change now and go, quickly."

"I will never forget your kindness," Shawn said, and did as he was told.

∽

Shawn looked up, mentally trying to refocus his gaze back to the safety of his living room. As he did, he was looking into the face of his own father. Mrs. Fortini and Miss Townsend were staring at him, their eyes wide open, almost in disbelief. Patrick was sound asleep. Shawn had told them almost everything about this second half of the story. Except the details about killing the German officer. He left the vague impression that *they* had to kill him, hoping no one asked any questions. Thankfully, no one did.

"That must have been horrible," Katherine said. "Having to hit the father like that."

"You only did what had to be done, Shawn," said Mrs. Fortini. "God understands."

Shawn looked into his father's eyes and saw tears. "I'm so sorry, Shawn. But I am so glad you had the courage to do what you did. And I think I understand Mr. Beekman. Were you able to help his son get to England?"

"The trip across the North Sea was uneventful. Johan really knew how to run that boat. We got off within the next fifteen minutes, and within an hour we were beyond sight of land. It was a dark and cloudy night, no moon or stars. We didn't see a single ship until daybreak. By then we were in sight of England. A big fishing trawler came near enough to get their attention. They helped us get into a small port north of London. By the end of that same day, we were all back to our base, except Anderson, who was taken to the hospital."

"What happened to Johan?" Miss Townsend asked.

"We said our good-byes as we left his boat. He refused to leave it. The English fishermen seemed to understand and promised to take care of him. They said a number of Dutch refugees lived nearby and said they would get him set up with them. I took down a bunch of names, so I could follow up on him later."

"What an amazing story," said Mrs. Fortini. "Patrick will be sad he fell asleep . . . at least for most of it anyway."

"I am exhausted," said the elder Collins. He got up and began to carry his cup toward the kitchen. "Oh Shawn, I almost forgot. Just before dinner, an Air Force colonel called and asked you to call him back as soon as possible. I wrote the number down by the telephone."

"Did he say why?"

"He wouldn't tell me, but he said it was very important, and that it was some kind of good news. I told him the only good news I wanted to hear was them letting you stay home and take care of Patrick."

"Thanks, Dad. I'll call him first thing in the morning." He walked over to Miss Townsend and gently lifted Patrick into his arms. "I'll take him up to bed."

"I don't think I'll ever forget this story," she said.

"I'm sorry if I upset you. I haven't talked about this with anyone before tonight."

"No, don't apologize. You just never imagine what's really going on over there when you watch the newsreels."

Shawn told her good night and headed up the stairs, wondering how to get these images out of his mind long enough to keep them from invading his dreams.

Ten

It was just after 8:30 in the morning. Shawn was already showered and dressed, wearing his finest uniform. A half hour ago, he'd dialed the phone number his father had written down, the Air Force colonel who'd called yesterday. Colonel Simmons couldn't have been more pleasant, but Shawn knew it wasn't a social call. He'd just ordered Shawn to take the 10:00 a.m. train to Union Station in Washington DC, unwilling to give any details, other than to say they would discuss his next assignment, and that Shawn would be glad he made the trip. Colonel Simmons said he'd have a driver there at the station to pick him up.

Well, Shawn thought, guess I can consider my request for a permanent discharge denied.

He took a sip of coffee as Patrick sat down at the table, carrying a hot bowl of oatmeal. "I can't believe I fell asleep during your story last night," Patrick said.

"Well, it was way past your bedtime."

"But I wanted to hear how it ended. What did I miss?"

Shawn wished the coffee wasn't lukewarm. "I don't know, what do you remember last?"

Patrick swallowed a big spoonful; a dab of oatmeal rested

on his chin. Shawn smiled. "Your plane had just been shot at," Patrick said, "sounded like it was real bad. You were talking like you knew it wouldn't be able to make it back to England. Then you started telling the other guys about a plan you had to fix everything."

Fix everything, Shawn thought. To Patrick he was still Superman. "That the last you remember?"

"I think I fell asleep while you were telling your plan. Why you all dressed up?"

Shawn took a deep breath. What should he say? He heard loud thumps behind him, his father coming up from the basement. Shawn turned as the door opened.

"Just putting some coal in the furnace. Supposed to get colder again today."

"I could have done that, Dad."

"I know. But I saw you getting that uniform on, heard you talking to that colonel."

Shawn looked at Patrick, still happy with his oatmeal. "Still, while I'm here, Dad, I wanna help with things like that."

"While you're here?" his dad asked, closing the basement door.

"Where you going, Daddy?"

Shawn sat back. "Well . . . I have to meet this colonel I talked to on the phone a little while ago."

"Where?"

"To Washington, you know, where the president lives."

"You gonna see the president?"

"No, silly. I'm just going to the same city."

"Today?"

Shawn put his hand on Patrick's shoulder. "It's just for today. I'll be home tonight."

Patrick dropped his spoon. "But you just came home yesterday, and you're going away again?"

"I'm sorry, Patrick. I don't have a choice."

"I don't understand," Patrick said, looking down at his bowl. "I thought you were home from the war."

Shawn reached over, put his finger under Patrick's chin, and gently lifted his head. "I am home from the war, son. I'm just not out of the army yet."

"What does that mean?"

"Maybe today I'll find out," said Shawn, trying to sound hopeful. Patrick got up and ran toward the stairs. "Patrick," he called out to him. But in a moment, he was up the stairs.

⁂

Katherine stared at a big fat file on her desk. Familiar office sounds drifted over the walls of her cubicle. Typewriters clicked away. Telephones rang every few moments. She could hear Shirley in the cubicle next door giving out details of last night's date with another co-worker. Katherine was glad the other noises muffled the details. She rolled a blank sheet of paper into her typewriter then heard an unfamiliar noise over her shoulder. She looked up, startled to see her boss, Bernie Krebb, staring down at her.

"You started those reports yet?" he asked.

She couldn't see his mouth; he wasn't tall enough to get his entire face above the cubicle wall. He looked like that army cartoon, *Kilroy*, peeking down at her, complete with the big nose, bald head, and fingers. He looked absolutely ridiculous. She turned away to keep from laughing. "It's what I'm working on now, Mr. Krebb."

"That the *first* one?"

"You just gave me the assignment an hour ago."

He didn't reply. She looked up at him. His nose was actually resting on the cubicle wall. "I promise, I will get every one of them done before my last day."

"You better, if you want a good reference from this office."

His eyebrows moved up and down as he spoke, sending wrinkles up his forehead. She had to look away. She wanted to say, *I couldn't care less what kind of reference you give me, little man.* "I will get them all done, even if I have to work overtime."

"Not paid overtime."

You are so pathetic, she thought. "No, I wasn't thinking I'd be paid. If you would leave, I could get right on it." She started typing quickly, anything that came to mind, pure gibberish. She kept it up until she heard loud footsteps walking away.

Truth was, she had no motivation for any of this. The assignment was to create a detailed background summary for all her client families, starting with her first visit right up to the current status for each one. According to Krebb, this would make things easier for her successor. But Katherine knew it was just busy work. Any woman with half a brain could gain as much by reading the existing reports in each family's file. This was the little weasel's way of punishing her. Dig the ditch. Fill up the ditch.

Well, she'd do whatever she had to, if it kept the final two paychecks coming her way.

"How'd it go last night?"

Katherine looked up. Shirley was standing by her desk.

Katherine leaned back. "I've never heard anything like it."

"Really?" said Shirley. "Tell me about it."

"Captain Collins is a bona fide hero," said Katherine. "I couldn't believe what he went through."

"A hero and a looker to boot."

Katherine restrained a smile. "It's not like that."

"What's not like that? You don't think he's gorgeous? I saw his picture on your desk back at Christmas."

"Shirley, the man just lost his wife a few weeks ago."

"So . . . what . . . that did something to his looks?"

"You're terrible. I wasn't even thinking about him that way."

Shirley walked over and grabbed Katherine's wrist.

"What are you doing?"

"Looking for a pulse."

Katherine pulled it away. "Oh, stop."

Shirley headed back toward her cubicle. She turned and said, "I'll stop, but you really need to lighten up."

"I've got to get back to work."

"We're going out after work for drinks," Shirley yelled over the wall. "Want to join us?"

"I better stay on this. Krebb is breathing down my neck about these reports."

"Suit yourself."

Katherine didn't know what to make of all that. Of course, she found Shawn—Captain Collins—handsome, but it just wasn't right to think of him that way. Not now, anyway, and not for a long time. What she was far more aware of was the troubling thought that she might never see him or Patrick again. There just wasn't a legitimate reason to think she would.

The case was closed, and it was not like Patrick could keep finding reasons to get her invited over. She stared at the jumble of nonsense she had typed on the paper, then yanked it out of her typewriter and put a clean one in its place.

Patrick, she thought, you have ruined my life.

Eleven

The train ride down from Philadelphia to Washington had been uneventful for Shawn. Crowded, noisy, smoky, but uneventful. About every third passenger wore a uniform. The rest were businessmen reading newspapers or moms with small children, trying to keep them from disturbing everyone else. Shawn had tried to read the paper, then a book. His eyes had read the words, line after line, but no thoughts or images would form.

He felt numb.

In the last twenty-four hours a trio of emotions had fused together inside, like a wave rushing over him. First was the ever-present grief for Elizabeth, then last night revisiting all the details of his last battle, and now, this morning, he must add Patrick's disappointment to the list.

Nothing Shawn said this morning had eased Patrick's sadness. This was supposed to be the day Shawn drove Patrick to his first day at his new school. He had promised to be there when Patrick got home this afternoon to hear all about it. Instead, he was leaving him again, and he wouldn't be home until well after Patrick's bedtime. The best he could offer Patrick was to let him stay home another day and say they'd try again tomorrow. But would he be able to do that? The army could order him to do anything, go anywhere, for almost any length of time.

Shawn stared out the window. He didn't notice that the scenes outside had stopped flashing by or that the click-clack sounds of the train wheels had ceased.

"Excuse me, Captain?"

"Huh?" Shawn looked up into the smiling face of a black Pullman porter.

"Sir, you did say Union Station was your stop."

"Yes."

"We're here."

Shawn looked around. Almost all the passengers in his car were already gone. "I'm sorry."

"No problem, sir. We gonna be here for at least twenty minutes. You ever been to Washington?"

"No, I haven't," Shawn said as he got up. He grabbed his brief bag and slung his overcoat across his forearm.

"Then you in for a treat. Got the fanciest buildings I ever saw. And I travel all up and down the East Coast." He started to walk down the narrow aisle.

"I'm supposed to meet someone, a driver. Any idea how I'm supposed to find him?"

The porter turned. "You just follow the crowd. Got two big halls to go through. You get to the second one, can't miss it—got the biggest ceiling I ever saw and got all these big Roman soldier statues up on the walls, with shields guarding their privates—I expect your driver be somewhere in there, near the doors in the front or on the side to the right. That's where all the cabbies come in. Folks mostly get picked up around there."

"Thanks."

"Well, make sure you stop and get your bags first."

"This brief bag here's all I've got. I'm not staying overnight."

"Can I get that for you?"

Shawn smiled. "No, you don't have to do that. You've already been a great help." As Shawn walked past, he shook the porter's hand and gave him two dollars.

The porter looked down at the money. "Sir, you don't gotta pay me for answering a question. I give answers out for free."

"I insist," Shawn said as he turned and headed down the aisle. An average tip ran more in the order of fifteen cents or a quarter, but after what Ezra Jeffries had done, saving his son's life at Christmas, Shawn had resolved never to take a black man for granted again.

Shawn stepped down from the train and followed the line of passengers heading into the terminal. He made his way past the first big room and then into the second. Immediately his eyes were drawn upward to the ceiling of the cavernous room. The porter had not exaggerated. It was one long massive series of stone arches, perhaps the most impressive ceiling he had ever seen. The white arches were trimmed in gold; between each, large octagons connected them together. The whole place reminded him of the elegance of Wanamaker's department store in downtown Philly.

Someone bumped into him from behind, almost knocking him down. "Sorry, soldier," the middle-aged man said. "Not a good time for sightseeing."

He kept walking but looked up again at the life-sized Roman statues around the perimeter, where the walls and ceiling met. He smiled as he noticed their shields, remembering what the porter had said. It did appear they were naked below the waist, except for those shields. What kind of idiot would sculpt warriors without pants? Shawn thought. He looked to the right. The ceiling gave way to a smaller set of arches separated by a series of glass doors.

"That looks like the place," he mumbled to himself and threaded a pathway through the crowd in that general direction. As he neared, amongst the throng he noticed a young soldier wearing an overcoat standing against the flow of the crowd, holding a sign, waving in Shawn's direction. As Shawn looked at the sign, he was surprised to see his name. "I guess you're my driver," Shawn said.

The young man instantly converted his waving hand to a salute. "Corporal John Miller, sir. At your service. It's an honor, Captain Collins. Can I take your bag?"

"That's all right," Shawn said. The salute he expected, but why would anyone consider meeting him an honor? "Do you know me?"

"Colonel Simmons showed me your picture and told me who you are. He was very emphatic, said if I was late or lost you, I'd be shot. I've got a car parked just outside. If you'll follow me."

"This is quite a place," Shawn said. "I've never seen anything like it."

"It really is, but wait till you see the rest."

"The rest?"

"The colonel said I was to give you the grand tour before I take you back to the Pentagon. The Capitol Building, the Supreme Court, White House, and the Lincoln Memorial. Then we'll grab some food at the Pentagon cafeteria. Pretty good chow."

Shawn followed Corporal Miller's hurried pace. What was going on? He thought he was coming here for a quick meeting to find out his next assignment. But a private driver? A grand tour ordered by a colonel? And then on to the Pentagon? He had read about the Pentagon, a monstrous project finished just last year, supposed to be the biggest office building in the world. But he never dreamed he'd see it up close.

"Where is the Pentagon?"

"Across the Potomac a ways," Miller said. "Now there's an impressive place. Not as fancy as Union Station, but way bigger. Here's the car, sir." He opened the back door for Shawn.

Shawn threw on his overcoat. Before getting in, he stood a moment and surveyed the scene. First the car, the longest car he'd ever seen, had to be a staff car for generals and top brass. Straight ahead, a few blocks away through some empty trees, something else caught his eye. "Is that the—"

"Capitol Building? Yep, sure is, sir. Our first stop."

∽

Corporal Miller had driven Shawn slowly around the Capitol, then past the Supreme Court Building. They were now riding down Constitution Avenue, headed toward the White House. It amazed him to see all these historic buildings, things he'd only seen before in newspapers or black-and-white newsreels. And Miller could have been a tour guide, filling the empty spaces with all kinds of facts and trivia. Shawn was glad for the distraction.

Every few moments he couldn't help but look up at the top of the Washington monument, which he could see at any angle. The city seemed to boil over with people and traffic, much busier than downtown Philly. "Is it like this every day?" Shawn asked, looking out the window as a hundred people hustled across the intersection.

"Pretty much," said Miller. "I came here in '42. Three times as many people here now than then, and it just keeps growing. About a block up here on the left, you'll see one of the nastier side effects. See those rows of boxy two-story buildings lining the Mall area? Don't think the founding fathers had those in mind."

"I don't see any granite steps," Shawn said.

Miller laughed. "Exactly, sir. It's temporary housing they threw up in a hurry for all the thousands of workers they brought in to support the war. Ugly as sin, you ask me. The president promised they'll all come down after the war."

Shawn stared at a string of white sheets and towels blowing on a clothesline as they drove slowly past the apartments. The whole scene seemed so out of place.

"If you look to your right, Captain, just up ahead you'll see the White House." He looked in his rearview mirror. "I'm going to slow down. It's set back a ways, but I like the view back here on Constitution Avenue. I'll drive around the whole thing, nice and slow. On the other side, we'll get real close."

As they drove past, Shawn noticed two anti-aircraft gun emplacements, one on each corner, manned by three soldiers apiece in full battle gear. Their guns pointed to the sky. Shawn had seen several others at the Capitol Building. "Had many German bomber attacks, Corporal?"

Miller laughed. "No, sir. Not since I been here. Kind of crazy, isn't it. Think by now, we'd let it go. I know a few guys on that duty. Bored out of their minds."

As Shawn gazed at the manicured lawn and shrubs leading up to the majestic steps and pillars of the White House, he thought about how different Washington was from London. There, surrounding all the historical and architectural landmarks, were dozens of bombed-out buildings and rubble strewn all about. Once, while Shawn was on leave, a wave of German bombers had flown over the city, sending everyone fleeing to underground bunkers and the subway tubes. As the bombs fell and exploded, Shawn could hear the anti-aircraft gunners firing right back. "The gunners in London are never bored," he said.

"Yes, sir."

Shawn was still not totally used to the idea that he was no longer in mortal danger. After they drove around the White House, they headed over to the Lincoln Memorial. Miller suggested they park and get out. "Gotta see this one up close, sir."

Shawn was glad they did. He took his time as he read the Gettysburg Address etched in the granite wall. Then he walked to the edge of the steps and looked out toward the Washington Monument and, beyond it, the Capitol. Elizabeth would have loved this, he thought. She would have loved everything about this place. They had talked about visiting here when Shawn came home from the war.

"Looks like we better head over to the Pentagon, sir. I need to get you there by 2:00 p.m. If we leave now, we'll just have time to grab some lunch."

"Whatever you say, Corporal. Lead the way." Shawn still couldn't understand this VIP treatment. It didn't make any sense. He knew better than to ask Corporal Miller anything. But it was clear, something was up. They crossed the Potomac on the Arlington Memorial Bridge. Shawn noticed Robert E. Lee's home high on the hill as they turned.

"The Pentagon's just a few blocks ahead on the right, sir. Colonel Simmons said he's very anxious to meet you."

Shawn could not begin to understand why.

Twelve

"What do you think, Captain? Ain't she something?"

Shawn was already staring. The Pentagon was massive. Not that tall—maybe four or five stories—but it was so thick, all of stone and windows, like a modern-day castle fortress.

"Just a year old this week," Miller said. "Before they built it, we were spread out in seventeen buildings all over the city. Got over twenty thousand people working here now. That's more than we got in my hometown back in Ohio."

As they got closer, Shawn felt a sense of pride he didn't expect. He thought about all the buildings he'd seen today. *We have to be doing something right,* he thought, *to be able to make all this.*

"I gotta check the car back in the pool, sir. I'll drop you off right up here. Just wait for me at the curb, and I'll join up with you in a few minutes."

"Any chance they got a pay phone nearby? I'd like to call my son."

"Tell you what, sir . . . they got one on the curb around the next side. I'll drop you off there instead."

"Thanks, Corporal."

Shawn got out by the telephone booth and watched Miller

drive off into the sea of cars. The wind had picked up, so he hurried inside and slid the door over. The phone rang, must have been a dozen times. He hung up and dialed again. He looked at his watch. It wouldn't be like his father to go anywhere. After the third attempt, someone finally picked up.

"Hello?" It was Patrick.

"Hey, bud, it's me."

"Daddy!" Patrick yelled. "Are you home?"

"No, silly, if I was home I wouldn't call you on the phone."

"When are you coming home?"

"Remember what I said this morning? I'll be home tonight, but it will be after your bedtime."

"I remember," he said, dejected.

"Hey, how come it took so long for you fellas to answer the phone? I tried three times. I was starting to worry."

"We were up in the attic. I told Grandpa the phone was ringing, but he didn't believe me. Then he heard it and let me come answer it."

"What are you doing up in the attic?"

"Grandpa is letting me help him put all the Christmas stuff away."

"He is?"

Patrick whispered the next part. "And he hasn't yelled at me one time."

"That's just what I was going to ask," said Shawn. "You having fun?"

"A lot. What are you doing? Are you having fun?"

Shawn laughed. "No, I'd rather be with you and Grandpa. I'm just going to some old meeting with a colonel, to talk about my next job in the army."

"They're not going to let you stay home?"

"I don't think so, Patrick. But I'm going to try my best.

Uh-oh, here comes the soldier to take me to my meeting. Gotta go. Love you."

"I love you too," said Patrick.

"I'll come in and kiss you when I get home."

"Will you wake me up?"

"We'll see. Be good for Grandpa."

They hung up. Shawn exited the phone booth. "Okay, Corporal . . . let's see the colonel."

"You don't want to eat first, sir?" Miller asked.

"I forgot. No, let's eat. I'll follow you."

❧

Ian Collins sat on a large wooden chest in the attic, waiting until he heard Patrick's footsteps coming back up the stairs. He took a deep breath and groaned as he stood up. He felt so tired. He walked to his workbench near the back wall, choosing his steps carefully. The last time up here was Christmas Eve. He was finishing the wooden soldier he'd carved for Patrick. He knew then that soldier would be his last project. He picked up the worn leather pouch that had held his carving tools all these years and opened the flap.

He heard Patrick clear the last step. He turned and walked toward him when a wave of dizziness washed over him. He felt light-headed; his legs seemed to give way. He reached back for the workbench to keep from falling.

"Grandpa, you okay?"

Collins shook his head and wiped his forehead with a rag. "I'm fine, Patrick. I almost tripped, that's all."

Patrick walked toward the Christmas decorations. "Are we almost done?"

"Yeah . . . almost done."

Patrick waited a moment. "Are you coming over?"

It seemed his head was clearing. He set the leather pouch

down. "Be right there." The pouch had just given him an idea, something he and Patrick could do together while Shawn was away. He decided to bring the pouch down to his room, to avoid having to climb the attic stairs again.

"Here I come," he said. The dizziness was gone, but he took short steps, just to be safe. "Just one more boxful and then we're done. Who was that on the telephone?"

"My dad. He said he was just going to a meeting with a colonel. But he promised he'd be home tonight."

"Then I'm sure he will," Collins said. He wondered what this so-called good news was that the colonel had in mind. From what he remembered, the army wasn't in the business of passing out good news.

Thirteen

"Colonel Simmons's office is just around the next bend, sir."

Shawn followed Corporal Miller's double-quick pace, still trying to comprehend the enormity of the Pentagon. It wasn't as fancy as Union Station but nicer than any military facility he'd ever seen. They walked through a maze of hallways that seemed to go on forever, passing door after door, department after department. Each step went deeper into the complex, through even wider corridors that led to what looked like separate buildings, built inside the main structure. "How do you find anything in this place?" Shawn asked.

"They got this thing down to a system, sir," Miller replied. "Think of it like five little pentagons, each one built within the other. They call 'em rings, connected together by ten corridors, like spokes in a wheel."

That didn't help. "Just don't lose me," Shawn said.

"I do that, Captain, and my life is over. Colonel Simmons said you're my only project all day. Here we are. Colonel said he only needs about twenty minutes. I'll make myself scarce and be back to pick you up in plenty of time."

They walked through a tall brown door into a living-room-sized office area, a row of straight chairs lined against one wall, a secretary's desk in the center. A gray-haired woman about fifty years old smiled pleasantly as they stepped inside. She stood up. "Corporal Miller, you're back. Is this our guest of honor?"

"Sure is, Miss Hart. Captain Shawn Collins." Miller looked at his watch. "Two o'clock sharp."

She held out her hand. "Captain Collins, it's an honor to meet you. I'm Abigail Hart, Colonel Simmons's secretary."

Shawn shook her hand. An honor? he thought. "Very nice to meet you," he said.

"Can I get you some coffee?"

"That'd be great."

"How do you take it?"

"Just a little cream, if you have it."

"I'll just tell the colonel you're here." She sat down and pushed a button on the bottom of her telephone. "Colonel, Captain Collins is here . . . I will, sir." She looked up at Shawn. "He said go right in. I'll bring the coffee in just a moment."

"And I'll be back in twenty," Miller said as he turned toward the hallway.

"Thank you, Corporal," said Shawn. "I really mean it. That was an experience I'll never forget."

"My pleasure, sir."

Shawn walked up to the closed door on the right side of Miss Hart's desk, took a deep breath, and went in. Covering the back wall were three large War Bond posters, big as life, the kind you'd see hanging in a storefront window. On the right wall, a framed black-and-white photo of FDR. In the center of the room behind a wide gun-metal desk sat the colonel, head down, writing something. He instantly looked up, smiled, and stood. Shawn stood at attention and saluted.

Colonel Simmons returned the salute then held out his hand. "At ease, Captain Collins, it's an honor to meet you." They shook hands. "Please, have a seat." The colonel was taller than Shawn, with broad shoulders, dark hair, slightly graying on the sides. He smiled as if they were good friends.

None of this made any sense to Shawn. *I'm at the Pentagon, driven here in a general's staff car. A full-blown colonel has just said he is honored to meet me.* "Colonel, if I may, sir. I don't understand."

"What do you mean, Captain?"

"This VIP treatment I'm getting. I don't . . . get it."

"Then it's time someone explained things to you. That's partly why you're here. When was the last time you spoke with any crew members from your bomber?"

"Not since I left England. Have you heard from them? Everyone all right?"

"They're all doing fine, Captain, still in England. But they've been doing a lot of talking since then. In fact, they've all submitted detailed reports about your last mission to Bremen. They think pretty highly of you, to put it mildly."

"Best crew I ever had, sir. It was especially hard losing Bosco and Hastings on that last one. I left England in such a hurry. If there's any way I could get their home addresses, I'd like to send letters to their family."

"I'll see that you get them."

"Any word on how Hank Anderson is doing?"

"Let me see here." He looked down at the file open on his desk, shuffled a few papers to the side. "He's healing up nicely in a hospital near London. Well, enough to turn in his own report about the mission. I've been reading them carefully. So have a lot of people. You've become something of a legend back at your base, really throughout Bomber Command."

"What?" Shawn asked. "Why?"

"Captain . . . well, let me correct that . . . it's *Major* Collins now. Congratulations, you've been approved for a promotion."

"Really?" Shawn tried to sound excited. But he knew this meant the army had no intention of letting him go.

"There's more. We are recommending you for the Medal of Honor, Major. What you did on that last mission was nothing short of extraordinary."

Shawn could hardly believe his ears. "Sir, I was just trying to get us all home in one piece."

"You did that, Major, and a whole lot more. I don't think you understand. We've never had a bomber shot down like yours, crash-land in enemy territory, and then have the captain get himself and his entire crew safely across the English Channel in a single day. Most of our crews don't even survive what you went through, and those who do for the most part wind up getting killed or captured by the Germans in a matter of days. Those who do escape often take weeks or even months to make it back to England."

It had never once crossed Shawn's mind that he had done anything heroic, certainly nothing that deserved consideration for the Medal of Honor.

"And the way you dispatched that German officer in Holland?" the colonel continued. "Saved the lives of your entire crew, as well as the father and son who helped you escape. Unfortunately, for the father's sake, we're going to leave the details of that part off the record. But the whole plan you came up with, and the execution of that plan? That was some brilliant soldiering, Major. I had to fight to keep you in the States. Several generals in Bomber Command wanted you back right away, to be part of their staff."

There was a brief knock on the door. Miss Hart came in and served them coffee. Shawn thanked her and took a sip.

His hand was trembling. The Medal of Honor. It didn't seem right. All he'd thought about the entire mission was getting home to Elizabeth and Patrick.

"Major," the Colonel continued, "at the very least you'll get the Distinguished Service Cross, our second-highest medal. But I feel pretty certain from what I've read that they're gonna give you the big one—perhaps put on by the president himself—once we go through all the formalities and approval procedures."

The president? Shawn thought. He couldn't believe what he was hearing. He could tell the colonel had more to say. "Sir, I am very grateful for your kind words, but I really don't . . . I don't know how to respond. I don't think I did anything heroic. And to be honest, I'm not really looking for anything else at this point in my military career. Certainly nothing like this. I don't know if anyone mentioned this to you, but I actually put in a request to be permanently discharged."

"I know that, Major. I read your request. I'm very sorry to hear about your wife. A terrible loss. And if this were a peacetime situation, we'd probably grant it. But we're still in the thick of it, Major. The war's at a critical stage. Every week bombers are still crossing the Channel. Men are still dying. We got thousands of men right now, making their way north in Italy. We're still months away from the big invasion of Europe. We just can't let you go right now. You're far too valuable."

"But how, sir? If I may speak freely . . . I'm just a pilot. And from what I've heard, you can't even send me back on missions into Germany anymore. They say when you get shot down and escape, they take you off combat duty."

"You're correct, Major. The concern is, you get shot down again and captured, under torture you might give out critical intel about how you escaped the first time."

"So, what can I do then?"

"That's the best part, Major. I am putting you on a dream assignment. You are a bona fide war hero. As such, you get to serve your country in a totally different way."

"Doing what, sir?"

"Helping us raise millions of dollars to fund the war effort."

Shawn couldn't believe it. He'd had a feeling that's where this was going.

"You heard of the War Bond rallies we've been doing here, right?"

"A little, sir, but not much. I see signs all over the place saying 'Buy War Bonds' like the ones on your wall."

"Well, some of the biggest names in Hollywood have signed on for an East Coast tour. You'll be joining with them, traveling to twenty major cities by train. Boston, New York, your hometown of Philadelphia."

This was starting to sound like a nightmare.

The colonel continued, looking out his window now, a gleam in his eye. "This thing is going to be huge. We're going to raise more money than anything we've done so far. We got Greer Garson, Hedy Lamarr, even Bette Davis signed on to this, and a whole bunch of others." He turned back to Shawn. "Can you imagine, Major? You are being assigned to work alongside some of the most beautiful actresses in Hollywood. No bullets, no bombs . . . just beautiful women everywhere you look."

This meant nothing to Shawn. "And do what, sir? What could I possibly do?"

"Major, it's like this. We've been doing these bond rallies now a couple of years, even with the Hollywood types. More and more of them are getting involved. Their agents are even calling me now, asking to let them sign on. Does great things for their image. But there's the rub. They draw a huge crowd, but regular people don't trust 'em. Everyone else is on rations and struggling to get by. These stars are rich and famous. People can't relate. Sure, they want to see them in person, but that's all. Once we started having guys like you—legitimate war heroes—get up after the stars draw the crowds . . . the people loved it! And boom—the money starts pouring in. It's a perfect combo. And Major, from what I've read of your story, you'll be a big hit with the crowds."

It sounded like some sick exploitation scheme. And Shawn was being ordered to help it succeed. "Sir, I'm really uncomfortable with this."

"What part?"

"All of it, sir. I don't like any of it. I'm no movie star. I wouldn't even know what to say. I joined up to fly bombers and fight Germans, not this."

"Major, I'm not sure I like your tone."

"I'm sorry, sir, but you did ask. All I want is to go home and grieve in private and take care of my son."

"That's just not possible, Major Collins. We all have to do our part. Your part *was* to fly bombers and fight Germans. Now your part's changed. My part is to raise money so we can fight this war. I don't know if you've ever given a thought about where the money comes from to buy all those bombs and planes you and your buddies used. It's costing us millions of dollars every week to finance this war. Where do you think the money comes from for all this?"

"You're right, sir. I've never thought about the money."

"It comes from the good people of this country buying war bonds, Major. The Japs attacked us by surprise, if you recall. We didn't have a big military machine before that, and no money in the budget to pay for one. Believe it or not, Major, I know what I'm talking about. I ran a large marketing firm in

New York City before this. This War Bond tour—combining Hollywood stars with real-life war heroes—it's going to buy us a whole lot more planes, and tanks, and ships . . . you get the idea."

"Yes, sir."

"So are we clear?"

"Yes, sir," Shawn said, a sigh escaping involuntarily.

"C'mon, Major, you're going to have the time of your life here. I can think of a million fellas in Europe right now would give their right arm to be in your place."

How Shawn wished any one of them would. "When's all this going to take place, sir? Do you know how long I'll be gone?"

He handed Shawn a folder. "All the details are in there. You can read it on the train on your way home."

"Is that all, sir?"

"For now, Major. But we'll be in touch, and members of my staff will be with you every step of the way."

"Thank you, sir." Shawn stood up.

"You are dismissed, Major." They exchanged salutes. As Shawn walked out the door, the colonel said, "Major, you better prepare yourself for some big changes. I'm getting ready to issue a press release about you to the local radio stations and newspapers in Philly. I know what happens after this. You'll be as big as Jimmy Stewart or Clark Gable, least in your neck of the woods."

That's just great, Shawn thought. "Yes, sir" was all he said and closed the door. He tried to smile sincerely as he greeted Miss Hart and Corporal Miller, who was all ready to escort him back to Union Station.

He realized what the colonel had said was true . . . most men would be jumping out of their skin to receive a promotion, the Medal of Honor, public acclaim, and a chance to travel up and down the country with beautiful Hollywood actresses.

I don't want any of this, thought Shawn as he followed Miller down the Pentagon hallway. *How am I going to explain this to Patrick?*

Fourteen

"Enjoy your trip to Washington, sir?"

Shawn looked up into the smiling face of the same Pullman porter who'd helped him as he exited the train at Union Station. He was sitting in the dining car, eating a fairly tasty pork chop. "DC was amazing. You were right, the fanciest buildings I've ever seen."

"Told you. I'm from North Carolina, but I got kin live in DC. See 'em every chance I get."

Shawn turned in his chair to face the man. "What's your name?"

"Harrison James, sir. Friends call me Harry."

Shawn held out his hand. "I'm Captain—well, Major Shawn Collins. You can call me Shawn."

As they shook hands, the porter looked around nervously. "Don't think I can do that, sir. But we'll pretend your first name's Major. How about that?"

Shawn smiled. "I understand. Well, Harry, looks like I better get used to riding trains. I'm going to be doing a lot of this over the next few months."

"Trains is wonderful, sir. Been working on 'em for near

twenty years, this one here almost ten. Know it like my hometown."

"Bet you got a lot of great stories."

"That right, Major. But I better get moving. Got some errands to run a few cars up ahead. Just passing through, saw you there, thought I'd say hello."

"Glad you did, Harry. Maybe I'll see you in a few weeks."

"Don't know about that," said Harry. "They fixin' to reassign me to some big USO train coming up soon."

"No kidding," said Shawn. "Got a lot of Hollywood stars on it?"

"Yessir, I believe it do." He smiled extra wide at that.

"Then we might see a lot of each other. See this folder here? I just found out the army's putting me on that same tour. Start off in Boston?"

"Yessir."

"Got to be the same one."

"I declare," said Harry. "Then we will be seeing each other a bit."

"Hey, darkie, how long you gonna just stand there yakking? Refill my drink."

Harry froze, still looking at Shawn; his smile quickly evaporating. Shawn looked across the aisle toward the loud voice. A white businessman about his age was holding up an empty glass from the bar in Harry's direction. It was clear he'd already downed quite a few. A few of the nearby passengers stopped talking and turned to face the scene.

"Hey, George, or whatever your name is, I'm talking to you. Get me another drink."

Harry turned toward the man and said politely, "I'm sorry, sir. I don't work here in this car, but I will get you a waiter directly."

"I don't wanna hear excuses. Just go to the bar and tell the boy there to put another gin and tonic in this glass." His voice was getting louder. Now most of the tables in the dining car were watching.

Harry hesitated for a moment, then reached out for the man's glass.

Shawn stood up and got in between Harry and the drunk. "Sir, you're disturbing all the nice folks that came in here for a quiet meal, me included, and you've just insulted this gentleman."

"Gentleman? I don't see no gentleman. Just this darkie here gabbing when he should be working. Just go back to your chair, army man. This isn't any of your business."

"I'll go back and sit down as soon as you apologize to my friend Harry here, and to all of the rest of these folks for upsetting their dinner."

"Apologize? Why you—" He stood up quickly and took a swing at Shawn's face.

In one instant Shawn ducked the fist, grabbed the man's wrist, and twisted, sending his face crashing to the table.

"Ow . . . ow, you're hurting me!" he screamed, his face mashed into his napkin.

"It can hurt a lot more than this," Shawn said, and twisted an inch more.

The man screamed again. "Let me go."

"I'll be happy to, sir. Just as soon as you apologize to Harry here, and the rest of the dining car." Shawn heard a commotion at the front end and looked up to see a waiter and another Pullman porter who rushed in to see what they could do.

"It's all right, Johnny, Willie," Harry said. "We all right in here."

"I ain't gonna apologize to no negro," the man said. "I didn't do anything to apologize for."

Shawn twisted his wrist another half inch. The man yelled again in agony. "One more turn, and you will hear a loud popping sound," Shawn said in a menacing voice.

There was a brief pause, and the man said, "All right, all right. I'm sorry."

"Who are you apologizing to?" Shawn asked.

"Your friend Harry here."

"And . . ."

"And to everyone else."

"A little louder, please."

"AND TO EVERYONE ELSE."

Shawn released his grip, and the man's arm flopped to his side. He instantly grabbed his shoulder and started rubbing it. He shot Shawn a glance, half hatred, half fear. Then stood up and staggered toward the back of the train. As the doors closed behind him, the dining car erupted into applause.

Shawn smiled and nodded and went back to his seat.

"Thank you, Major," Harry said. "No one ever done anything like that for me."

"You don't need to thank me, Harry."

"Well, I gotta go 'fore I get in some more trouble." He started walking down the aisle, then turned. "When we on that tour, Major . . . you need anything, anything at all, I'm your man."

"Thanks, Harry."

And off Harry went down the narrow aisle.

A moment later, the waiter took Shawn's half-eaten plate of food away and set a fresh plate down. "My compliments, sir. The name's Willie. Look like your food got a bit cold."

"Thank you, Willie." Shawn looked up at the much younger man's smiling face.

"That man you helped . . . Mr. Harry. He's my dad. You

ever need anything while you on this train, you just ask, sir. You hear? You just ask."

"Thank you, Willie."

At that Willie walked down the aisle to attend to another table.

Shawn looked down at the fresh new pork chop and sawed off a bite. It was cooked just right, nestled in a puddle of piping-hot brown gravy. He followed it with a forkful of mashed potatoes and a swig of Coca-Cola. He looked around the dining car again, everything back to normal. It was quite a place as he thought about it, as if someone had put together a fine, upscale restaurant then stuck it in a big hallway. Linen tablecloths and napkins on every table, a nice vase of flowers, elegant curtains framing every window. He turned and looked out his window, past his reflection to the sun already setting in the west, thinking about what he'd just read a few minutes ago, the details of his new assignment.

They were giving him two more weeks to get his affairs in order, then he was to report to a military office near Boston for a briefing. An aide to Colonel Simmons, some lieutenant— he'd already forgotten his name—would serve as his personal secretary throughout the four-month tour. He read something about the possibility of the assignment being extended beyond that, but no specifics. All his expenses would be covered. When not on the train, he would be staying at the same hotels as the Hollywood stars, eating at the same restaurants. He was told to expect to give newspaper and radio interviews. He would receive briefings instructing him what to say and, more importantly, what *not* to say.

Only one part of all he'd read kept replaying in his mind, though, the part about being gone for four months. That would kill Patrick, he thought. Patrick already struggled when Shawn was gone a single day. And what would he do with

Patrick all that time? He couldn't see his father taking care of him, even with their relationship doing better. Shawn could tell he wasn't well. You could see it in his face and his eyes; they looked so tired and worn, even in the middle of the day. How could he possibly endure four months of feeding Patrick, cleaning his clothes, getting him back and forth to school?

Maybe he could bring Patrick along with him, hire someone to watch him. Immediately, he realized it was a dumb idea. This was no kind of life for a little boy, especially one who'd been through all Patrick had been through. He needed order and routine. School, recess, playing ball in the neighborhood. A normal kid life. He stared out the window, searching for an answer.

Then it came. *A nanny.*

Someone who could do all the work, so his father could just be the grandpa. And Shawn could afford it; he wouldn't need any of his military pay while he was gone. He suddenly remembered a conversation at dinner the other night. Miss Townsend had said something about losing her job at Child Services. She needed a job; Patrick needed a nanny. She was clearly fond of Patrick, and he seemed to adore her. So much so, that it annoyed Shawn. Elizabeth had always quoted that verse in Romans about God working all things together for good. Maybe Shawn was looking at this the wrong way. Maybe God had brought Miss Townsend into the picture for this very reason. If she agreed to become Patrick's nanny, that might ease the blow about Shawn being gone four months.

But where would she live? Certainly not in his father's house. It was obvious that Dad just barely tolerated her.

Mrs. Fortini.

She seemed to really like Miss Townsend, and she had two spare rooms right next door. This might just work, Shawn thought. He took out a sheet of paper and began to hammer out the details.

∞

Shawn arrived at the Philadelphia station at 8:30 p.m., then rode another train out to Allingdale. Walking home in the bitter cold, he turned onto Chestnut Street forty-five minutes later. He decided to stop by Mrs. Fortini's first and tell her the plan. If she didn't agree, there'd be no point in taking it any further.

He neared the house, glad to find lights on in the living room. Mrs. Fortini as a rule was in bed every night by 9:00. He walked onto her porch and knocked on the door.

"Who is it?" she yelled through the door.

"It's me, Mrs. Fortini. Shawn."

"Shawn?" she asked as she opened the door. "Is everything all right?"

"Everything's fine, I just had something I need to ask you before tomorrow."

"Come in," she said. "Can I get you some tea? Here, stand over here by the radiator. You want me to take your coat?"

"No, it's late; this should only take a few minutes."

She still had a worried look on her face. She sat down as Shawn explained the situation. He left out the detail about the Medal of Honor, simply mentioning them giving him a medal, but told her everything else. Her eyes widened with each new segment. When he got to the part about asking Miss Townsend to be Patrick's nanny, she jumped out of her seat.

"Shawn, that's a wonderful idea. I think she will make an excellent nanny. If you could have seen her, the way she cared for him while you were gone. And now that she has no job, I think she will say yes in an instant."

"Well, Mrs. Fortini . . . there's a little catch. That's really why I'm here. The only way I can see this working is if she could . . . live here with you. I'd pay you room and board," he added quickly. "Whatever you need."

She sat back down on the sofa. "I see." She was obviously giving it some thought. "How long did you say it would be for?"

"Right now they're saying four months. But it is the army."

She stood back up. "Then that's it," she announced. "Katherine will stay here with me. I'm sure we can make it work. She's a lovely girl."

"Thank you, Mrs. Fortini." Shawn gave her a hug. "This is such a load off my mind."

"Don't you worry about a thing," she said as they walked toward the front door. "I can't believe you're going to be rubbing elbows with Bette Davis and Greer Garson. Could you get me their autographs?"

"I sure will. The folder they gave me said Bing Crosby and Danny Kaye are also going to be on part of the tour. I'm not sure which part just yet, but—"

"Oh, Bing Crosby. I love Bing Crosby. You've got to get me his autograph."

Shawn laughed. For a moment she looked like a teen girl. "I will certainly try." Shawn walked out to the porch.

"When are you going to ask Katherine?"

"I'm going to talk to my dad right now. If he's okay with it, I'll ask her tomorrow. If she says yes, I'll tell Patrick about it. He's the one I'm most concerned about."

"I understand," said Mrs. Fortini.

Fifteen

Shawn walked into the vestibule of his father's house, banging away the mud that had gathered on his shoes. He was bone tired. His father must have heard him, because he came to the door before Shawn unlocked it.

"You're home, son. C'mon in. I put some more coal on the furnace." The elder Collins was smiling, the all-familiar cigar hanging out of his mouth.

"Thanks, Dad." Shawn still wasn't used to his dad greeting him this way, after all the years of hostility. He set his brief bag down and laid his overcoat across the armchair.

Ian turned the radio volume down and retreated to his favorite chair. "You don't look too happy," he said. "I take it they're not letting you out."

"Nope, they're not. But I didn't really expect they would." Shawn unbuttoned his uniform coat and sat on the couch.

"So what they say?"

"You're never going to believe it. It hasn't really sunk in yet. They're putting me on the craziest assignment you could possibly think of." Shawn tried to sound optimistic.

"What is it?" His father let go a long puff of the cigar; the familiar smell actually soothed Shawn's nerves a bit.

"First, this colonel—the one you talked to on the phone— tells me they are promoting me to major, effective immediately."

"That's great, Shawn." Noticing Shawn wasn't smiling, he added, "That is a good thing, right?"

"That's only the beginning. He tells me all the guys in my crew have turned in these reports about me, what we did on that last mission, and now they're recommending me for the Medal of Honor."

"What?" Ian's face lit up. "The Medal of Honor?" He leaned forward in his chair. "My gosh, Shawn. That's . . . that's wonderful." Shawn thought he saw tears forming in his eyes. "It's a good thing too, I'm telling you. After hearing your story the other night, I went to bed thinking . . . they don't give my son a medal for what I just heard, someone's gonna hear about it from me. If only your mother could hear this."

"Right now, it's just a recommendation. There's all sorts of procedures and protocols they gotta go through first. But the colonel felt certain it would happen, said the president would probably put it on me himself."

At that his father shot right up. "The president? FDR?" He paced back and forth across the living room. Shawn had never seen him so excited. "We've got to call somebody. This, this is the biggest thing that's ever happened to a Collins. To think . . . my boy getting the Medal of Honor. The president. The newspapers will wanna hear about this. I'll call them first thing in the morning."

"Actually, Dad, it's already happening. This colonel already sent the story to all the radio stations and newspapers all over town. We've probably only got a few days left of peace and quiet before things get a little crazy around here."

Ian sat down again, on the edge of his seat. "My boy's

going to be famous," he said, looking up at the ceiling. "A war hero, Ida, right here in our house." He looked back at Shawn, tears now rolling down his cheeks. "We've had Collinses in the military since the Civil War, no one has ever done what you've done, Shawn." He stood up, walked over to Shawn, and held out his hand. When Shawn took it, he pulled him to his feet. "I'm so proud of you, boy," he said and pulled him close.

Shawn had not expected anything like this. It was the first moment he considered that anything he'd heard today could actually be a good thing. After they hugged, his father walked out into the dining room. "This calls for a celebration. I've got a nice bottle of whiskey here. Just one shot for the both of us, warm up your insides to boot."

Shawn sat back on the sofa. "There's actually more to this story. A pretty big thing actually."

"I don't think I can take any more," Ian said, walking back with the bottle and two glasses in his hands. "You've got me feeling dizzy and I ain't even took a drink yet."

"You know those big War Bond rallies they have, the ones with all the Hollywood actors and singers?"

"I think I heard a few on the radio last year," his father said.

"Well, they're having another one start up in two weeks, going to twenty different cities by train, up and down the East Coast. Starting in Boston. They want me on it."

"You're going to be on a train with all those famous people?"

"Yep. I guess the plan is to have a big rally in each town. They'll put on some kind of a show, and at some point they're going to stick me out in the middle of the stage and have me tell a little bit about that last mission. Guess the idea is to get people to give money and buy bonds."

"My gosh, Shawn! But you know . . . I can see that. I went out and bought ten dollars worth at Hodgins's the morning after you told us your story. Shawn, you're going to be famous."

"Maybe for a little while, anyway."

"This is . . . it's just so much to take in. Patrick's going to be so proud when you tell him."

Shawn let out a long sigh when he heard Patrick's name.

"What's the matter?"

"It's Patrick. I'm going to be gone for at least four months on this thing."

Ian sat down in his chair. He let out a similar sigh. "I didn't think about that."

Shawn could tell the implications were beginning to click.

After a few moments, his father said, "Well, son. We'll make it work somehow. We're family. We'll get by. You've got your duty. And I'll do my best to do mine."

"Dad, I'm glad you feel that way, but to tell you the truth, I think it might just be a little much. I know you could do it, and I know you're willing. But I've been thinking about a plan on the train, a way this all could work, so it won't be so hard on you, or on Patrick. I want your time with him to be full of grandpa stuff, not cooking and cleaning and laundry."

Ian lifted his head up and looked at him. "What do you have in mind?"

Here goes, thought Shawn. I hope he's ready for this.

✤

When Shawn awoke the next morning, he didn't feel like a major. He didn't feel like a man who'd just been handed a dream assignment. And he didn't feel like a Medal of Honor winner. One part of him knew these were big things, huge things. The kind of things that should provoke awe and wonder and gratitude. But without Elizabeth there to share them, it all felt so empty.

He was glad the plan was coming together so well. Mrs. Fortini was on board and his father was surprisingly open to the idea of hiring Miss Townsend to be Patrick's nanny, after they talked it through. But even that . . . they talked it through. No yelling, no bickering. In the end, his dad even offered to pay her salary and the board money to Mrs. Fortini.

Only two obstacles left. Miss Townsend and Patrick.

Patrick was still upstairs getting ready for his first day at his new school. He was so excited. Yesterday before Shawn got home, Mrs. Fortini had walked Patrick to the school, about six blocks away. She'd timed it so he could watch all the kids as the school bell rang, ending the day. He hadn't been around any kids his age since he'd left their old neighborhood on Clark Street. That's what he needs, thought Shawn, kids his own age. He'll be fine after he gets over the disappointment. At least that was the plan.

Shawn looked down at the notepad by the telephone, smiled as he read Miss Townsend's name and number, in huge letters and numbers, obviously written by Patrick. He dialed her number and waited nervously as it rang.

"Good morning, Child Services, Katherine Townsend speaking. How can I help you?"

"Hi, Miss Townsend. This is Shawn Collins, Patrick's father."

"Captain Collins, what a surprise."

"Actually, it's Major Collins now."

"Congratulations . . . Major. When did that happen?"

"Just yesterday. They asked me to take a train down to DC to find out about my next assignment."

"I remember your father saying something the other night about a colonel calling."

"Well, that's part of what he wanted to talk about."

"Oh?"

"Yeah. Well, the rest of it is why I'm calling. It's a bit complicated. I was wondering if we could meet sometime this morning to talk."

"You want to meet? With me?"

"If that's possible. I know it's short notice. But I'm going to take Patrick to school in about a half hour. I don't suppose you have any free time this morning."

There was a pause. "I . . . guess I could get away for a bit. Mind if I ask what this is about?"

"Not at all, but I think I'd rather go over it in person. Didn't I hear you say you gave your two-week notice?"

"Yes. The clock's already ticking," she said. Sounded like she was almost whispering.

"So you haven't found another job?"

"Not yet."

"Well, that's what this is about. I may have one for you."

"Then I can definitely get away. Just say where and when."

"How about you meet me at the Eagle in Wanamaker's, say at 10:30? We can go upstairs for a cup of coffee, and I'll go over my proposal with you, give you a few days to think it over." Shawn instantly regretted calling this a proposal.

"I will definitely be there."

"Do you need more time?" Shawn asked.

"No, really. It's not a problem. Meet you at the Eagle, 10:30."

Sixteen

Katherine walked down the 13th Street sidewalk, carried along by the flow of the crowd, her hands stuffed deep in her coat pockets and her collar pulled up as high as it would go. The wind whipped through the canyon of tall buildings, stinging her cheeks. But she hardly noticed; she was almost beside herself with excitement. She couldn't believe Shawn had called her, that he'd wanted to talk to her about a job, that she even had a chance of getting involved with the Collins family again.

It wasn't hard to get away from work; she had simply whispered to Shirley what happened and said, "Cover me?" Shirley was on the phone, but she'd nodded and said with her eyes and eyebrows that she'd take care of Bernie Krebb.

Katherine looked up ahead at the Wanamaker's Building on the corner of Market Street, twelve stories tall. She loved going there for any reason and was so glad Shawn had picked the Eagle as their meeting place. She'd left fifteen minutes early, giving herself time to walk slowly past the storefront windows, taking in all the things she could never afford. But that's what store windows are for, she thought. For dreaming.

As she neared the corner, she noticed that every trace of Wanamaker's Christmastime transformation had already disappeared. Everything was back to normal. But for Katherine, normal at Wanamaker's still held out an almost magical appeal.

She crossed the street and stood before the first window. A woman about her age wrapped a mink stole around the shoulders of a mannequin. What a job that must be, she thought. Imagine dressing up all these storefront windows every day and getting paid for it. As her body drifted past the other windows, her mind drifted to Shawn's job idea. What could it be? She couldn't begin to guess. Anything would be better than her dim prospects. But it had to be something significant for him to call her, then want to meet with her right away.

She looked up at a clock on a building across the street. There was just enough time to browse past the perfume and jewelry counters. She preferred coming in the Juniper Street entrance, because it was closest to the Grand Court. A smiling middle-aged man with a moustache held open the front doors.

She never tired of the sight. Her eyes were instantly drawn toward the magnificent pipe organ. It looked like a mini-cathedral made of gold. Its presence seemed to fill the Grand Court. She looked up at the beautiful arches in the ceiling, rising 150 feet from the marble floor.

She walked several steps inside and turned slowly in a circle. The first floor was rimmed by more marble arches, the remaining floors supported by thick Roman pillars trimmed in bronze and gold. Shoppers peeked down at the elegant scene below over white ornamental railings. It was as if the entire place glistened and gleamed with treasure. Katherine knew that almost everything in the store was beyond her reach, but the merchandise was said to be reasonably priced and the store was always crowded, not with the rich but with mostly ordinary shoppers.

It saddened her to think she didn't even dwell in that bracket of society. So . . . don't think about it, she told herself. Who knows? Someday she might even buy that beautiful black purse with silver trim, sitting over there in that glass box. She walked over to see it more closely. It could happen.

She turned toward the massive bronze Eagle statue, the centerpiece of the Grand Court. It had become the perfect downtown rendezvous place ever since John Wanamaker brought it by train from the St. Louis World's Fair in 1911. About a dozen people were standing around the Eagle, looking past Katherine toward the front doors. Undoubtedly, looking for whomever they were supposed to meet. She looked up at another wall clock. Shawn would be here in less than ten minutes. She couldn't wait to see him again. Instantly she scolded herself. It was not as if they were meeting at the Eagle for a date.

She walked to the perfume counter through an invisible dome of lavish smells hovering over the entire area. A small crowd of ladies gathered around a saleswoman. Occasionally they offered a free spray or two of something on sale. She walked around the corner to join in but glanced back at the Eagle.

There was Shawn.

He must have just come in the front door and walked straight to it. She saw him studying the faces of the people standing around, then at his watch, then toward the front doors. She had to admit, he looked so handsome in his uniform and cap and matching overcoat. No, stop it, she told herself. What are you doing? She took a deep breath and walked over to join him.

Shawn checked his watch once more; she wasn't late, he was five minutes early. He needed to calm down. He was just edgy from the tension of this whole thing. Earlier, when he'd dropped Patrick off at his new school, Patrick had been so happy and excited, talking about all the things they could start doing together now that Shawn was home. Had he already forgotten their conversation the day before? Shawn told him he wasn't out of the army yet. Maybe in his little mind, if he didn't say it out loud, it wouldn't happen. But it worried Shawn. How would Patrick handle things two weeks from now when he had to leave for four months?

"Major Collins?"

Shawn heard Katherine's voice. He looked around.

"Over here," she said.

He turned and saw her weaving through a group of elderly women. He smiled and waved, then removed his cap. "Have any trouble getting off?"

"Not really," she said, now standing in front of him. "I'm dying to find out what this is about."

She smelled very nice. "Let's get a cup of coffee, and I'll tell you."

"We could go to Linden's around the corner. I go there a lot."

"We could," Shawn said, "but it's so cold out. Ever been to the Tea Room upstairs?"

"The Crystal Tea Room? No, but I've heard it's very nice."

"It is," said Shawn. "It's got crystal chandeliers and linen tablecloths. It's as fancy as anything down here in the Grand Court. Best part is . . . cup of coffee up there just costs a dime."

"You mean I could have afforded the Crystal Tea Room all this time?"

Shawn laughed. "Follow me."

He led Katherine toward the elevators that took them to the ninth floor, ever-so-slowly and after so many stops. They walked across the marble floor to the Tea Room entrance. Shawn paused to gaze up at the tall mahogany doors, the smooth mahogany pillars standing like sentries on either side, and the half-moon wooden arch across the top. This had to be the most upscale diner in the world. As they stepped through the doors, Shawn watched Katherine's eyes get very big, like those of a little girl opening a present.

"Table for two?" the hostess asked, picking up some menus.

"That's right, but we're just here for coffee."

She put the menus back. "I'll tell your waitress. Right this way."

As they walked toward their table, Katherine stared at the beautiful chandelier hanging in the center of the room. The rest of the ceiling was quartered off by large squares of white ornamental trim. The whole ambiance was that of a restaurant catering to the wealthiest clientele. The waitress stood off to the side of a small round table, right next to one of the many mahogany-trimmed pillars throughout the place.

Shawn held her chair out, and Katherine sat down. Suddenly, she seemed nervous. She took the white linen napkin and spread it across her lap. "I've never been in a place like this." She said it as if she didn't belong.

"It's okay, Miss Townsend. Look around, it's the same people who shop downstairs. I've eaten here a lot over the years."

"I guess. It's just so . . . fancy."

The waitress walked up and filled their coffee cups. She smiled and walked away. Shawn decided to just jump in. "I'm not sure where to begin. Maybe I'll just start with the biggest part of the thing, and fill in the blanks after that. I don't want to keep you in suspense."

"I appreciate that," she said, taking her first sip.

"I already told you I went to Washington yesterday to find out what they want me to do next." Shawn took a deep breath. "This is just so crazy, I still don't believe what I'm about to say."

"What? What is it?" she said.

"I have been ordered to report to Boston in two weeks. Shortly after that, I'm to join some big War Bond tour that will travel up and down the East Coast by train with a number of Hollywood stars."

"Really?"

"Yes."

"Like who?"

"People like Greer Garson, Hedy Lamarr, and Bette Davis—"

"Bette Davis?"

"She's supposed to be a part of it, and at some point Bing Crosby and Danny Kaye are joining in."

"That's incredible, Major. Are you excited? You don't seem like it."

Shawn looked down and sighed. "I'm not, not even a little bit. I mean, I'm glad I'm not getting sent back to England, but this thing's going to last at least four months."

"Poor Patrick," she said, sounding instantly sad. "He was so excited to get you back. How did he take it?"

"I haven't told him yet."

"Oh."

"I'm going to tell him when he gets home from school today."

"He started back to school? I'm so glad. That should really

help him start to adjust. So you're going to live at your dad's for a while?"

"Well, for two weeks anyway. The plan is for Patrick to stay there while I'm gone. Which brings me to the reason I asked to meet with you. Okay, I'll just say it. Would you consider becoming Patrick's nanny, working for me that is, but being his nanny while I'm gone?"

Katherine was clearly stunned by the question. She almost dropped her cup.

"You can take some time to think it over. I know it's a huge—"

"Yes."

"What?"

"I'll do it. I don't need to think about it. I would love to be Patrick's nanny. I'd do it even if you didn't pay me."

"Really?"

"Yes. Well, I guess I would need a little money, maybe for expenses, but—"

"I'm going to pay you. In fact, I want to pay you at least what you're getting now. And I've already talked with Mrs. Fortini. She loved the idea and said you could move into one of her guest rooms upstairs."

"Really? Mrs. Fortini said that? She loved the idea?"

"Yes, she did." Tears began streaming down Katherine's cheeks. "What? I'm sorry, did I say something wrong?"

She reached down at her feet for her purse. "Where's that stupid handkerchief?"

"Here," Shawn said, holding out a linen napkin. "Use this. Is everything all right?"

She took the napkin and dabbed her eyes. "I don't know what to say, Major. I love your little boy, and I thought after the dinner the other night I would never see him again. And I have absolutely no job prospects. And pretty soon, no place to live. What you're offering me feels like a dream. How long did you say it's for?"

"They said at least four months, but with the army there's no guarantees. We can say for at least four months right now, take another look at it after that."

She dabbed her eyes again. "Well, I can start whenever you want me to."

"Don't you need to finish out your two weeks?"

"Not really. I can finish what they've asked me to do by the end of this week. And my rent is paid weekly, so there's no problem there, either."

"Didn't you say at dinner you had to turn in your car also?"

"Yes, it belongs to the agency."

"Well, you can use my dad's car. He never drives it anymore. Excuse me—I can't believe it." Shawn looked across the room. "There's a pilot buddy of mine over there. We trained together in Arizona but got sent to different bases in England. I haven't seen him for months." Shawn stood up. As he did, his friend saw him too and jumped out of his chair. He walked right over and they embraced. "I can't believe it's you, Al. What are the chances we'd bump into each other here?"

"I ain't even from Philly," Al said. "Just visiting my aunt and uncle a few days. Say, who do we have here?" He looked down at Katherine with obvious interest.

"I'm sorry, let me introduce you. This is Miss Katherine Townsend. Miss Townsend, this is Captain Albert Baker, the worst pilot in the Army Air Force."

"Hey." He feigned a punch to Shawn's stomach. Then he and Katherine shook hands. "So are you two, uh . . ." He made a gesture with his hands, asking if they were a couple.

"No, Miss Townsend just agreed to be my son's nanny."

"Nanny? Really? We don't do that over here, do we? Isn't that a Brit thing?"

"Well, it's a long story. Excuse me, Miss Townsend." Shawn put his arm around Al and began guiding him back to his table. He stopped about halfway, so he wouldn't be overheard. "Hey, Al, I know we haven't talked for months. A lot has happened since then."

"Looks like you've got a swell setup." He looked over Shawn's shoulder at Katherine. "She's like Rita Hayworth meets girl next door."

"It's not like that. I don't have time to explain."

"So you're really not a couple?"

"No."

"Mind if I get her number?"

Shawn immediately regretted bumping into Al. "Please, Al, just leave it alone."

"You don't have to get sore."

"Al, my wife died last month. The army's got me on some four-month War Bond tour. I'm talking with Miss Townsend about watching my son while I'm gone. Okay?"

Al's expression turned instantly serious. "Shawn, I'm . . . I'm so sorry. I had no idea."

"I know, don't worry about it." Shawn stepped back and held out his hand. "No hard feelings, right?"

They shook hands, and Shawn went back to his table. Katherine had been looking but quickly turned away as he came back. He looked at Katherine as if seeing her through Al's eyes. He'd never considered how attractive she was. At this point, still in the depths of grief, he didn't see women that way. It never dawned on him that people might get the wrong impression about their relationship.

This could make things extremely difficult.

Seventeen

"Is everything okay?" Katherine asked.

"Yeah, Al's a great guy. I just had to clarify a few things." Shawn sat back down. The waitress came up and offered to refill their cups. Both nodded and thanked her.

"Major, there's something I feel I must tell you, before we go any further." She looked away a moment. She didn't want anything to kill this dream. "I just don't want you to have a wrong impression about me."

"What do you mean?"

"People could think—well, you could think—that because I work for Child Services I've got all kinds of experience with kids. But really I don't."

"Oh?"

She looked at his face. What kind of "oh" was that? "I mean, I care deeply about children, Patrick most of all, but I have no . . . nanny-like experience. My job didn't really allow me to spend much time with the kids, beyond making sure they got in a decent situation. The amount of time I spent with Patrick actually got me into a little trouble."

Shawn smiled. That reassured her a little. She took a sip of coffee.

"Honestly, I didn't even think about that," he said. "I don't care if you've never been a nanny. I'm sure you've got good instincts from just growing up in a family. Besides—what . . . did I say something wrong?"

Katherine tried to hold back the tears. Why was she being so emotional? Sometimes she hated being a woman; men could just will things like tears into submission. What must he be thinking? She took a deep breath and blinked several times. "I didn't grow up in a family."

"What?"

"I'm an orphan. Well, I was an orphan. I mean, I still am, but—" *Oh, would you stop*, she scolded herself. "I was abandoned might be a better way of putting it. The people running the orphanage would never tell me if my parents were dead, but I think I figured out that one of them, or both, just dropped me off there when I was three. I was clothed and fed, but there were no kind, motherly women in my childhood. More like wicked stepmothers."

"Katherine," Shawn said. "I don't care if you were orphaned or abandoned. I'm sorry, that didn't come out right. I do care, but I mean it doesn't affect my decision. Here's what I know . . . Patrick thinks the world of you. After what he's been through, that matters more to me than twenty years of nanny experience. And Mrs. Fortini was a great mom. I spent most of my childhood with her right next door. After my mom, she's top on my list. You have any questions, she'll have the answers. Besides, she backed this idea completely. So don't worry about your lack of experience."

Katherine smiled. What a relief. And she loved the way he'd said everything he had just said. "I will do my very best, I can promise you that."

"I know you will," he said. "I don't have to report to Boston for almost two weeks, so you could probably finish out your two weeks at your current job. I'd like to spend as much time with Patrick as I can until then."

Katherine understood. If she started early, she would create a distraction. And she really could use next week to take care of some loose ends and get freed up from her apartment. "I'll start whenever you think best, but I think I'll probably leave at the end of this week. My boss is making life pretty difficult for me since I turned in my notice."

"I understand," Shawn said. "I'll take some time this week writing out your duties, so there won't be any misunderstanding."

"That will be helpful, thank you," she said.

Shawn looked at his watch. "I guess I've got to start heading back, but there's one more thing I need to mention." A worried look came over his face. "I'm not exactly sure how to bring this up."

"What is it, Major?"

"Well, you calling me Major for one."

"You want me to call you Shawn?"

"Actually, no. I think it would be better if you did call me Major. How should I say this? You know my wife has just been gone a little more than a month."

"I know, I'm so sorry."

"Under any other circumstances, if I were going to hire a nanny right now, I'd probably hire someone who . . . I guess I'm saying someone who looked more like a nanny, someone older."

"I think I understand."

"Well, I don't want you to have to guess at what I mean. I need to be very clear. I realized something a few minutes ago when Al came over. He thought you and I were a couple. I can see a lot of people making that mistake. So I think it's going to be very important—if this is going to work out—for you and I to keep this relationship very professional. Calling me Major, or Major Collins, would probably help."

"I understand, Major. I can see what you're saying."

"And we're also going to have to figure out a way to keep your relationship with Patrick on a somewhat professional level. I mean, to keep it from drifting into more of a mommy role. I can see Patrick already starting to look to you that way, and I don't think it's a healthy thing. He's very vulnerable right now, just losing his mom, and let's face it—little boys need their moms. But if we let that happen, and we have to end this nanny role a few months from now, it would devastate him. I can't let that happen. Do you understand what I'm saying?"

Katherine thought she did, but it saddened her. "I will definitely do anything you ask or think is best, but . . . do you have any ideas about what that should look like? I'm not sure I'd know how much is too much or how far is too far."

"Right now I don't. That's what I've got to work on. I just wanted to be upfront with you so we have the same expectations."

"Well, I'll abide by any guidelines you come up with."

"Thank you, Miss Townsend. I appreciate the way you're taking this. It's just very important to me to keep Patrick from suffering any more heartache."

"That's the last thing I want."

Shawn waved to the waitress walking by. "Could we get a check? Thanks." He turned back to Katherine. His expression softened, back to where it was before his friend Al came over. "I am so glad you said yes, Miss Townsend. I hate leaving Patrick again, but it will be so much easier telling him with this piece of news thrown in."

"Major, I'll do everything I can to make Patrick feel safe and cared for while you're gone."

"Good," he said. "I know you will." The waitress set the check down on the table. Shawn picked it up and set down a generous tip. They stood up and made their way toward the door.

As they stepped into the elevator, Katherine tried convincing herself she was glad Shawn—Major Collins—had made the boundary lines of their relationship so firm and clear. And he was right. It was better to keep things professional. For Patrick's sake.

As she stood there next to him, she realized . . . for her sake too.

Eighteen

Patrick looked at the clock on the wall. His teacher was still talking, but no one seemed to listen. The other kids fidgeted in their seats, some already putting their books and pencils away. Some leaned forward, gripping the edge of their desks, like racehorses waiting for the bell. The school day was about to end.

It had been a pretty good day, for a first day at a new school. No one had picked on him or made fun of him. But none of the boys had invited him to play during recess. He'd stood on the edge of the playground watching, trying to look interested. One boy named Roy did talk to him, but afterward Patrick wished he hadn't. He led Patrick to the side of an old brick building and invited him to burn ants with a magnifying glass. Patrick had never done that before. He was pretty sure ants didn't make any noise, but he could almost hear them screaming. It was awful.

He looked up at the clock again. One more minute. Standing near the chalkboard was a little boy—Patrick forgot his name—waiting for his punishment to start. He'd been talking in class and had to write "I will not talk in class" fifty times, then clean the entire chalkboard. That would be terrible,

Patrick thought. First you'd be late getting home from school and then have to say why.

He looked over at the boy on his right and noticed a gold star on a paper sticking out of a book. *Miss Fitzpatrick gives out gold stars.* None of the teachers in his old school did that. They just wrote notes on the top of the page, red pencil if it was something bad, blue pencil if something good. Patrick decided he'd work hard to get gold stars every day. He'd bring them home and show them—

The next thought stung like a bee.

He couldn't show his gold stars to his mom. She was still in heaven. And she would always be in heaven. He could show them to his dad, but it wouldn't be the same. Dads didn't make half as much fuss. Besides, Patrick knew—even if he didn't want to think about it—the army wasn't going to let his father stay home. So who would ever see his gold stars?

Suddenly, all the kids rushed out of their desks and herded toward the door. The bell had rung. Patrick didn't even hear it.

⚮

Shawn eyed the doorway to Patrick's school from inside the car. The sky was dull and overcast. The temperature had dropped ten degrees since this morning. Had he sent Patrick out dressed warm enough? Elizabeth always listened to the weather report the night before. He'd have to remember that was his job now . . . at least for two more weeks.

A bigger wrestling match resumed in his mind: the big talk with Patrick. Should he lead with the news about Miss Townsend being his nanny, then slip in the part about being gone four months? Should he talk about the medal and the train tour with all the stars, then talk about Miss Townsend, and then tack on the part about being gone four months?

Any way he tossed it, he still had to talk about leaving home.

His job was to make it sound like it wasn't so bad, but it was. It could only come off sounding like it didn't bother him. But it did, a great deal. His thoughts were interrupted by a loud bell, followed moments later by the school doors swinging open as dozens of children fled the scene.

He thought about how his dad would have handled it. He'd just say it. *I gotta leave for four months. It's work. I don't have a choice. Stop crying.* It was a simple world. The world of duty. Don't let relationships interfere.

After a few minutes, the stream of fleeing children slowed to a trickle, but still no sign of Patrick. Shawn was just about to get out of the car when Patrick finally came out. "Patrick," Shawn yelled. "Over here." Patrick looked down from the top of the stairs, then waved. He walked down the steps, holding on to the rail like he was told.

"Hey, buddy," Shawn said as they connected at the base of the stairs. "You warm enough?"

"Huh?"

"Pretty cold out here."

"Oh, I'm fine."

Shawn put his arm around him as they walked. "What took you so long? I was starting to worry."

"My new teacher was just talking to me a few minutes."

"Anything wrong?"

"She was just making sure I had all the right books."

"What's her name?"

"Miss Fitzpatrick."

"You like her?"

"She's real nice. But she will punish you if you're caught talking."

"Were you talking?"

"Not me, another boy."

"They gotta do that, otherwise things get out of control."

"I know."

Shawn opened the door for him then walked to the other side. They drove a few blocks to a drugstore on Clifton Avenue. "Thought we could get a soda together, and maybe talk a little bit."

"What about?"

"Just stuff. About your day, what you think of your new school, then some other stuff."

"Could I have a cherry soda?"

Shawn smiled. "Sure."

Within a few minutes, Shawn pulled into an open parking spot near the store. He waited for a trolley to pass, then walked around to join Patrick, who'd already let himself out. They walked inside. He watched Patrick run up to the counter and hop onto one of the swivel seats. He gave it a spin, big smile as it rolled around. He was so happy. Shawn hated to spoil it. He looked around the diner area, glad it was mostly empty. Just an older couple in the corner and two teens sipping a milkshake near the door.

Less people to witness a little boy getting his heart broken . . . yet again.

"Hey, Patrick, let's sit in one of these booths."

Patrick spun around again. "Do we have to?"

"C'mon. Sit next to me."

Patrick obeyed. A waitress in her mid-thirties came to their table a few minutes later. She pulled a pencil out of her hair. "What can I get for you gentlemen?"

"Just a Coca-Cola for me," Shawn said.

"Can you put cherry in mine?" Patrick asked.

The waitress looked at Shawn, who nodded. "Nothing to eat?" she asked. "Lemme guess, too close to dinner."

"Right," Shawn said.

"Back in a jiff," she said.

"So you like your new school?"

"So far, I guess. No one would play with me at recess."

"They will, once they get to know you. Just give it a few days."

"I hope so."

"I know so. You had lots of friends in your old school, and all over the neighborhood on Clark Street, right?"

"I miss them."

Shawn gave him a hug. "It'll get better, you'll see. Look, it's getting better already." The waitress set their sodas down on the table. Patrick quickly picked out his, the one with the reddish tint. He smiled as he took his first sip.

Here goes, thought Shawn.

"Guess who I talked to today?"

"Who?"

"Somebody you really like."

"Someone I like? Billy, was it Billy?"

"No, it was an adult."

Patrick thought hard a moment.

"She was at our Christmas dinner," Shawn said.

"Miss Townsend?"

Shawn nodded.

"You talked to Miss Townsend? When?"

"This morning. I met with her to talk about something."

"You did? What was it?"

"Well, the same thing I want to talk to you about too."

Patrick looked confused.

"You drink your cherry soda and I'll explain." Shawn decided just to let the story come out however it came. He started with a reminder of their earlier conversation, about the army not being ready to let him stay home. Before Patrick could react, Shawn broke the news about asking Miss Townsend to be Patrick's nanny while he was gone. He barely got the words out before Patrick shouted "Yippee!" His excitement filled the diner.

Shawn added a few more details: about him getting the medal, the train tour, being home for two more weeks, and once even slipped in the part about being gone for four months. None of these things seemed to sink in or really bother Patrick at all.

Patrick asked a number of questions, but none were about Shawn; they were all about Miss Townsend. When was she coming, where would she live, would she be taking him to school, did his grandfather really say it was okay. Overall, Patrick seemed happy and excited about the conversation. No tears, no sadness. The day was ending for him much better than it had begun.

He got Miss Townsend and a cherry Coke.

As Shawn got up to pay the bill, he realized . . . it wasn't Patrick's heart being broken yet again.

∽

The house was quiet.

Shawn's dad was downstairs sitting in his favorite chair, reading the paper and smoking a cigar. Upstairs, Patrick lay safely tucked into his bed, looking up at Shawn with sleepy eyes. It was time for his bedtime prayers. Shawn sat on the edge of the bed. He'd just finished reading a few pages from *Make Way for Ducklings*.

"You gonna make it?" Shawn asked quietly.

"I'm not sleepy."

"You're not? Better tell those eyes. They're blinking pretty slow."

Patrick forced his eyes open wide, but they just wouldn't stay put.

"Well, let's say your prayers."

Patrick clasped his hands together and closed his eyes. What a beautiful boy, Shawn thought.

"Thank you, God, for my first day at school. Thank you for my new teacher being nice. Forgive me for helping that boy hurt those ants. Thank you for letting my dad pick me up at school and buying me a cherry soda."

Shawn smiled.

"Thank you for saying yes to my prayer about Miss Townsend. I kinda knew you were gonna say no about Daddy staying home from the army. Since I can't have Daddy, thank you for not letting me have to be all alone."

Shawn swallowed hard as he listened.

"Tell Mommy . . . tell Mommy I think about her a lot, and tell her about Miss Townsend for me. Bless Grandpa, and thank you for making him nice again today. Please help me make some new friends at school . . . in Jesus's name, amen."

Shawn looked toward the dresser, saw the picture of him and Elizabeth, then looked away. Seeing that image after hearing Patrick pray . . . he was about to lose it. He stood up.

"Are you okay, Daddy?"

"Sure, son, I'm fine."

"You didn't say amen."

"I'm sorry. Amen." He leaned over and kissed Patrick on the forehead. "Good night, son."

"I love you, Daddy."

"I love you too," Shawn said as he walked toward the door.

"Daddy?"

Shawn turned around. "What, son?"

"Why don't you pray after me like Mommy did?"

Why didn't I, Shawn thought. "Well, maybe I will tomorrow. Good night," he said as he turned the light out.

"Good night," Patrick said.

Shawn closed the door gently and turned toward the stairs. Was it possible? Had this whole idea about Miss Townsend come to him because of Patrick's prayers? He sighed as he walked down the steps, realizing it certainly hadn't happened because of his.

He knew he was avoiding God, and he knew it was because of Elizabeth. But he also knew it was not what she'd have wanted. In fact, it was the exact opposite. He could almost imagine what she'd have said, could almost see her beautiful face presenting her appeal, but before the thought formed into a sentence, he hurried down the stairs, leaving it to hover alone in the shadows of the stairway.

Nineteen

For Shawn, the next two weeks went by much too fast.

He managed to make *some* memories with Patrick: threw the ball in the backyard a few times, made two more trips to the drugstore for cherry sodas. Patrick had sat on his lap a full hour once, as Shawn read him the funnies. But most of the time had been spent dodging the press and numerous well-wishers throughout town, as his new hero status began to take hold.

The story had broken in the paper the day after Shawn told Patrick about Miss Townsend. They even included his picture. Now he couldn't walk down the street without stopping for handshakes and pats on the back. Every aging WWI veteran in Allingdale must have told him his own war story. He'd been interviewed on the radio three times, mostly trying to downplay the adulation. No one would let him pay for a thing. Not a sandwich, a movie, not even a loaf of bread.

His dad was loving it. It actually got him out of the house a little. Every other day, he'd let somebody buy him a beer at McHale's Tavern on the corner of Clifton and Elm. And every other night Mrs. Fortini would cook them dinner and bake a fresh pie in his honor. "I know you won't eat right on those trains," she'd say.

And Patrick now had plenty of friends at school, more than he knew what to do with. He said every day kids would argue over whose team got to pick him.

Everybody loves a hero.

At the moment, he walked the back roads of Allingdale toward Christ the Redeemer Church, about a half mile from his home. He wore his uniform under a civilian overcoat, trying not to draw any attention. It was just after 10:00 a.m., a bit chilly but thankfully no wind. It felt strange walking the neighborhood as an adult. During his childhood, the church stood on one of the four corners that outlined the borders of his world. It was as far as his mother allowed him to roam on his bike.

Yesterday he'd called the number on a card given to him by his former pastor, Jonathan Barnes, when they'd bumped into each other at Penn State two weeks ago. Shawn couldn't hide his grief from the discerning pastor, and after a brief but encouraging conversation, Pastor Barnes recommended this man and this church to Shawn, since it was so close to his father's home.

He read the name on the card again, to make sure he got it right. *Pastor Donald Harman.* When Shawn called, he said he'd just wanted to introduce himself, set things up for Patrick and Miss Townsend while he was gone. He really didn't want to talk about Elizabeth.

He turned the final corner, and the church came into view. He didn't remember it looking so small. It was surrounded by mature elms and firs. The shingles on the steep roof were stained with age. To the left of the arched front doors, a thick bell tower rose to match the height of the trees. The walls and bell tower were covered with a dull gray fieldstone. As he drew near, it was obvious the property was clean and well maintained. A date, 1891, was etched in the cornerstone. Near the sidewalk, a church sign announced Pastor Harman's last sermon title, or maybe it was this Sunday's: "Our Times Are in Your Hands."

Shawn realized he wouldn't be there this Sunday or any Sunday for the next four months. He was leaving tomorrow for Boston.

"Can I help you?"

Shawn looked up and saw a short elderly man coming out a side doorway.

"You can go in to pray if you'd like," the man said. "Church isn't locked."

"Thanks," said Shawn. "But I'm here to see Pastor Harman. I have an appointment at 10:15."

"Was it here or at the parsonage? That's about three houses down on the right."

"I'm pretty sure it was here. Is there an office?"

"Round the other side. Can't miss it. Just follow the walkway. Dark brown door. Got a sign right on it."

"Thank you." Shawn started to walk around the front steps toward the other side.

"Aren't you . . . aren't you that officer been in the news lately? The one getting that big medal?"

Shawn sighed. "Yes."

"An honor, young man. Lost my boy last year over France, a gunner on a B-24."

"No, the honor is mine," Shawn said. He walked over to shake his hand. "What was his name?"

"Jimmy . . . James. Jimmy's what we called him. My name's John Rigley, take care of the place."

"Sorry for your loss, sir. I'm Shawn Collins. I lost a lot of good men and good friends."

"Wished you were Jimmy's pilot. Might've made it back home."

"You're very kind . . . truth is, I have no idea how we got out of the scrape we were in."

"Lord had a reason, always does. I believe that . . . most days, anyway. Well, an honor to meet you."

"You too."

In a few moments, Shawn stood before the office door. He took a deep breath and knocked. He tried to blot out the unsettling thoughts stirred by what Mr. Rigley had said, about God having a reason for everything, and about the pathetic answer he'd given, as if he had no idea how he'd survived the battle. Not long ago, he would have been telling anyone who'd listen that God's mercy and providence had made the difference.

His heart was hardening. He could almost feel it. And he hated the feeling.

The door suddenly opened. "Hi," a smiling middle-aged man said. "You must be Shawn Collins." He looked at Shawn's lapel. "Major Shawn Collins." He held out his hand.

"Thanks for taking time to see me, Pastor."

"Come in, come in. No need to thank me. Any friend of Jonathan Barnes is a friend of mine."

Shawn walked in to a cozy reception area. There was no one seated at the desk. "So you talked with Pastor Barnes?"

"Just briefly," said Pastor Harman as he walked past the desk toward an open door just beyond. Shawn followed. "About two weeks ago. He said you might be calling."

Pastor Harman sat at his desk, which made Shawn a little nervous. He didn't want a long conversation. The room was fairly small, crowded with bookshelves loaded with books. Not arrayed in some neat order, like a man looking to impress, but like a man who simply loved books and couldn't part with a single one. Shawn stood just inside the doorway.

"Do you have time to sit down a minute?" the pastor asked.

"Uh, not really, sir. I'm leaving for Boston tomorrow. I got a lot of things to check off my list today."

"I understand. Mind if I do? These middle-aged bones are always looking for a chance to sit."

Shawn smiled. "Not at all."

Pastor Harman had a pleasant face, and he looked right at Shawn as he talked. But his eyes were gentle, instantly putting Shawn at ease. His auburn hair still covered most of his head, surrendering at the borders to a creeping invasion of gray. Shawn thought the wrinkles around his cheeks and eyes looked like they'd been formed by years of smiling.

"Major, I am so sorry for your loss. I can't begin to imagine the pain of it." He looked to a picture frame at the edge of his desk. "Mary and I have been married for thirty-five years. I'd be lost without her."

"Thank you, Pastor." Shawn felt sincere empathy from the man. "That's partly why I'm here. I wished I could have attended your church the last two weeks left on my leave, but it has been crazy for me, trying to get everything done . . . all the distractions."

"Well, you are quite a celebrity in this town. People are looking for something positive to cling to in times like these. It's one thing to read about the war in the paper or watch the newsreels, quite another to meet someone like you face-to-face."

"I'm trying to get used to it. It looks like it's going to be my life for the next four months. Anyway, I've hired a nanny to take care of my son while I'm away. Her name is Katherine Townsend. My son's name is Patrick. He's seven."

"Well, we'll do our best to make them feel right at home. Our church isn't very large, just about two hundred. But they are a caring bunch, doing their best to stay centered on the gospel. We have quite a few moms with husbands fighting overseas, even a few widows. I'll speak to two or three I have in mind about Miss Townsend and Patrick. Is there anything I can do for you?"

"Thanks, but I don't think so."

"Well, if you can think of anything, or while you're away, if Miss Townsend makes you aware of anything we can do to help her or Patrick, please call and let me know."

"Thank you, that's very kind." Shawn reached out to shake the pastor's hand before the conversation went any deeper.

The pastor stood up and followed Shawn to the door. As Shawn reached for the knob, the pastor asked, "Can I pray for you?"

"Sure," Shawn said.

He laid his hand gently on Shawn's shoulder. "Lord, I thank you for Shawn, for all you've done to bring him home safely to his son. I can't begin to fathom your wisdom or your reasons for taking his wife, Elizabeth, home so suddenly. Thank you that he has at least the assurance of her salvation to comfort him, and the knowledge they will one day meet again. Please, Lord, sustain him by your grace for the challenges he will face over these next four months. Protect him and keep him and give him your peace as he entrusts his son to the care of others. In Jesus's name, amen."

Shawn exhaled and said amen. As the pastor lifted his hand off Shawn's shoulder, the warmth remained. His words, at least for those few moments, imparted something that used to be familiar to Shawn—rest in his soul.

"Thank you, Pastor," he said. They exchanged good-byes, and Shawn quickly walked away. The wind had picked up; the sky was a little grayer. At the intersection he looked up at the bell tower pointing toward the sky, then down the tree-lined road in the direction of his father's house.

For a moment, it seemed unfamiliar, like a road leading nowhere.

Twenty

The cab carrying Katherine and all her worldly goods pulled up to the curb just outside Mrs. Fortini's home. She'd driven out to this neighborhood maybe a dozen times before, but now—and for at least the next four months—it would be home. She could barely contain her joy.

"This it, ma'am?" the cabbie asked.

"Yes, it's perfect."

"What?"

"I mean, yes . . . this is it." She stepped out and twirled slowly around. She'd never lived in the suburbs before. The cab driver got out and walked past her. He pulled her two suitcases and a cardboard box out of the trunk. "I'll get the box," she said.

He followed her down Mrs. Fortini's driveway and up the porch steps. Mrs. Fortini burst through the front door. "You're here, Katherine. I'm so glad." She held the door open. "Come right in. I'm all ready for you." She looked at the luggage being carried in. "Is there any more?"

"This is it," the cabbie said.

He set the bags just inside the living room, walked out to the porch, turned around, and stared back. There was this "C'mon, lady" look. Katherine walked out and paid him. Now she had only fourteen dollars left in her purse. And nothing left in the bank. No car, no furniture. Just two mismatched suitcases full of clothes and some odd items taped up in a box.

She had never been so happy.

She walked back into the living room and closed the door. The sofa with the doilies, the photographs in the frames, the knickknacks on the shelves, the smiling Italian mother. It was like a dream.

"Got your old room ready," Mrs. Fortini said. "Remember where it is?"

Katherine looked up the stairs and nodded.

"That was some night," Mrs. Fortini said.

"I was so afraid we'd lost him," said Katherine, remembering the ordeal that happened just before Christmas. "But you weren't. You knew we'd find Patrick."

"God let me know somehow."

Katherine was glad to be here under much nicer circumstances. "I'm going to bring my stuff upstairs and get situated, if that's okay."

"Let me help you," Mrs. Fortini said.

"No, I had to carry all this down three floors. I'm sure I can manage carrying it back up one."

"Then I'll make us some coffee. Would you like that?"

"Very much."

"Take your time. If you're not done, I'll bring it up."

Katherine climbed the first few steps. "Mrs. Fortini?"

"Yes, child?"

Even that, so sweet. "I just want to thank you again for opening your home to me."

"Think little of it, dear. I've been looking forward to this since the moment Shawn mentioned the idea. After coffee, I'll show you where everything is in the kitchen."

A few minutes later, Katherine had all three pieces up the stairs and in her room. Mrs. Fortini had the closet empty and full of hangers. The dresser drawers were all empty too. Plenty of room. She might have enough money in a month or so to replace some of these neatly folded rags she was unloading. Major Collins had insisted she be paid the same salary she got at Child Services, then included Mrs. Fortini's room and board. The money she used to pay for rent and food was now . . . *extra*. What must that be like, she thought, to have *extra* money at the end of a month?

She finished unpacking and slid the empty suitcases under the bed. The cardboard box could wait until after coffee. She looked at her watch, the main reason she was down to fourteen dollars. She'd bought it at Wanamaker's, the first thing she'd ever bought there. It was almost 2:30. Patrick would be getting out of school in thirty minutes. She wasn't responsible for Patrick yet, but all day she kept checking her watch, memorizing the schedule Major Collins wrote up for her. The watch wasn't fancy, but it was nice, the nicest thing she'd ever owned. After buying it, she'd walked it right up to the Crystal Tea Room and stared at it over a cup of tea.

At the head of the stairs, the smell of fresh coffee greeted her just a moment before Mrs. Fortini's voice. "It's ready, Katherine. Shall I bring it up?"

"I'm coming right down. It smells wonderful."

"You like cream and sugar?"

"You have cream and sugar? Real cream and sugar?"

"I'll take that as a yes," Mrs. Fortini said as she walked back to the kitchen.

Katherine walked down the steps. She noticed the floral wallpaper, how perfectly the patterns connected, even at the seams. She rounded the stairway and followed the aroma back to the kitchen. Mrs. Fortini poured the coffee into two matching china cups. "It's so beautiful," she said as she sat down.

"My Anthony bought them for me on our fortieth anniversary. People say you should use your china for special occasions. This is a special occasion." She sat in the little chair, just one of two in the kitchen.

"It's very special for me." Katherine sipped her coffee, careful not to drip it on the linen tablecloth as she set the cup in the saucer. She looked over Mrs. Fortini's shoulder at the corner section of white metal cabinets, with little ivy stencils stuck on the center of each door. Beside them a General Electric icebox and Magic Chef gas range. They almost matched, and neither had any rust. What kind of appliances did Mr. Collins have? She didn't remember. That's where she'd be cooking for him and Patrick next door. "I'm a little nervous," she said.

"I can see why. There's a lot to be nervous about."

That's not what Katherine wanted to hear.

"I'm only kidding you, dear."

"I thought you were serious."

"My, you *are* nervous."

"I've just never been a nanny. I've never taken care of a home. I've never cooked for others. Major Collins made out three pages of instructions for me, but there's nothing on the list about running a home. I said yes so quick, I never thought through all the home things I'd have to do. I'm not ready."

Mrs. Fortini reached over and patted her wrist. "You'll do fine, Katherine."

"I don't even know where to begin."

"Katherine, guess what I've been doing for the last forty-five years? Taking care of a home, cooking for others, all kinds of home things. I was hoping you'd let me help you."

"But I don't know anything."

"Then we'll take it nice and slow, one day at a time. Anthony and I never had any girls. I thought . . . who will I pass on my family recipes to? Then God sent me you."

"I can't imagine ever making a dinner Mr. Collins will approve of."

"Katherine, Mr. Collins loves my cooking."

"How do you know?"

"A woman knows. He shuts up the whole dinner. He cleans the plate. He asks for more. Where's the mystery? You'll never hear him say it, but you get those three things in the same meal . . . he loved it."

Katherine laughed out loud.

"We'll do fine, you'll do fine. Patrick will love it—everything you do—and he will tell you. So do it for Patrick."

Do it for Patrick, Katherine thought. That she could do.

⁓

Shawn folded the dish towel over the towel bar to dry. He was exhausted, but before dinner he had managed to check every errand off his list. Tomorrow he wanted to spend every remaining moment with Patrick before boarding the train. Patrick's teacher had agreed to give him the day off from school. Shawn walked into the dining room then turned back for a final inspection. His mother would have been proud. After dinner he told his father to rest in his chair with the paper. When Shawn came home from his errands, his father had looked winded and weary. Far as Shawn could tell, he hadn't done a thing all day.

Shawn walked past him on his way to the stairs. His father's chin was planted firmly on his chest, which moved up and down as he breathed, deep in sleep. The paper had fallen to the floor. Fortunately, the cigar had burned itself out in the ashtray. Better put the first one to bed, he thought, then come back for him.

Patrick was already upstairs, taking his bath, putting on his pajamas. He could do the whole routine now on his own. Shawn was sad it was already his bedtime on the last full day they'd spend together in months. Maybe he could prolong things a bit by reading him a book. He tiptoed up the stairs, careful to sidestep the squeaky spots. As he cleared the landing, he looked to the left, but Patrick was already finished in the bathroom. He turned the bathroom light out and walked toward Patrick's room straight ahead. The door was closed but not latched.

As he neared the door, he heard Patrick crying, muffled as if trying to hide. His first thought was to rush in, but then he heard Patrick's voice, speaking through tears. He pressed his ear to the edge of the doorway and listened.

"God, why is Daddy leaving tomorrow?" More muffled sobs. "I'm trying to be strong, so Daddy won't be sad, but I can't do it anymore." It sounded like he'd buried his face in the pillow. Shawn could bear it no longer.

"Patrick." He ran in and lifted him in his arms.

"I'm sorry, Daddy," he cried, burying his face in his chest. "I didn't want you to be sad. I know you can't stay. I tried to be strong."

"It's all right, Patrick. You're just a little boy. You don't have to be strong." He stroked his hair, then held him close and let him cry.

"I don't want you to leave me, Daddy." Patrick looked up, eyes peering through little puddles. "I like Miss Townsend. She is very nice, but I need you." Patrick tried to hide his face.

"I'm glad you feel that way, son." Shawn put his finger under his chin and lifted his face. "Listen to me," he said softly. "I *hate* leaving you. I don't want to do this." Tears began streaming down his face. "Don't think for a single minute that I'd rather be doing anything else but be here with you."

"Really?"

"Really. I don't care about being famous or being anybody's hero. I don't care about meeting Bing Crosby or Danny Kaye. I told the colonel that two weeks ago. But he said the army needs me to do this, and he wouldn't let me stay home. That's the only reason I'm going. When you're in the army, you have to do what you're told."

"Will you call me?"

"Every chance they let me."

"Will you write me? I can read lots of words now."

"Every chance I get, and you write me too. Miss Townsend will help you mail it."

"Okay," Patrick said. He wiped the tears from his face.

"Listen, Patrick. You let me be strong and let Miss Townsend be strong and let God be strong. You just be a good little boy, okay?"

"Okay."

Shawn laid him back on his bed.

"Will you pray for me, Daddy?"

Shawn swallowed hard. "Course I will. Close your eyes." He stroked his finger across Patrick's brow. "Dear Jesus, thank you for loving us so much that you died on the cross for us. Thank you for being willing to help Patrick right now. Your Word says, 'Weeping may endure for a night, but joy comes in the morning.' Please let Patrick fall fast asleep now, have good dreams, and wake up tomorrow without any sadness. In Jesus's name, amen."

Patrick was already asleep before Shawn finished praying. He stood up quietly and walked toward the door, then looked back. The dim glow of the lamp rested gently on Patrick's face, lighting up his cheeks and eyes. What a beautiful face,

Shawn thought. So full of innocence and wonder. He faced the same measure of uncertainty as Shawn, but with such hope and simplicity. Shawn saw something of Elizabeth just then. She looked at life that way. He remembered how much he used to love watching her sleep. Patrick had her eyes. But more than that, he had her heart.

Elizabeth had done such a wonderful job with him while Shawn was away. Now he was going away again. "God, keep my little boy," he said, choking back tears as he made his way downstairs.

Twenty-one

The dreaded moment had arrived.

Shawn was driving; his father sat next to him. Patrick was sandwiched in the backseat between Miss Townsend and Mrs. Fortini. Everyone bundled up in overcoats, scarves, and hats. It wasn't far to the Allingdale train station, just a few more blocks. That morning, they had all enjoyed a breakfast feast at Mrs. Fortini's. Everyone seemed in good spirits, so Shawn pretended to be too. It was hard not to smile downing fresh scrambled eggs, fried scrapple, and homemade biscuits. Somehow, she had even managed a small bottle of fresh orange juice. His dad winked at him when Shawn asked how she'd pulled that off. He loved using his money making shadowy little deals down at Hodgins's Grocery.

"Sure seems crowded for this late in the morning," the elder Collins said.

Shawn noticed it too. Cars were parked end on end for several blocks as they approached the train station. Shawn suddenly had to put on the brakes. Everyone shifted forward.

"What's wrong, Daddy?"

"Nothing, Patrick. Just some unexpected traffic."

"Are we there yet?"

"Just another block or so."

"I wonder what's going on?" Mrs. Fortini said.

"Maybe an accident up ahead," said Shawn's father.

"I don't think so," Shawn said. "I don't hear any sirens. Road looks clear up ahead all the way to the stone bridge." The traffic was moving, just very slowly. As they got within eyesight of the train station parking lot, Shawn noticed a steady stream of people turning in.

"Look at them all," Miss Townsend said. "Must be hundreds."

"Parking lot looks completely full," Shawn said. "I don't think we're going to find a spot. You might have to drop me off at the curb and keep going."

"No, Daddy. We wanna see you get on the train."

"I know, Patrick. But what can we do?"

Just then Shawn's father rolled down his window. "Excuse me, chief," he said to a man walking with two kids on the sidewalk, about the same speed as the car. "Know what's going on? Why the big crowd?"

"We're here to see the war hero off on the train to Philly. Didn't you hear? The mayor was on the radio last night, asked everyone to come out if they could. Heard him again this morning. Gave all the city workers the morning off so they could be here. Never had a Medal of Honor winner from around here. Wanted my kids to see him."

"Daddy, they're talking about you," Patrick yelled from the backseat.

"Oh no," Shawn muttered.

"Shawn, you should be proud," said Mrs. Fortini. "We're proud of you."

"Excuse me, sir," his father yelled to the man. "The war hero? You're talking about my son here, Shawn Collins."

"Yeah, that's his name, Collins. Is that him?" He started pointing at Shawn.

"He's my son."

"Hey, everyone," the man yelled. "Major Collins is right here in this car." The people nearby all stopped and turned. Everyone started pointing; some began to clap.

Shawn looked down at the floor. He just wanted a few quiet moments to say good-bye.

"Think you could make a way for us to get into the station?" Mrs. Fortini yelled out her window. "Major Collins doesn't want to miss his train."

"Sure thing," the man yelled. Others nodded and instantly started yelling for people to get out of the way.

Shawn heard his name tossed about by the crowd. Each time the cheering got louder. In moments, the crowd parted like the Red Sea. Shawn drove slowly through the opening path. People waved, pointed, and applauded as they drove by. As he turned into the parking lot, he saw the entire platform around the train station covered with people. He recognized the mayor and several members of the town council. At the base of the steps there was even a high school band.

"Can you believe this?" Mrs. Fortini said. "Isn't it wonderful?"

"They're all here to see your daddy, Patrick," Miss Townsend said.

"I know," he said excitedly.

Shawn wished he could share their joy. He smiled and waved. Just then the mayor and others on the platform started pointing at the car. "Is that him?" the mayor yelled. "Is that Major Collins?" Everyone near the car yelled back that it was. "Make way, everyone! Make way for Allingdale's favorite son."

The car edged forward until it was literally surrounded by people; there was no room for people to move. "Guess this is it," Shawn said. He turned toward Patrick in the backseat. "Grab hold of Miss Townsend's hand and don't let go."

"I will," Patrick said.

He handed the keys to his father. "Stay close to me," Shawn said to Katherine.

"I'll be right behind you."

"Dad, Mrs. Fortini? Maybe we should say good-bye here."

"Don't be silly," Mrs. Fortini said. "You think I wanna miss this? Maybe you should let me and my purse lead the way."

Shawn laughed. "All right then, let's go."

As soon as they got out of the car, they were surrounded. Everyone reached out to touch him or pat him on the back. Shawn kept looking back, to check on Patrick and Katherine. Each time, they were right there. Katherine was pretty tough. She had no problem pushing people out of the way. Fortunately, the mayor intervened. "Okay, everyone, let them pass. You'll all get a better chance to see him if you let him by."

This opened a narrow line to the steps. Patrick and the others pushed through. The mayor actually helped them up the steps. He walked over to a small clearing on the platform. At that moment, everyone heard a loud train whistle coming from the west. "Quiet down, everyone, let's hear what Major Collins has to say. His train is almost here." He motioned for Shawn to join him.

"Major Collins," the mayor announced, more to the crowd than to Shawn. "As you can see, you've made all of Allingdale proud by your heroic service to your country." The crowd erupted in applause. "We have many brave men serving in the Armed Forces, some who've even given their lives. But having you back with us, after barely escaping from the Germans the way you did . . . well, it's just such a wonderful thing." Again the crowd cheered. "Please know our thoughts and prayers will be with you as you leave us today for your War Bond tour with all those Hollywood stars. Please tell Bette Davis and Bing Crosby I said hello, will ya?" The crowd laughed and clapped. The mayor stood aside. As he did, the train pulled into the station, drowning out all other sounds for the moment.

"Thank you, Mayor, and members of the town council," Shawn said. "And all you fine folks who've come out here on this chilly morning to send me off." Shawn looked back at the train. "As you can see, I need to be going now. But thanks so much for all your care and support." He turned and saw Patrick leaning up against Miss Townsend. Next to them were his dad and Mrs. Fortini, all smiling brightly. He turned back to the crowd and said, "Guess I better get used to saying this . . . let's show our support for all our brave boys by going out and buying War Bonds." The crowd yelled out their approval. Shawn shook the mayor's hand and walked over toward Patrick and Katherine. "Let's go," he whispered.

He picked up his duffel bag, and they followed him down the walkway toward the front of the train. The mayor gave a signal, and the marching band started playing "God Bless America." Shawn waved as they turned a corner around the little brick building and out of sight. They walked past a luggage cart then down the sidewalk until they saw a conductor standing at the stairs of one car, ushering passengers inside.

"All aboard," the conductor yelled.

Shawn put down his bag and bent down to face Patrick. He couldn't hold back his tears. Instantly Patrick started to cry, then Miss Townsend, then Mrs. Fortini. "I'm sorry, everyone, look what I started." He picked Patrick up and gave him a big squeeze. "I love you so much," he said.

Patrick kissed him on the cheek. "I love you too, Daddy."

"Now don't you worry about a thing, okay? Miss Townsend

will take great care of you, and so will Grandpa and Mrs. Fortini."

"I know."

"I'll call you every chance I can."

"And write," Patrick said.

"And write." Shawn set Patrick down and reached out his hand to Miss Townsend. "Thanks again for taking care of Patrick."

"Thank you for giving me the chance. I will guard him with my life."

"Hope it doesn't come to that," Shawn said. "But I know you'll do just fine. Mrs. Fortini?" He walked over and gave her a big hug. "I'm going to miss you . . . and your wonderful cooking."

"Well, you just come home to us as soon as you can," she said. "Don't you worry about a thing."

He stepped over to his dad. There was an awkward moment as they looked in each other's eyes. A thought flashed through Shawn's mind about whether to hug him or shake hands. His father ended the debate by grabbing him and giving him a big hug. As they pulled apart, his father leaned close and whispered. "Shawn, I am so proud of you. Not because of all this," he said, nodding back to the crowd with his head. "It's not the medals or the fame. I'm proud of the man you've become."

Shawn was speechless. "I love you, Dad," he said, and they hugged again.

"Like Mrs. Fortini said, don't worry about a thing. We'll get along just fine. There is one last thing I'd like to ask, a favor." He looked away as he finished the sentence.

"Anything, Dad, what is it?"

"You can say no, and there won't be another word about it."

"What is it?" Shawn asked. The train whistle blew again. Shawn looked over his father's shoulder at the conductor, who gave Shawn a nervous look.

"I'd like to teach Patrick how to carve, just very basic things. It would give us something to do together." His father was talking even quieter now. He looked back at Mrs. Fortini, as if to make sure she couldn't possibly hear him.

"I don't know, Dad. He's so young."

"I will be very careful and make sure he knows all the safety matters. I've never cut myself in all these years."

His dad's face and eyes, almost pleading. Shawn had never seen him like this.

"Okay, Dad. But please . . . really lay on the dangers with him. Make him almost afraid of those tools."

"I will, I will. Thanks, son." He gave Shawn another hug.

Shawn walked over to Patrick and hugged him again. He picked up his bag and walked up the stairs. "Good-bye," he yelled and walked through the doors. The train started to pull away. He ran to a window and kept waving until they could see each other no more.

∽

Ian Collins stood in his driveway, waving to Patrick as he walked with Miss Townsend onto Mrs. Fortini's porch and into her home. On the drive back from the train station, they had discussed Patrick eating lunch with them. Collins said he hadn't slept well last night and thought he might lie down for a nap.

That was partly true.

He felt tired enough to need a nap, but he had slept fine. He felt so sluggish and out of breath and not at all up to being with company. He walked slowly up the steps to his vestibule and into his living room. He knew he'd left the heat running, but he didn't feel any change in temperature. He walked over to the radiator to make sure it was working.

It was. He was the problem.

He knew something was wrong, could feel it in his bones. He knew the difference from fighting a cold or some kind of bug and having something bad wrong with you. He was afraid of going to the doctor, had always been afraid of those quacks. He grew up seeing friends and loved ones being one kind of sick, then going to the doctor and coming out five times worse. Some got so sick they just died, way before their time, seemed like to him.

Ida always thought the best of people, even her doctors. But they had never done a thing for her, far as he could see. Just kept her holed up in that sick ward, day after day, as the life ebbed out of her.

So he wasn't going to call any doctor. Not now anyway. He walked over to the telephone in the dining room and pulled out a little white card with all his important numbers. He would call his lawyer, then maybe his accountant. He wasn't going to say much. They'd try to talk him into all kinds of things he wanted no part of.

He would just tell his lawyer he wanted to change his will as soon as possible. Make sure Shawn and Patrick got everything he owned. Maybe a little bit for the church.

As he dialed the number, he was glad he got to say what he said to Shawn just before he left. Been meaning to say that to him for weeks. Now, if something did happen to him before Shawn finished this fancy train ride of his, Shawn would always have those words to hold on to.

Course, he could do all this and live another ten years. But that didn't matter. This was the right thing to do. The phone picked up on the other end, his lawyer's secretary, Betty something.

"Hey, this is Ian Collins. I need to set up a time right away with your boss, I'll pay extra if he can make it this week."

"Well, I'm sure we can get you in, Mr. Collins. Can I ask what this is in reference to?"

"Well, I just want to change my will. That one he wrote up for me a few years ago, you can tell him to throw it out. I don't even wanna see it. Tell him I want to start off from scratch, and I want to do it soon as he can."

Twenty-two

What a strange day. Katherine had no reference point for all the conflicting feelings going on inside. For starters she was a nanny. What was a nanny anyway? A mom, but not a mom, with the added warning from Major Collins not to get too close to Patrick over the next four months. But it was too late; she already loved him like a mom would. At least the way she thought a mom would love a child.

She was a nanny working for a real-life war hero. She had never seen anything like the scene at the train station this morning. They treated Shawn like a celebrity, and he looked the part. And he deserved the part. After hearing about his last mission, she wasn't at all surprised about the medal, the promotion, or the War Bond tour with the Hollywood stars. But seeing and feeling the thrill of that crowd up close . . . how would he handle all this adoration over the next four months? Would it change him?

But then, why should she care if it did? There was no relationship, no understanding between them. She was the nanny; right now, the four-month nanny. He had never given her the slightest notion that he cared about her on any other level. And why would he? He was a grieving husband, mourning the loss of a woman he clearly loved with a passion. To even think this way made her feel stupid.

But she did care. Every time she was around him, she cared a little more.

She sighed.

"Katherine, are you all right?"

She turned from the living room window, where she had been staring out at nothing. "I'm fine, just a bit overwhelmed by all this."

"I know," said Mrs. Fortini from the sofa, "you're going through a lot of changes right now. Losing your job, starting a new one, moving to a new place. Why don't you take your coat off and relax. I could make us a cup of coffee."

"I told Patrick I'd take him for a walk. School's out for the day, so he wants to take me there, show me where his classroom is, where I need to drop him off and pick him up. I thought I'd let him play on the swings a bit. Maybe by then Mr. Collins will be through with his nap and I could go over and start dinner."

"Do you have the recipe I gave you?"

"In my purse. You sure he has everything I need over there?"

"Checked it all myself yesterday. Tomorrow morning we can plan out the meals for the next few days, then go shopping. Don't forget to get his coupons."

"I am so glad you're here."

"It'll be fun."

Just then Patrick came running down the stairs.

"You wash your hands?" Katherine asked.

"Oops." He turned and ran back up. "We still going for a walk?" he yelled at the top of the stairs.

"Soon as you're finished. I'm all ready." She heard the water in the bathroom sink turn on.

"What a delightful boy," Mrs. Fortini said. "I think you are going to like your new job."

"I know," she said, then thought, *As soon as I can figure out how to stop caring.*

◦◦◦

Shawn sat comfortably in his seat on the train, heading north from Philadelphia to Boston. When he'd stepped on board the first train at Allingdale, the passengers had stared at him for the first few miles, trying to make sense of all the fuss at the station. Soon everyone returned to their book, newspaper, or conversation. But every few moments, Shawn had caught someone looking at him, like they were trying to figure out who he was. They'd instantly look away, but it got on his nerves so he walked back to a different car.

When he'd arrived at the 30th Street Station in Philadelphia, he half-expected to find another crowd gathered to welcome him, then laughed at his paranoia. No one cared, no one even said hello. He was just one of hundreds of GIs mingling in the crowd, trying to find the right train to their next destination.

He was happy to be a nobody again.

The car wasn't crowded. Shawn had the aisle to himself. To get his mind off the aching loneliness, he picked up a newspaper. He'd been out of touch for most of the last two weeks. As usual, war news occupied the headlines. Apparently, General Eisenhower had been made Supreme Allied Commander in Europe a few days ago. Shawn saw that coming. He read another article about the war raging in Italy. The 36th Infantry Division was attempting to cross the Rapido River. Sounded like an Italian river. They were meeting stiff German resistance. The article was very upbeat, highlighting all the positives, but Shawn knew how to read between the lines. Didn't sound like things were going well there at all. He looked out the window. His train was crossing a river just north of Newark, meeting no resistance at all.

It didn't seem right that he was traveling on a leisurely train ride to stay at a high-end hotel in Boston. To be wined and dined with celebrities and stars. To have almost no duties other than to smile and say a few words about war bonds. What a shocking contrast to the contribution he'd been making just five weeks ago.

He wondered what his crew had been doing over the last five weeks. Or his buddies back at Bassingbourn airfield in England. How many missions had they flown? How many planes had been shot down? How many of his friends had been killed or captured? What would they say if they knew what he was doing right now?

He looked up as a heavyset man almost tripped into the seat beside him, trying to navigate his way through the narrow center aisle. "Excuse me," the man said. "I'm such an oaf."

"No problem, sir. Here's your hat."

"Thanks," the man said and kept walking.

Shawn looked at his watch. The train should pull into Boston in about three hours. He opened his briefcase, noticed an unopened letter addressed to him. As he read the return address, he remembered getting it a few days ago. It was from Captain Albert Baker, the pilot buddy he'd bumped into at the Crystal Tea Room. He'd slipped it in his briefcase intending to read it later but had forgotten all about it. He opened it and read it.

Dear Shawn,

Really sorry about being so insensitive there at the restaurant (couple of weeks back, when you were there with Miss Townsend). It had been so long since we last saw each other. I even forgot

*you were married. I'm really sorry for your loss.
Can't imagine how it must feel. Anyway, you were
always a good friend.*

*I wanted to ask your permission to contact
Miss Townsend. To be honest, I can't stop
thinking about her. I'm being sent back to England
in a month, thought I might touch base with her
before I go, see where it leads. But if you have
any objections, I'll drop it like a rock.*

*You can write back to me at the return address.
Hope you're doing okay.*

Your friend, Al

Shawn slipped the letter back in the envelope. For some
reason it annoyed him. Why should he care if Al wanted to
ask Katherine out for a date? And why was Al asking him
for permission? He wasn't her father.

He reached back into his briefcase for the folder Colonel
Simmons had given him at the Pentagon. He decided to read
about the lieutenant who would serve as his aide on this tour.
He was supposed to be picking him up in Boston. The least
Shawn could do was find out a little more about him, like
maybe his name.

As he flipped through the papers, he stopped at one he
hadn't noticed before. It was a schedule for their time in
Boston. It said the first War Bond rally was January 21st at
3:00 p.m. *That's tomorrow afternoon.* It was at Fenway Park,
where the Red Sox played. There was a list of big bands that
would play and the times for each, then the Hollywood stars
who would come out, some doing song and dance numbers,
some just stirring up the crowd.

Then he saw his name. And beside it the words "War Bond
fund-raising speech."

Speech, Shawn thought. What speech? Colonel Simmons didn't say anything about making a speech. He quickly thumbed through the rest of the pages, looking for anything that might resemble a fund-raising speech. There wasn't anything. The few sentences he'd said at the train station this morning were the first words he'd ever uttered in public. And that was before a small crowd of hometown fans.

How could he face thousands of strangers at a major league baseball stadium, coming after a string of famous celebrities, and give a speech?

What would he say?

Twenty-three

Katherine set the kettle to boil, added a pinch of salt. A nice white sauce was already simmering. Soon she'd add the pasta. Where was the garlic and pepper? She looked quietly through the cabinets to find the spices.

"You sure you got this?"

She turned to see the elder Collins as he popped his head through the kitchen doorway. "I'll be fine. Mrs. Fortini checked all the ingredients. Got the recipe right here on the counter. She promised me you will love this. Now go do something for about thirty minutes, and I'll have it ready."

"I'm going to take Patrick with me."

"Where are you going?"

"Nowhere, just out to the garage."

"He's all clean; don't get him dirty."

"We won't get dirty."

She looked at the water in the kettle. Little bubbles were already starting to form at the bottom. "Better be back in twenty-five minutes. Give yourselves time to wash your hands."

"Let's go, Patrick."

Collins walked past her in hurried steps toward the back

door of the kitchen, wearing an overcoat. The door led out to the backyard, down a few wooden steps, to a freestanding garage. Patrick was right behind him. Collins had this look on his face. Hard to place it. Maybe . . . mischievous. She walked over to the window and pushed the sheers to the side. She couldn't help smiling as she watched them disappear into a side door of the garage. What a difference, she thought, between now and the way things were before Christmas. The old man really had changed. Almost a Scrooge-like transformation.

Almost.

She quickly walked back to the stove to check on things, glanced down at the recipe lying on the counter to the right, held down by a salt shaker. She'd already studied it a half dozen times. That exchange with Mr. Collins went rather smoothly, she thought. Once again, the wisdom of Mrs. Fortini had been vindicated.

Her last words to Katherine as she'd left to come over here were about how to handle the old man. "It's really very simple," she had said. "Use gentle tones but be very firm. Like you're talking to a child just a bit older than Patrick. I watched Ida handle him for years. He'll fall right in line."

It worked.

❧

"Watch your step, Patrick. It's a bit messy in here. Boards all over the floor. Stand there by the door till I find this light."

"Okay."

"There it is." He grabbed it and pulled. "Still not much light."

"I can see okay."

"All right, come on in then. But watch your step. I got something to show you."

"What is it?"

"A surprise."

"Really?"

"Come here. Stand right there and close your eyes."

"They're closed."

"No peeking."

"I won't."

Collins pulled the leather pouch from his coat pocket and held it right in front of Patrick's face. "Okay, open 'em."

Patrick did. "Wow," he said then looked puzzled. "What is it?"

Collins untied the leather strap and unraveled the pouch. "They're my wood-carving tools."

"They what you used to make my wooden soldier?"

"Yep, and a whole lot of other things."

"But why you showing them to me?"

"That's the surprise." Collins was glad Shawn had said yes. He decided to get started right away, give Patrick a diversion, get his mind off his dad leaving. "How would you like to make something like that wooden soldier yourself someday?"

"I could never do that."

"You could if I taught you. Before your dad left, I asked him if I could teach you how to carve things with wood."

"You did? What did he say?"

"He said I could . . . but on one condition. That I teach you all the safety things I've learned so that you don't get hurt."

"How would you get hurt?"

He really doesn't know anything, Collins thought. Better take this real slow. "These tools are very sharp. Here, let me show you something. Come over here right under the light." Collins held out both hands. "Tell me what you see."

Patrick looked closely. "Fingers and thumbs."

"That's right, fingers and thumbs. How many?"

Patrick counted. "Eight fingers and two thumbs."

"And how old am I?"

"I don't know, a hundred?"

"No, but I'm real old," Collins said. "And I've been carving things in wood all these years, and I still have all my fingers."

Patrick didn't seem to get it. "See, Patrick, some of these tools are sharp enough to cut the ends of your fingers right off if you're not careful."

A look of horror came over Patrick's face. "That would be awful."

"Yes, it would. It would hurt really bad; it would bleed a lot, and you'd have to go to the hospital."

"I would?"

"And your daddy would be so mad at me, he wouldn't let me ever teach you another thing about carving."

"That would be bad."

"Look again at my fingers, even closer this time. Tell me what you see."

Patrick got his face within a few inches of his hands. "Lots of lines and cracks."

Collins laughed. "But do you see any scars?"

"No."

"That's your goal. To be so careful you never even get cut with these tools. For your whole life."

"I already don't want to get cut now."

"That's good, you're on the right track. Just one more lesson and we'll go in and get washed up for dinner. Bring me that little stick over there, the one with the bark still on it."

Patrick obeyed.

"Now, push down on that stick with your finger, real hard. Then push down on a finger on your other hand. How hard is that compared to the stick?"

"My finger's real smushy and the stick is real hard."

"Bring the stick here."

Patrick handed it to Collins, and with one motion, Collins sliced off a big section with one of the knives. "See that?"

"Wow," said Patrick.

"See what this knife can do? Imagine what it could do to your finger."

Patrick winced. "I don't want to. It scares me." He took a few steps back. "Maybe you shouldn't teach me yet."

"No, Patrick. It's okay to be afraid when danger is present. That's a good kind of fear, the kind of fear God gives us so we don't do stupid things."

"You'll teach me how to carve so I never get cut?"

"That's the plan. But just a little at a time. Right now, we better get ready for whatever Miss Townsend is cooking." He reached over and pulled on the light chain. As they walked toward the door, Collins said, "Let's keep this a secret, just between us for now."

"But I thought you said my dad said it was okay."

"He did. But I gotta think of a way to tell that to Miss Townsend and Mrs. Fortini."

"Okay," Patrick said. As they walked toward the kitchen, Patrick reached up and grabbed hold of Collins's hand, giving it a gentle squeeze.

Collins looked down, smiled, and squeezed back.

Twenty-four

The train arrived at Boston's South Station right on time. It was already dark. Shawn's instructions were to make his way through the terminal toward the center. There he should find his liaison officer, Lieutenant James Winston. He didn't have a picture, but the paper said Winston knew what Shawn looked like and would be holding a sign with his name. Shawn weaved his way through the multitude in that general direction.

He saw a number of military personnel, but no one standing still or holding a sign. He looked at his watch to confirm he wasn't late or early. He set his bag and briefcase on the floor, then laid his overcoat over them.

As he looked around, he noticed a photo machine off in the corner, one of those little booths where you get three pictures for fifteen cents. He suddenly remembered he'd forgotten to bring a picture of Patrick. He'd have to call Miss Townsend and fix that.

Fifteen more minutes passed.

He was just about to head to the men's room when he heard someone call his name from the front of the terminal. He turned and saw an officer waving, slicing his way through the crowd. Shawn smiled weakly and picked up his things.

"I'm so sorry, sir," the man said when he made it to Shawn. "Lieutenant Winston, James Winston." He looked to be about thirty, very fit and trim.

Shawn was just about to hold out his hand when Winston saluted. Shawn saluted back.

"It took me a little longer than I planned to grab a car from the pool. Thought it would give us more freedom than riding cabs everywhere. I've got it double parked out front, so we better hurry."

"Lead the way, Lieutenant."

"Better put on that coat, sir, it's a bit nippy outside."

As they made their way toward the doors, they heard a commotion behind them. Shawn turned and saw the crowd parting as they murmured and pointed. An MP led a number of shackled German soldiers through the terminal, shouting for people to clear the way. Most of the crowd just stared, some jeered and shouted insults. The Germans ignored them, their eyes fixed straight ahead, almost in defiance. Shawn noticed they were marching, though not doing the goose step he'd seen in so many newsreels.

Shawn backed out of the way to let them pass. Just then he noticed one who instantly reminded him of the young officer he'd killed back in Holland. He turned away.

"C'mon, sir. Let's follow them out the door."

When they got outside, Shawn saw two army trucks at the curb. "Where do you suppose they're from?" Shawn asked, pointing at the Germans.

"They're infantry guys. My guess is from the fighting in Italy."

"I didn't know we kept POWs in the States," Shawn said.

"They got a base filling up with them just outside of town a few miles. My car's just over there."

A minute later, Shawn and the lieutenant were at the car, a shiny black Studebaker Coupe. As Shawn walked his things to the trunk, a yellow cab pulled in behind them.

"Here, let me take that, sir." Winston tossed Shawn's bag and briefcase in the trunk and walked to Shawn's side to unlock the door. Shawn got in. It was freezing outside, but inside it was warm. The cabbie beeped his horn. "Don't blow a fuse, mac," Winston shouted. He got in, turned the car on, and inched his way into the flow of traffic around Dewey Square.

Shawn detected an accent. "From Chicago, Lieutenant?"

"Very good, sir. You been there?"

"No," Shawn said. "Just bunked with a guy from Chicago for a few months." Lieutenant Winston had a very engaging smile, one of those optimistic faces, a born salesman.

"I grew up there," Winston said. "Went to college there, but after I graduated I went to work for Colonel Simmons's marketing firm in New York. Course, he wasn't a colonel then. When the military asked him to sign on, he talked me into coming along. We've got uniforms and different titles, but it's like we're doing the same thing as before."

This sounded strange to Shawn. He wondered if Winston had ever even fired a gun. "I guess we all have to do our part."

The car stopped suddenly. Shawn grabbed the dashboard. "I'm sorry," Winston said. "The traffic around this place is nuts." He looked in the rearview mirror, then started moving again. "I know what you mean, what you said about doing our part. I thought about joining the navy or some infantry outfit, but Colonel Simmons talked me into this job. Said I've got a gift for this kind of thing, and it was my patriotic duty to do what I'm best at. I don't feel like that when I get around people like you, even when I watch the newsreels. But he can be pretty persuasive."

"I know," Shawn said. "So where we going? The hotel?"

"I'm hungry, thought we'd get a bite to eat, maybe have some fun at the same time."

Shawn liked the eating part of his answer. "So where we going?"

"Just a couple more blocks, a place called Scollay Square. Great night spots and bars, the whole place caters to the military. Dinner and a show, you know?"

"Lieutenant, to be honest I'm pretty tired. Know of any places that serve dinner without the show?"

"We won't stay there long, sir. Man's gotta eat, right? It's just a few more blocks from there to the hotel where we'll be staying."

How could Shawn say this? "When you say 'show,' are we talking about girlie shows?"

"Some of them. That a problem?"

"I'm guessing you haven't done any reading about me."

"Sir?"

"The colonel gave me a folder with a page about you. I guess he didn't give you one on me."

"He did, sir. But it didn't say much about your personal life. Mostly covered your war record."

"Okay. Let me explain just a couple of things. I'm not trying to make you feel bad here, but I'm a Christian. I mean . . . more than a guy that just goes to church. Girlie shows are something I try to avoid. And I'm not really interested in picking up girls. I just lost my wife in a car accident about a month ago—"

"I am *so* sorry, sir. I had no idea. If I did, I would have never considered bringing you here."

Winston turned right onto a wide road; cars seemed to be going every which way. The place was lit up like a miniature Times Square. "Scollay Square's just up ahead. I'll find a place to pull over. There's got to be someplace here that just serves a good meal."

"I appreciate it, Lieutenant."

He pulled up beside a gray Packard, left the car running, and got out. He talked to a fellow on the sidewalk dressed in navy garb, nodded several times, then smiled. He ran back to the car and got in. "Bingo, Major. That guy's been on leave here for over a week. Told me about a place up ahead on the left that's just about food, a cafeteria called the Waldorf. Let me park this thing and we'll be eating in no time."

"I really appreciate you going out of your way here."

"Don't thank me, sir. I'm here to help make things smooth. Now that I know the lay of the land, I'll plan accordingly."

After a few minutes riding around, someone pulled out. Winston wasted no time grabbing the spot. "That sailor said the food here's not the best but there's plenty of it. I'm picking up the tab, so order whatever you want."

"Sounds good," said Shawn. It really did. Two themes dominated his thoughts at the moment. He was starving and exhausted. "Where we staying tonight?"

"The Hotel Kenmore, sir. A really swank place, close to Fenway Park. It's where all the visiting teams stay when they play the Red Sox."

Winston was just about to turn the car off. "Before we go in," Shawn said, "I was reading over the schedule tomorrow on the train."

"Big day, our first rally."

"Right, but it said something about me giving some kind of fund-raising speech. There wasn't anything else about it in the folder."

"Don't sweat it, sir. That's my specialty. Got the thing written out, really just a single paragraph. I'll give it to you at the hotel."

"So what, I just get up and read it?"

"No. We don't have anything else scheduled tonight. I figured you could take some time to memorize it. Not word for word, just close. I'll be introducing you to the crowd before each rally, then you just come out and say your bit. Won't take five minutes."

"Any other surprises I should know about?"

Winston thought a moment. "Don't think so. You read about the radio and newspaper interviews tomorrow, before the rally?"

"No."

"Not a big deal. I've written up some things you can say, and I'll be giving all the interviewers the skinny on what questions they can and cannot ask. It will all be very controlled. But we'll make it come off like it's all spontaneous and patriotic. After doing a few of these, you'll be able to pull it off in your sleep."

Great, Shawn thought.

Let the games begin.

⸎

A few hours later in Allingdale, Shawn's father was ready for bed. It was early, a full hour before his usual bedtime. Miss Townsend had already cleaned up the kitchen, got Patrick ready for bed, and headed next door. Collins had to admit, it was a passable dinner. Not quite up to Mrs. Fortini's cooking, but it gave him a good feeling about his immediate future.

He had planned to get comfortable in his chair and listen to *The Burns and Allen Show*, but he was just too tired. He stood at the foot of the stairs and gave the living area a quick once-over. Everything was in place. Patrick was already asleep upstairs. He eyed the top of the stairway. Lately it seemed further and further away, like climbing a steep hill. Some nights he entertained the idea of just sleeping downstairs on the davenport.

He took a deep breath and started putting one foot in front of the other. Only way to do it. About halfway up, he couldn't believe it, but he had to stop and catch his breath. He held the banister with one hand, the other hand on his knee. His head was down. He could feel his chest beating hard, like he'd just run a city block. This is ridiculous, he thought.

He looked up, tried to clear his head, but the stairway was moving. He waited a moment, straightened up, then lifted his foot toward the next step. Instead of moving forward, he felt himself falling back. He *was* falling back. He reached for the banister but only brushed it with his fingertips.

"Oh no."

For a moment he was in the air, a sickening feeling. The next moment he hit hard on the wood landing. His head banged against the closet door. Something cracked. From the inside. He didn't hear well, but he heard that. An excruciating pain rushed up from just below his hip, filling his whole body.

He yelled out loud, there was just no stopping it.

As he lay there, he wondered . . . was he about to die? He couldn't imagine ever moving from this spot. Just then, from the top of the stairwell, a light turned on.

"Grandpa? Are you all right?"

Twenty-five

The hospital smelled terrible. The seats were hard. The waiting room cold. The look on every face one of fear or dread. Katherine was sure hers was no exception. The waiting was killing her. She got up to check with the nursing staff again. They had said the doctor would tell them something over an hour ago.

"Where you going, Miss Townsend?" Patrick asked. He had such a rough night. None of them slept a wink.

"I'm just going to ask the nurse something. I'll be right back. See them right over there?"

He nodded.

"Don't worry, Patrick," Mrs. Fortini said, patting his hand. "Would you like something to eat?"

"No, thank you."

"You haven't had any breakfast."

"I'm okay. I just wanna see Grandpa."

"Well, you remember, dear, they don't allow children in," said Mrs. Fortini. "Which is really very stupid, if you ask me," she whispered. "Especially nice ones like you."

Katherine walked toward the nurses' station. They had rushed Collins to the hospital last night, the poor thing. He was in so much pain. She'd felt so helpless. When the ambulance came, it awakened the entire neighborhood. Everyone came out to view the spectacle. When they started wheeling the stretcher down the driveway, Collins pulled the sheet over his head so he wouldn't have to see them staring. The neighbors out by the sidewalk, seeing this, were certain he had died, and that rumor had begun to spread.

She, Mrs. Fortini, and poor little Patrick followed the ambulance to the hospital until it lost them going through a traffic light. They'd gotten there just in time to see two men in white coats rolling him past a set of swinging double doors.

That was the last they had seen of him.

After an hour, a doctor had come out, but only to say Collins had suffered a concussion and a severe break in his left leg. The doctor said he had to go, they were set to work on his leg in a few minutes. The three of them were left stranded in the waiting room until after midnight. Finally a nurse insisted they leave. She said there'd be no more news about Collins until morning.

That morning they had rushed back to the hospital just after sunrise.

"Excuse me, ma'am," Katherine said, "could I speak with you a moment?" Katherine saw the head nurse eyeing her from the side, pretending she wasn't there. Katherine waved her hand and leaned over the counter. "Hello? I'm sorry to be so bold, but we've had no word about Mr. Collins since last night."

The nurse spun in her chair and stood up. She was way too tall for a woman, had to be in her late forties, Katherine thought. She had dark hair, poorly dyed, and a face that looked like it had never smiled.

"Since you called him Mr. Collins, can I assume you're not a member of the family?"

"Well, no," Katherine said. "But I—"

"Hospital rules. Can't give out patient information to non-family members." She seemed to enjoy saying this. "That his wife over there?" she asked, pointing to Mrs. Fortini.

"No, his wife passed away. That's Mrs. Fortini, his next-door neighbor."

"So Mr. Collins has no family members present?"

It may have been the dim lighting, but her eyes looked black as night. "That's his grandson sitting next to her."

"Well, we can't likely give out information to a small boy, can we?" She started to turn, heading back to her chair.

Before she did, Katherine saw the name "Connelly" stitched above her pocket. "Listen, Miss *Connelly*, we're all the family Mr. Collins has in town. His son is Major Shawn Collins, a big war hero. Perhaps you've heard of him? He's been in the newspapers and on the radio almost every day the last two weeks. Right now, he's in Boston doing a big War Bond rally with a bunch of Hollywood stars. What do you think the press would say about you treating his father and son this way?"

"I beg your pardon?"

"No . . . I beg *your* pardon. I could call the press right now and just mention Major Collins's name and what happened last night. The lobby downstairs would be filled with reporters. Do I need to do that to get you to walk through those double doors and get a doctor out here to talk to us?"

Anger flashed across the nurse's face, but only for an instant. She quickly forced an insincere smile. "I'm sure that won't be necessary. Let me go see what I can find out."

Katherine saw the two other nurses whispering as their commander hurried away. When she smiled at them, they both looked away. She headed back to the waiting room. When she cleared the doorway, Mrs. Fortini stood and clapped gently.

"Very nice, Katherine. You do have a way of getting things done."

She looked at Patrick. He just smiled. He looked so tired. "Well, let's see if we get anyone to finally get out here." She sat down and looked toward the double doors.

"Were you ever able to get through to Shawn?" Mrs. Fortini asked.

"No. I don't know where he's staying in Boston. I've asked my friend Shirley at work to call that colonel Shawn visited two weeks ago at the Pentagon. He must know."

"He'll feel terrible not being here," said Mrs. Fortini.

"You think Grandpa is going to be all right?"

"I'm sure he'll be fine," Katherine said. Mrs. Fortini put her arm around Patrick and drew him close.

Katherine hoped she sounded convincing. He'd looked so terrible last night.

✑

By lunchtime they had still not been able to reach Shawn, but at least they knew what hotel he was staying at—the Kenmore. Katherine was about to place the call. They were back at Mrs. Fortini's. Patrick was upstairs taking a nap, Mrs. Fortini cleaning up the kitchen.

Before they'd left the hospital, the doctor finally did come out but only revealed a few more details than they had learned the night before. There was nothing life threatening about Collins's injuries, but then the doctor paused in an unsettling way. When Katherine asked about it, he admitted there was something else, something unexpected that came up, but he insisted he would only talk about it with Shawn. He quickly changed the subject, talking about the broken leg, saying he'd be in a cast for at least two months; because of his age, maybe longer. His concussion was less serious than they'd feared, but something they still needed to monitor closely over the next few weeks. He said the nurses would go over a list of things someone must take responsibility for if Collins were to heal properly once he came home. They allowed Katherine and Mrs. Fortini in for a brief visit. Neither thought he'd ever remember; he was so sedated.

His leg was wrapped in a cast from his toes to his hip, and his head covered in bandages like a mummy. His left eye was swollen and bruised. Shawn would be so upset to see him like this. She dialed the number Shirley had given her.

"Hotel Kenmore, front desk, how can I help you?"

"I'm trying to reach a Major Collins, he's part of the War Bond tour. I was told he was booked into your hotel last night."

"Let me check . . . yes, I see it, room 504."

"Could I please speak with him? It's very important. I'm his nanny."

"Excuse me?"

"I don't mean *his* nanny, I'm his son's nanny. Anyway, his father fell down the steps last night. He's in the hospital."

"How awful."

"I really need to speak with him."

"I'll ring you through to his room."

Katherine waited for what seemed too long a time. "I'm sorry, ma'am, there's been no answer. I tried twice. Want to leave a message in his box?"

"I guess we'll have to."

"Ready whenever you are."

"Just say . . . Major Collins, please call Mrs. Fortini's right away. Your dad fell on the stairs last night. In the hospital. Broken leg and concussion. Everyone else is fine. Doctor wants to speak with you about something else but won't tell us what. Sign it 'Miss Townsend.' Got it?"

"Think so, let me read it back." She did.

"Close enough. Thanks so much."

Katherine hung up and went into the kitchen to update Mrs. Fortini, then wondered again what the doctor was hiding from them.

⁂

One moment later, Lieutenant Winston stepped out of the Hotel Kenmore elevator into the crowded lobby. Shawn was right behind him. Almost everyone was headed out the front door, on their way to Fenway Park for the big rally. The War Bond folks occupied the top three floors, the finest suites reserved for the stars.

They followed the stream of band members and dancers moving slowly through the lobby. Things got a little less congested when he got to the center as various ones headed to the front desk.

"Where you going, Lieutenant?" Major Collins asked.

"I'll be right there, sir, just checking for messages."

"Can I help you, sir?" a blonde at the front desk asked.

"Any messages for room 505?"

"Let me check."

Winston watched her touch her finger on an empty slot with his room number right below it. But he saw a white slip of paper in the slot beside it, Major Collins's room. "Say, could you give me the message there in room 504?"

"But that's not your room, sir," she said.

"No, it's Major Collins's. I'll take it to him. I'm his aide."

"I guess that would be okay."

"Sure it is, that's him standing right over there by that plant."

"Here it is."

Winston stepped off to the side, then turned so that his back faced Major Collins and read the note from Miss Townsend. "That's just great," he muttered. He folded it and put it in his coat pocket. He walked quickly toward the major, all nonchalant.

"Any messages?" the major asked.

"Nothing that can't wait. We better go." They waited for a break in the crowd then headed out the door. Winston had worked with the colonel long enough to know how he'd react to this news.

The show must go on.

Twenty-six

War Bond rally. Need to raise millions for the war effort. Your country needs you now. Big bands. Patriotic songs. Hedy Lamarr and Bette Davis . . . who wouldn't want this assignment. War hero. These thoughts tried to occupy Shawn's mind, but he didn't let them in. He had barely begun this new tour of duty and was already tired of it.

Lieutenant Winston was driving the last few blocks from the Hotel Kenmore to Fenway Park, chatting all the while about something. "We'll be parking and entering the field at the same place the celebrities are," he said.

Wasn't that something.

As they pulled alongside the big brick entrance, the crowd forced the caravan into a single lane. The two Cadillac limousines they were following came to a stop. The crowd went wild. Everyone waved little American flags, smiling, laughing, pointing. They looked in Shawn's car with the same enthusiasm as they did the limos. He took some joy at the instant disappointment on their faces as they realized there was no one in the car worth looking at.

He wished he could have talked with Patrick back at the hotel, but no one had answered when he called. Patrick was probably still at school, but Shawn hoped he could at least have talked with his dad, if only a minute. He smiled at the thought. He'd never talked with his dad for an entire minute on the phone before. His dad hated the thing.

"So how'd you do with the speech, sir, you know the bit I wrote up for you?" asked Lieutenant Winston.

Shawn couldn't believe what he'd read. There wasn't a single phrase that sounded like him. Winston had actually put the word *swell* in the paragraph three times. "Got it memorized," Shawn said.

"You did just fine with the interviews this morning, sir. Yes and no answers, and a few well-placed clichés. Let them do all the talking. Now, don't get spooked about the crowds when you first take the stage. We go out near the end of the rally. By then, they'll be so worked up they'll clap at everything you say."

"How will I know when it's my turn?"

"I go first, introduce you, then call you out. It'll be over before you know it. Then we head back to the hotel, grab some chow, and you can either join me tonight back at Scollay Square or just hang out at the Kenmore. They got radios in every room, a movie theater a block away. Tomorrow we get on the train with everyone else and head for Providence, Rhode Island."

The car stopped, and they got out. Shawn heard the crowd roar to life up ahead. The limousine car door opened, and out stepped Bette Davis. Shawn couldn't believe it. There she was. Bette Davis in a big fur coat, standing right there, not fifty feet in front of him. She smiled and waved to her fans. People held out programs and slips of paper for autographs, but a well-dressed man blocked the way. Sorry, but they were in a hurry, he said over and over. The people in line beside Shawn's car pressed forward, trying to get a glimpse.

"Believe it or not," Winston said, "a lot of folks will be treating you that way after today."

"Hope not," Shawn said. It sounded absurd. They followed the entourage of stars and staff along a walkway leading into the stadium. Shawn could already hear a band playing "Don't Sit Under the Apple Tree"; the crowd inside instantly reacted with applause.

"Sounds like the Andrews Sisters are about to sing," said Winston, hurrying forward. "I love this job."

∽

A temporary stage had been built between the pitcher's mound and second base, facing the stands. The stage was surrounded by posters featuring all the popular War Bond slogans and dozens of American flags. To get to the area set aside for performers, they had to walk onto the field and come in behind the platform. But no one paid any attention to them. All eyes were on the stage.

Shawn had listened to so many Red Sox games on the radio, almost every time they played the Phillies. But he'd never been to Fenway Park before. As they neared the holding area, he stopped and took a panoramic view. So many things he'd only imagined in his mind. The odd shape of the field itself, the way the bleachers didn't start until centerfield then swooped upward like a hill. The famous clock in right field, the covered stands that wrapped back around toward home plate. He looked up to the press boxes where they called the games.

The stadium was only half full, but Shawn guessed there were still ten thousand people here. Some comedian Shawn didn't recognize followed the Andrews Sisters and was now working the crowd.

"Over here, Major," said Lieutenant Winston. "Behind

this curtain. It's out of the chill. You can still see everything going on, maybe even better."

Shawn followed. As he got closer, Winston whispered, "Look over there . . . can you believe it? Hedy Lamarr. What a dish."

Shawn looked to the opposite backstage area. She was a beautiful woman, dressed in a stunning black gown. Her eyes looked toward the stage, watching the comedian. Several men dressed in tuxedos and top hats surrounded her. Her act must be next.

"Can you believe we get to do this?"

"How much longer till we go on?"

Winston looked at his watch. "We're right on schedule. Miss Lamarr will go out, then Bette Davis, then some other singer—I forget who—then us."

Shawn found a seat off to the side and pulled out his speech. It really wasn't very long. He should be able to pull it off. It was just . . . not him. But this was supposed to get the good people of America to part with their money, and that was his new assignment. On one level, Shawn had made peace with the idea that raising money was a necessary task. Before talking to Colonel Simmons, he'd never given it a second thought, but obviously somebody had to do this. He just wished it was somebody, anybody else but him.

What were MacReady and Manzini doing right now, he wondered.

Without effort or intention, his mind returned to England. The sights and sounds around him faded to the fringe. He replayed the moment on their last mission when he and MacReady knew their plane was doomed. Felt the tension and fear mount as they pulled away from the formation. Heard the staccato sounds of machine gun fire smacking into the fuselage, the screams of his men wounded by cannon shells and shrapnel.

The scene switched. He was coming in for the beach landing in Holland, the uneasy feeling when he cut the engines and the plane glided in silence just inches above the sand. Followed by the wrenching, crunching sound of grinding metal as *Mama's Kitchen* tore into the beach, the roar of water washing over the starboard wing, the feeling they might start cartwheeling and break apart any second.

Now he was peeking in Mr. Beekman's window, watching the German soldier beating on the poor old man. A moment later he was sitting on top of that same soldier, pulling his own knife out of his back. Then with tears in his eyes, he was hitting Mr. Beekman. He could actually feel Beekman's face give way beneath his knuckles. How could he have done such things?

"Major?"

These were the images of war. These were the things men do when forced to fight for liberty and freedom. There wasn't anything swell about it.

"Excuse me, Major."

Now Shawn felt the tapping on his shoulder. He looked up. It was Lieutenant Winston. The next thing he heard was an eruption of laughter followed by applause. An announcer's voice proclaimed, "Isn't she something, folks?"

Where was he?

"We're on in just a minute, sir. Are you okay?"

Shawn inhaled deeply and stood up. "Fine. I'm ready." He looked down at his speech.

"Bette Davis and that comedian surprised everyone with an encore," said Winston. "We're on. I'll go out. Just wait for my cue. I'll make it real obvious."

Shawn followed the lieutenant to the edge of the curtain. Bette Davis shouted some War Bond slogan into the microphone, then walked off toward the opposite side, turning and waving as the crowd cheered. The band kicked in with some transition music, and out walked Lieutenant Winston, facing the crowd like he had been born in showbiz. No script or notes.

He walked right up to the mike and said, "Good afternoon, ladies and gentleman. I'm Lieutenant James Winston, and I'm here this afternoon to introduce a very special guest." He looked down at the soldiers in the first several rows. "How many of you guys have seen combat yet? Anyone?" No one raised a hand. "I'm sure when the time comes, you'll do your country proud." The crowd applauded. "I have the privilege of traveling with a real-life war hero. Backstage is a man who has not only seen combat but been in the thick of things many times."

Looking up to the crowd, he said, "How many of you have watched our brave boys flying those big bombers on the newsreels?" Almost everyone raised their hands, thousands clapped to voice their answer. "Well, our special guest this afternoon was a pilot on one of those bombers. He's flown eighteen missions into enemy territory, taking the war to Hitler and the Nazis for you and me. He's seen the things you and I have watched in the safety of our theaters up close and firsthand . . . and lived to tell the tale. But just barely."

The crowd grew very quiet. "On his last mission, his plane got all shot up, but not before they'd dropped all their bombs and shot down several enemy planes. Two of his crew were killed, two wounded. One engine was smoking, the other completely dead. They had to pull out of formation; the plane that had served them so well just could not keep up anymore. Usually, this spells the end for any bomber crew. They either get shot down and killed or captured as POWs . . . if they're lucky."

Winston allowed a moment of silence to linger. "But not Major Collins. Single-handedly, he flew his damaged bomber safely out of harm's way, avoiding enemy planes, then crash-landed it deep within enemy territory. He guided his crew out of the plane, fought in hand-to-hand combat with a Nazi patrol, stole a boat, and led the rest of his crew safely across the English Channel. And he did all this in a single day." The crowd started to applaud. "Please join me in welcoming Major Shawn Collins of the United States Army Air Corps, a candidate for the highest military honor our nation bestows—the Medal of Honor."

The applause was deafening. People were standing on their feet. Lieutenant Winston motioned for Shawn to come out, and Shawn obeyed.

He was shaking as he stood next to Winston, who quickly backed out of the way, leaving Shawn alone at the microphone. Shawn looked around, up and down, back and forth, trying to catch each area of the crowd with a glance. He repeated the first several lines in his head as the noise from the crowd finally subsided and people began to take their seats.

"I don't know what to say," he began. "Please understand, I don't feel like a hero. To me, I was just doing my duty." The crowd cheered and clapped. Shawn tried to get back to his prepared speech. "All the men I served with were heroes, a really swell bunch of guys. All doing their duty for God and country. You would be proud of every single one of them." Some light applause. "But they can't fight this war alone. Every one of us has to do our part. We're in this thing together."

It all sounded so hollow and unreal, and what followed was just more of the same. He paused as he looked down at the soldiers directly in front of him. None of these guys knew what they were getting into. He couldn't fill their heads with a string of empty slogans and clichés.

"You guys here in the front," Shawn said. "I do believe when the time comes you will do your part. You know why? Because you love this country and you believe in what we're fighting for." He looked up into the stands. "I know you folks care just as much, and if you could, many of you would be right there, fighting the Nazis with us overseas. You're probably worried sick about your sons, and brothers, and uncles, and—some of you kids—your dads. I got a little boy at home who was worried sick about me, and praying every night."

The crowd got very quiet again. "We don't know how long it will take to win this war. I hope it's soon. But we will prevail. We have to, because justice is on our side. And I believe God is on our side. We're fighting an enemy that hates freedom and wants to take our freedom away. Wherever they go, they kill and crush and destroy anything that stands in their way. Now you can't be over there fighting the Nazis or the Japanese with us. That's our job. And our boys overseas are doing their job every day. Just like these boys down here will do when their time comes." Shawn saw all the soldiers in front of him nodding their heads in agreement.

"But I didn't realize until I came home a little while ago just how much you folks here at home are doing. All the sacrifices you're making with the rationing and going without so many things for us. So that we can have the things we need to fight this war. And believe it or not . . . buying War Bonds is part of that fight. The money you give goes to buying us the guns and ammo and bombers and bombs we need to take this war to Hitler and Tojo. You keep giving . . . as much as you can spare, and our boys will keep giving . . . even their lives if they have to."

He was done.

He stepped back from the mike. Every single man, woman, and child in the stadium instantly rose to their feet, cheering and clapping louder than they had all afternoon. Lieutenant Winston walked back up to the microphone and shouted, "Didn't I tell ya? What a guy. Thank you, Major Collins, for serving your country so well."

The band began to play as the applause continued. Winston led Shawn off the stage. Shawn noticed every eye backstage was glued on him: the female dancers, the men in tuxedos and top hats. Even the movie stars.

Lieutenant Winston loudly whispered, "I hope you can remember everything you just said. I think we should go with that from now on." The band continued to play as the emcee wrapped things up with a few more patriotic thoughts.

Backstage, Shawn walked over to a chair where he laid his overcoat. Reporters rushed the platform steps, flashing their cameras over and over again, yelling out his name, firing off a string of questions. As he turned from the cameras, he was stunned to see Hedy Lamarr and Bette Davis standing right in front of him. Behind them a half dozen dancers still in their costumes.

Miss Lamarr reached out her hand and took hold of Shawn's, then said, "Major, I just want you to know . . . it's an honor to share the stage with you. Thank you for all you've done for our country, and for what you just said." Miss Davis patted him on the shoulder and smiled.

Suddenly, more camera flashes.

"Thank you," Shawn said. "I don't know what to say . . . I love your movies, both of you." They smiled and walked away, and several reporters followed after them.

"I might need some help getting you out of here," said Lieutenant Winston. He started to put his overcoat on.

Shawn did the same. As the lieutenant whipped the coat around his shoulders, a piece of white folded paper fell out of the pocket.

When it landed, Shawn noticed something written on it. His name.

Twenty-seven

Lieutenant Winston quickly reached down and snatched the paper. He looked at Shawn as he straightened up. Shawn was furious. Now wasn't the time to confront this, but he walked right up to him and whispered, "Get me out of here . . . now."

"Yes, sir, Major."

Shawn walked to the rear edge of the platform. The stairs were still crowded with reporters and fans. Some actually held out programs and pens, asking for his autograph. Winston came up behind him and whispered, "How about you just sign a few, then I'll pull you away?"

Shawn looked at their faces, so full of enthusiasm. It felt bizarre, but he reached out and began signing his name, over and over again. Each time he did, more papers were thrust in his face.

"Thank you, Major."

"We're so proud of you."

"A real hero."

"Your parents must be so proud."

Just then, Winston came up and said loudly, "Sorry, folks, duty calls. Gotta get Major Collins on to his next stop. Sorry."

He gently pushed Shawn forward, and Shawn feigned reluctance as he gave back the last signed program of the day. Winston walked past him, clearing the way, and Shawn followed right behind.

A few minutes later they were in the car. Shawn waited until they drove away from the ball field. "No messages, eh, Lieutenant?"

"I didn't say that, sir. I said nothing that can't wait."

"I thought you were talking about messages for you."

"I didn't say that."

"So that's how it's going to be? You're mincing words, Lieutenant. In the future, I'll get my own messages, is that clear?"

"But Major—"

"That's not a suggestion. Now hand it over."

"I think you should wait till we get to the hotel, sir."

"I think you better give me that message right now."

Winston hesitated.

"Lieutenant!"

"Sir, I've read the message, I know what it says."

"But I don't."

"Let me pull over."

"Why?"

"So you don't punch me while I'm driving, and we crash the car."

∾

After Shawn had read the note, he did have to get out of the car to keep himself from smacking Lieutenant Winston. They had pulled onto a neighborhood street. Shawn looked up at a woman rocking a baby on a porch and smiled.

Lieutenant Winston yelled through the open door. "I'm sorry, Major. I really am, but I'm just doing what Colonel Simmons would have wanted."

Shawn bent over and yelled back through the window, as quietly as he could, "The colonel would have wanted you to keep an urgent personal message from me? That's what you're saying?"

"That's exactly what I'm saying, sir. At least until after the rally. I was going to give it to you as soon as we got back to the hotel. I promise."

"Lieutenant, my father has been lying in a hospital and my family has been trying to reach me, since who knows when."

"Exactly. And look how upset you are."

"I'm upset because of what you did."

"Sir, can you really imagine doing what you just did back there and saying what you just said if I'd given you this note before the rally?"

Shawn stood up so he wouldn't have to see Winston's face, but he knew he was right.

Winston continued. "What difference would it make if you found out about this an hour ago or a few minutes ago? There's nothing you could have done differently."

"I could have called."

"I thought you said you did call home but no one answered."

That was true. "All right," Shawn said as he got back in the car.

"You're not going to hit me?"

"Let's just get back so I can call. I'm going to need to make arrangements to get back to Philly right away."

Lieutenant Winston did not immediately reply. They drove in silence for several minutes. Shawn saw the Hotel Kenmore come into view.

"Sir," Winston began, "may I suggest you call Colonel Simmons first before you call home?"

"Why, Lieutenant?"

"Because I can't see him granting that request. In fact, I know he won't."

"What request?"

"He won't let you go home."

℮

Shawn asked the hotel operator to try one more time. He'd been calling his father's house for over an hour. He was glad to have some time alone in his room to cool down.

Lieutenant Winston had been right about Colonel Simmons. It had been a very short conversation. Shawn made his appeal and was immediately shot down. Simmons reminded him that his orders at this moment were no less binding than when his CO in England sent him out to bomb a factory. It didn't matter what Shawn thought about the difference. He'd pointed out that his father was not dead. He had a broken leg and a concussion. He was in good hands at a decent hospital and Shawn had a capable young woman looking after his son.

End of discussion.

The operator came back. "I'm sorry, Major. Still no answer."

Shawn got an idea. "Thank you, but listen . . . I've got a five-dollar bill here with your name on it, if you can solve a problem for me."

"Really? What can I do?"

He gave her Mrs. Fortini's information and asked if she could somehow get ahold of her. Five minutes went by. Shawn couldn't stop pacing. Finally, the phone rang.

"Major, this is the operator. I have a Miss Townsend on the line. She says she's at the woman's house you asked me to reach."

"Thank you so much. I wasn't kidding about the money."

"Happy to help, sir. Here she is." Shawn heard a click.

"Major Collins?"

"Katherine, is that you?"

"Yes, we've been trying to reach you. Did you get my note?"

"I did, just about an hour ago. How's my father? Any more news?"

"We went back to see him just a little while ago. Mrs. Fortini is still there. She wanted to stay until visiting hours were over, at about 6:00. I brought Patrick home to get him some dinner."

"How's he holding up?"

Katherine didn't respond.

"Are you okay?"

"I'm sorry, sir. He's seems to be doing just fine. I'm not so sure I am."

"What's wrong?"

"I felt so bad for him. Patrick found him at the foot of the stairs last night. He must have been so scared. But you would have been so proud of him, the way he handled everything."

Shawn was relieved to hear it. "He bounces back pretty quick."

"He does," she said. "Right now, he's upstairs washing his hands. They're keeping your dad a few nights, mainly because of his head injury, so we're keeping Patrick here with us."

"That's a good idea."

"Are you . . . are you coming home?"

Now Shawn hesitated. A wall of emotions welled up inside him. Anger, guilt, fear for his father, some more anger, some more guilt. "They won't let me," he said.

"What?"

"I've been told since it's not life threatening, it's not an emergency. Katherine, I'm . . . I can't stand being stuck up here right now."

"I'm sorry, Major. That is just so wrong."

"It feels wrong to me."

"Did you call the doctor yet?"

"No, I wanted to call you first . . . see how you all are doing."

"You want me to get Patrick?"

"No, I'll call back a little later, when I'm not so upset."

"He will be so glad."

"I wish I could be there . . . but I'm glad you are. And Mrs. Fortini. Well, I better go so I can call the doctor."

"There's something he's not telling us about your dad," she said. "He said he'd only talk about it with you."

"I'll call right now, then let you know what's up when I call Patrick later."

Before hanging up, Shawn asked Katherine to get a picture of Patrick for him. He dialed the hospital number, and in a few minutes was talking with his father's physician, Dr. Matthews.

"Thank you, Doctor, for taking my call. Did the operator tell you who I am?"

"She did, Major. Sorry to interrupt you with bad news. Miss Townsend told me about the War Bond tour."

"Is the news really that bad? She said you wouldn't tell her or Mrs. Fortini."

"It's just hospital policy, especially with news like this." Dr. Matthews paused. "I haven't even told your father yet."

"What is it, what's wrong?"

"It's his heart, Major. He didn't have a heart attack, not exactly. But he's on the verge of one. I'm still running tests, but my preliminary findings are not good."

"Is he . . . dying?"

"In a way, yes. Maybe not today or tomorrow, but I don't think his heart can hold out too much longer. Maybe a year if he behaves, a few months if he won't."

 perm

After Katherine hung up with Shawn, she felt so much better. At first, she wasn't sure why, because, really, nothing had changed. She cleaned up the kitchen, replaying the telephone conversation in her mind. Then her mood change became clear.

Several times as they talked, Shawn—Major Collins—had called her by her first name. He hadn't done that since their conversation back at the Crystal Tea Room in Wanamaker's, when he'd announced he wanted to keep the relationship strictly professional. But she was certain . . . he had only called her Miss Townsend one time in the conversation. His first words: "Katherine, is that you?"

Oh, you idiot, she thought. Sometimes you are so pathetic. Just then, the telephone rang again. Could it be Shawn calling back? She picked it up quickly.

"Is this the Townsend residence?"

Townsend residence? she thought. "No, this is the Fortini residence. May I ask who's calling?"

"It's Al Baker, Captain Albert Baker. Who's this?"

"I'm Katherine Townsend, but this isn't my place." She wondered, *Who is Al Baker?*

"Must have gotten my lines crossed. Anyway, Miss Townsend, I don't know if you remember me. We met at the Crystal Tea Room a little while ago. Shawn introduced us."

Now it was beginning to click. "I do remember you, Captain."

"Please, call me Al."

She really didn't want to do that. "You and Shawn flew together or something, right?"

"That's right. I was at the Tea Room visiting some relatives who live in Philly. Anyway, I'm getting shipped back to England soon. But I'm just across the river here in Jersey. I was wondering if you'd like to join me for lunch tomorrow, back at the Tea Room?"

Katherine was not prepared for this. "Tomorrow's not a good time for me."

"How about the next day? Or if you'd like, I could pick you up for dinner. You name the place."

Katherine took a deep breath. "I'm really sorry, Captain Baker. But I'm really not interested in starting a relationship right now. It's nothing personal."

"I see. You seeing someone else?"

"No, it's not that. It's kind of hard to explain. Maybe when you're back in the States again, things will be different. But thanks for asking."

"Not a problem. It was great meeting you, Katherine. Hope we meet again."

After he hung up, she berated herself for not having the backbone to just say no, plain and simple, without leaving the door open for later. Maybe Captain Al Baker would get stuck in England for a long time.

Long enough to forget all about her.

Twenty-eight

It was Sunday morning. Katherine was as nervous as she could be. She was going to church, actually escorting Patrick to church per Major Collins's instructions. Katherine hadn't set foot in a church since she was a little girl. What few memories she had were not pleasant.

Over the last several days, Shawn's father had continued to mend, but he was still in the hospital. Now there was the added worry of his heart condition. Katherine had missed Shawn's call about this, but he'd told Mrs. Fortini what the doctor said. For now, they were to keep Mr. Collins in the dark. No point in upsetting him, and, between the cast and concussion, he couldn't get into too much trouble.

Shawn had called each day, mostly to talk to Patrick and check on his father. But he did share a few tidbits about his travels. The War Bond tour had already been to Providence, and the crew was now riding the train to somewhere else. Yesterday, he told Mrs. Fortini that Bing Crosby was supposed to join them in New York City. "You better get me that autograph," she'd said.

Katherine looked at her watch; it was almost time to leave. "Patrick, are you ready?" she called up the stairs.

"Almost, just one more thing."

She looked at a newspaper on the coffee table. Mrs. Fortini had bought a small stack the day after Shawn's first big rally in Boston. She'd already given most of them away. This last one was for the scrapbook. Shawn made the front page of the *Philadelphia Inquirer*. It was on the bottom half, but it included his picture.

She walked over and turned the paper upside down. She hated the picture.

It was silly, and she knew it. But there was Shawn, for the whole world to see, with Hedy Lamarr, one of the most beautiful actresses in Hollywood, holding his hands. Beside her stood Bette Davis. Behind them, six beautiful young women wearing feathery costumes, faces all smiley and full of excitement. Shawn was the reason. Katherine counted three of them looking at Shawn that certain way.

She heard Patrick's footsteps coming downstairs.

"All ready," he said.

Why is he so excited about going to church? she thought. You'd think he was going to the zoo. "You look very nice."

"I do?"

"A handsome little man. What's that book?"

"It's my children's Bible. The church I used to go to gave it to me."

"Your father said the church we're going to this morning is a lot like your old one. Is everyone supposed to bring a Bible?"

"I think so," Patrick said. "Don't you have one?"

"No, but that's okay. If I need one, I can get one before next Sunday."

"Want to use mine?" he asked.

She bent down and looked in his eyes. She wanted to hug

him but remembered Shawn's warning about getting too close. "Thank you, Patrick. But you keep it. I'll be okay."

"Where's Mrs. Fortini?"

"She's already left, to go to her church. We'll meet back here for lunch, then maybe go visit your grandpa in the hospital."

"I wished they'd let me see him."

"I know, Patrick. I wish you could too."

They put on their coats and hats and headed out the door. It was less than a mile to the church, but it was cold and overcast, so they drove. As they arrived at the intersection where the church stood, Katherine saw dozens of people heading there from all over the neighborhood. With so many walking, she quickly found a parking space a few houses down the street.

"Is this it?" asked Patrick.

"This is it." She had no idea what to expect and wished she possessed an inkling of the zeal she saw in Patrick's eyes. They got out and joined the flow of people walking toward the building. Several of them smiled and greeted them. As they climbed the front steps, a middle-aged woman with a pleasant smile walked right up to them and reached out her hand. "Is this your first Sunday?" she asked.

"Yes," said Katherine. "This young man is Patrick Collins. I'm Katherine Townsend, his nanny."

"I'm Sadie Robbins, and I've been coming here since I was his age. My husband's a deacon. He's already inside." They shook hands. "How old are you, Patrick?"

"Seven."

"Miss Townsend, if you'd like, Patrick could stay with you for the service, or he could go to our children's service."

"Where is that?"

"It's here, in another room around the corner. I could

take you there and let him see it, then you can decide what you'd like to do."

"Thank you," Katherine said. They followed the woman along a sidewalk toward another wing of the church. It looked like a small school.

Patrick tugged her hand. "I want to stay with you," he whispered.

"If that's what you want, that's okay," she whispered back.

But as soon as they walked through the doorway, Patrick saw about ten children his own age sitting around a large table. One little redheaded boy turned and saw them. His face lit up. "Patrick," he shouted.

"Tommy?" Patrick shouted back. "You go here?"

Tommy ran over and stopped just inches from them. "Yep. Are you coming here now?"

"Can I?" he asked Katherine. "Tommy's in my class at school."

Katherine looked at Mrs. Robbins. "They sing the same hymns we do," Mrs. Robbins said, "then one of the men in the church teaches them lessons from the Bible they can understand. Their service ends the same time as ours, and no one will release him until you come for him."

"Is that what you want, Patrick? Because you can stay with me."

Patrick nodded. "I'll be okay." He ran off with Tommy to join the others.

"Thank you, Mrs. Robbins."

"Well, I've got to get back," she said. "I'll see you inside."

Katherine watched her walk around the corner toward the front doors. It suddenly dawned on her: she could leave right now and just come back for Patrick when the service ended. Major Collins didn't say *she* had to go to church, just that she would bring Patrick. At the time, she didn't know they had a children's service. She assumed he'd be sitting next to her in the pew, forcing her to sit through the entire thing.

◦∕◦

After fumbling her way through the third song from the hymnal, Katherine sat down with the rest of the congregation. She had wrestled with herself in the car for five minutes then snuck in after the service had begun, found plenty of room on the back row. She just didn't feel right leaving Patrick alone at a strange place. What if he got nervous and came looking for her? He'd be terrified if she wasn't there. Besides, these people weren't all that bad. She could already tell they were nothing like the people at the church she'd visited as a child.

For one thing, most of them were smiling.

She'd grown up in a state-run orphanage. Some years, depending on who was in charge, they'd drag the kids to a church down the street. But that church had no special service for children. All she remembered was being scolded and punished for not paying attention or for fidgeting in her seat, while an angry old man up front talked for an hour about things she never understood. The only thing that seemed clear was that God didn't like people very much and those people didn't like her.

But already she sensed something different going on here.

Apart from the pronounced joy evident on most of the faces, she had been welcomed and greeted by at least a dozen other people before she'd taken her seat. When they sang, their joyfulness seemed to increase, as though they really believed what they were singing. She knew a little bit about Jesus but didn't quite understand all the imagery in the lyrics.

The cross of Christ, the blood of Christ, Jesus as a Lamb, Christian soldiers marching on. But everyone else sang like it all made perfect sense.

After the singing was over, a man got up and welcomed any first-time guests, then talked a few minutes about things going on in the church that week. He asked people to pray for all the soldiers, especially ones related to people in the church. He mentioned one corporal in particular who had been wounded two weeks ago in Italy. Then some men came up to the front with baskets, and they prayed about money.

She suddenly felt very nervous.

They began passing the baskets from aisle to aisle. She tried not to look obvious, but she had no idea how much the service cost. As the men came to the aisle in front of her, she tried to see what others put in but couldn't tell. She quickly reached in her purse and pulled out three dollars. It was all the cash she had.

As she dropped the money in, she enclosed it in her palm so no one would see. She hoped it was enough.

A few moments later, Pastor Harman went up to the pulpit and asked everyone to turn in their Bibles to a passage somewhere in the Psalms. She looked around, again feeling very uncomfortable. Everyone else had a Bible and instantly began turning pages. She was half-tempted to pull the hymnal out of the little rack and pretend it was a Bible. But a woman next to her leaned over and whispered kindly, "You can look at mine if you want." She shifted the Bible on her lap so Katherine could see.

"Thank you," Katherine whispered back.

The pastor read several verses, then prayed. Everyone closed their eyes, so Katherine did too. He talked for the next forty minutes. She found his voice fairly pleasant. He really seemed sincere. Occasionally he got loud, but it seemed more from genuine enthusiasm than anger, like someone getting excited when retelling a story. She couldn't follow everything he said, but it certainly wasn't hard to sit there and listen.

She smiled as she realized she hadn't fidgeted in her seat a single time.

Pastor Harman said, "As I close, I want to take just a few moments to explain how the gospel is revealed in this psalm."

She decided it was time to slip out. She wanted to be there waiting for Patrick when his service ended.

Twenty-nine

The train rolled down the tracks, the soft clicking sound always in the background, a nice rhythm, like a drummer playing the brushes. Shawn thought it oddly comforting, sitting there in the dining car. He looked out his window, trying to ignore the cigarette smoke drifting his way from three tables down. A table full of showgirls. He looked up at them then quickly turned from the stares of one blonde, Lana-something. She'd had him in her crosshairs almost since the tour began.

He looked back through the window. It was dark outside. The city lights flashed by in his face like a photographer's bulb. Another thing he wouldn't miss. *Where are we now?* he wondered. Every few days a different place.

Last night was easy to remember. New York City.

Bigger than all the other crowds combined, Lieutenant Winston had said. After the show, Colonel Simmons had even called to congratulate Shawn. The rallies were bringing in record numbers of dough. Shawn thought it didn't hurt adding Bing Crosby and Danny Kaye to the lineup. Both had flown in for the day.

Shawn had to admit . . . it was a thrill to see them perform up close. He loved their singing, the dance moves, and in between they kept everyone in stitches. It felt good to laugh. He kept thinking about Mrs. Fortini the whole time. She would have loved it.

"Say, Major. Saw you last night at the rally. Right after Mr. Crosby and Mr. Kaye done their bit. I was in the crowd, in the colored section. They sure was somethin'."

Shawn turned to see the smiling face of Harrison James, the Pullman porter who'd been so helpful on his train ride down to Washington last month. He was still being helpful every single day. "Well, Harry, you should have come up after and said hi. I could have introduced you."

Harry looked over his shoulder, as if someone was listening. "I couldn't do that, Major," he whispered. "But I sure liked hearing what you said when they was done. Made me want to go right out and buy some of them bonds."

"Thank you, Harry. So what you got there in your hand?"

"I was in the mail car, found this in your slot. Thought I'd save you the trouble." He handed a long envelope to Shawn.

"That was very kind, Harry."

"We gonna be in Philly by the end of the week. That where you're from, ain't it?"

"Sure is. I'm hoping to see my son and father if I can swing it."

"Well, I better get back before they come looking for me." He turned to head back the way he came. Shawn gently grabbed his sleeve.

"Where you going so quick?" Shawn asked, then discreetly handed him two dollars.

"Now, you don't have to do that, Major."

"You've got your way of being nice. This is mine."

"Well, thank you. Maybe now I can buy me some of those bonds," he said, winking.

Shawn noticed the address on the envelope. It was Mrs. Fortini's. He quickly opened it. Out popped a one-page note folded in half and a slip of paper with three photo prints. Shawn smiled. It was Patrick and Katherine; the pictures were the kind you get at a photo booth. Patrick was sitting on her lap. He smiled slightly on the first shot. Smiled much bigger on the second. Then Katherine—Miss Townsend—had picked up his hand, got him waving on the third. He looked so happy. Shawn wished he could somehow process his grief as well as Patrick seemed to be doing. To be able to be that happy this soon after . . .

Shawn noticed writing on the back and turned it over. There in huge letters he read: "I miss you Daddy." He looked at Patrick's face again. "I miss you too, my little man." He opened the note and read:

Dear Major Collins,

Found a place that does the photos like you asked. Had fun with Patrick taking them. Sorry I'm in the pictures, but he was too afraid to go into the booth alone. I don't mind if you want to cut me out. I sent all three, because I couldn't decide which one was the cutest (I liked them all).

Yours truly, Katherine Townsend

Shawn looked at the photos again and decided to leave them just as they were.

"Whoa . . . who's that?" Lieutenant Winston walked by from behind and sat at the table across from Shawn. "May I, sir?" he asked, pointing at the pictures.

Shawn reluctantly handed them over. "That's my son with his nanny."

"Nanny? You're kidding, right? When you said you had a nanny, I'm thinking old lady with her hair in a bun."

Shawn watched him as he ogled the pictures. "My son's in there too."

"Nice-looking boy, sir." Winston handed them back. "You and the nanny . . . are you . . . ? What I mean is—"

"No, we're not a couple. And I didn't pick her for her looks. She happened to be the lady who took care of Patrick after my wife . . . while I was in England. She saw him through a pretty dark time, and they became close. About the time I got stuck doing this, she lost her other job."

"I understand, sir. Didn't mean anything by asking."

"That's okay, Lieutenant."

"Say, sir, got a few more details about our time in Philly. Got a minute?"

"Fire away."

"After the rally on Saturday in the afternoon, the colonel lined up a huge dinner party with all the who's-who in town. They're each buying a thousand dollars of war bonds for a chance to meet the stars up close. After we eat, we'll do the show, then some dancing. Colonel said a number of them asked about you, whether you'd be there. Course he promised them you would."

Shawn sighed.

"But listen, sir. You don't have to get up and give a speech. I'll introduce you like I always do. But all you have to do is say hi, thanks for coming. Everyone there is already paying a ton of money just to walk through the ballroom doors."

Shawn had an idea. "Lieutenant, when they arrange the seating, leave room for two women and a little boy at my table."

"I can do that, sir."

"Also, in between the rally and the dinner, I want to borrow the car to visit my dad in the hospital."

"I don't know about that one."

"Lieutenant . . . he's dying. Once this train leaves Philly and heads south, we'll be gone three more months. This could be my last chance to see him."

"All right, sir. I'll make it happen somehow."

"Appreciate it."

Winston got up. He nodded at the three girls still sitting a few tables away. He pointed down at the photos of Patrick and Katherine. "The nanny coming, sir? To the dinner in Philly?"

Shawn nodded then signaled with his head for the lieutenant to beat it.

∽

At the next stop, someplace in New Jersey, Shawn found a pay phone and called Mrs. Fortini. It was after 9:00; he hoped it wasn't too late.

"Hello, Mrs. Fortini's residence."

"Katherine . . . Miss Townsend? It's Major Collins."

"Oh, hi. Are you looking for Mrs. Fortini? She's already gone to bed."

"Well, can you give her a message?"

"Did you get the pictures?" Katherine asked.

"They were great, thanks. I just have a minute. Here's what's going on. We'll be in Philly this Saturday, and I got permission for you, Patrick, and Mrs. Fortini to come to a big dinner they're having downtown."

"Really? They'll be so excited. Where at?"

"Believe it or not, it's in the Wanamaker's Building. They've rented out one of the top floors. Big affair with all the richest people in town coming. The dinner is at 7:30, but I'll meet you all downstairs at the Eagle."

Katherine paused. Shawn wasn't sure why. "Is that a problem?"

"Well, if it's for rich people, I imagine they'll be dressing in tuxedos and evening gowns."

"Probably," Shawn said.

"I don't . . . I don't have anything like that to wear. Just work outfits."

"Oh."

"Do you know if Patrick has a suit to wear? I could just drop him and Mrs. Fortini off then come back after."

"I don't know if Patrick has a suit or not. If he does, I doubt it would still fit him. I'm sorry. I didn't even think about clothes. But I don't want you to just drop him off. I'm planning to spend as much time with him as I can, but in these situations, my time's not my own." He thought a moment. "Tell you what, tomorrow when we stop, I'll wire you seventy-five dollars. That should be enough, I think. Fifty for you and twenty-five for Patrick."

"Oh, Major, I couldn't ask you to buy me a dress."

"Don't be silly. I *need* you to be there . . . for Patrick. Besides, they're paying all my expenses on this tour, so I've got plenty of extra money."

"Fifty dollars," she said.

"Is that enough?"

"It's too much."

"Look, I've got to get back on the train."

"Thank you so much. On the next stop could you call Dr. Matthews?"

"Is my dad all right?"

"He's about the same, physically. But he won't leave the hospital."

"What?"

"Dr. Matthews wants to release him to come home, but your dad won't leave."

"Why?"

"He won't say, not to us anyway. The doctor knows, but he said your dad told him not to tell us."

"That's crazy."

"I'm sorry to bother you with this, but Patrick really misses him. You know what the doctor said about his heart. It just seems like they should be together now as much as possible and—"

"Don't say another word. I'll take care of it."

They hung up, then Shawn fumbled through his pockets for the hospital's telephone number. He heard the conductor shouting just outside. "All aboard. Last call."

Thirty

Ian Collins sat in his hospital room listening to *The Adventures of Sherlock Holmes*, one of his favorite shows, but he was completely distracted. He stared at the bathroom door then down at his bum leg in its cast. Where was that Robert anyway? He'd told the nurse he needed him right away. They'd provided him a set of crutches, but he was too weak to use them. Over in the corner sat his wheelchair, too far to reach. Robert did that on purpose, to make sure he wouldn't even try to use it without help.

Robert was good to him that way. Robert was his orderly.

Collins was paying the hospital extra to get some extra attention. Figured he had that pile of money in the bank and never used it. Seemed clear that now was a good time to spend some. It had also gotten him out of that dreadful sixteen-bed ward down the end of the hall. All night long, all these strangers snoring and moaning. Couldn't put ten minutes of decent sleep together.

Shawn had called an hour ago. Collins didn't have a phone in his private room, but Robert had told him. Said Shawn had called Dr. Matthews and was on his way to the hospital right now. If Robert got the message right, Shawn had done one of his big War Bond rallies right there in Philly this afternoon. Had some other big shindig going on tonight. But they loaned him a car to come by for a quick visit.

Last thing Collins wanted was to waste the little bit of time Shawn had taking care of business in the bathroom. Took so long to do what needed doing, this stupid leg all busted up. Least the bump on his noggin had gone down, got that turban of bandages off his head.

Where is that Robert anyway?

He looked toward the hall, just about to shout Robert's name when he appeared in the doorway. The next moment, there was Shawn standing right next to him.

"Shawn!" he yelled. "My boy . . . Robert, you meet my boy Shawn?"

Robert walked in, big strong guy, had to be Italian by the look of him. Then Shawn. "Yes, I did, Mr. Collins. He and I been talking a little bit. Need some help getting to the john?"

"Keep your voice down," Collins said.

"Dad, he wasn't talking loud," said Shawn. He walked over and gave his dad a hug.

"I wanted to get this over with before Shawn got here," Collins said as Robert rolled his wheelchair to the bed. In one motion he lifted Collins up and sat him down.

"We'll be done in a minute, Major."

"Take your time, Robert. Dad, don't worry, I'll be fine out here."

In a few minutes, they were in and out and Collins was back in bed. That was why he liked Robert. Did what needed doing with no chitchat.

"Wow, look at you in that uniform," Collins said to Shawn. "All spiffed up. Thanks, Robert, we're all set here."

"Till the next time then," Robert said, heading for the

door. "Nice talking with you, Major. Just call me, you got my number." He turned right and was gone.

"What's he mean by that?" Collins asked.

Shawn took a seat in the lone chair next to the bed. "I'll get to that in a minute. How you doing, Dad? I'm so sorry I couldn't be here for you."

"Shawn . . . I'm okay. I don't want you feeling that way. You're doing your duty. I couldn't be prouder. I been bragging about you to everyone walks through that door."

"I've been so worried about you." Shawn reached out and put his hand on the bed next to his father's side.

Collins reached out and patted his arm. "Really, I'm okay, son. See? They got that bandage off my head. You should've seen me. Looked like an Arabian knight."

Shawn sat back and took a deep breath. "You do sound okay."

"I am . . . now what are you and Robert cooking up?"

"Dad, what's this about you not going home?"

"Miss Townsend tell you that?"

"It's true, isn't it?"

Collins looked away. "I don't feel ready to go home."

"Dad . . . I talked with Dr. Matthews. He thinks you'd heal better at home, and he needs this bed back."

"I'm just not ready."

"I been thinking about this, Dad, the whole drive over. I think I know what's bothering you."

"Nothing's bothering me."

"I just watched what's bothering you." Shawn said, almost in a whisper, pointing to the bathroom door with his head. "It's okay. I understand."

"What are you talking about?"

"You can't make it up the steps till you get that cast off. We only got one bathroom at the house, and it's upstairs."

"Son, I can't be going in one of those stinking bedpans. Who am I gonna get to clean up after me? Miss Townsend . . . Mrs. Fortini? I can't do it, Shawn. And where am I gonna sleep?" He looked away again.

"Dad, look at me." Shawn waited a moment. "Dad."

Collins faced his son but had the hardest time making eye contact.

"I understand, really I do. I've got it all worked out."

"What do you mean?"

"I've talked with Dr. Matthews and Robert, even made a few calls, one to your accountant then to a contractor. It's all set up."

"What is?"

"I'm going to spend a little bit of that money you've got stored away. Actually, what I'm doing will cost about the same as what you're giving this hospital every week for this room. And the contractor said he can get right on it, have it done in a week, maybe less."

"What are you talking about, Shawn?"

"I'm talking about getting you home, Dad, where you belong. I'm talking about you spending some time with Patrick. He misses you so much."

"He say that?"

"Katherine said that's all he talks about."

"Really?"

"He said somebody promised to teach him how to carve things out of wood."

Collins sighed. He'd forgotten all about that.

"So I've figured out a way to get you home. Just hear me out. The hospital is going to rent us a bed for you; we can put it right there in the living room. If we need to, we'll buy it. I got a contractor who's going to build a bathroom downstairs."

"People don't have bathrooms downstairs."

"Well, we're going to. He said he can put one right under the stairs. It won't have a shower, but it will have a sink and toilet. And he'll put all kinds of handles everywhere so you can keep your balance getting in and out. Robert said he could use some extra cash. So he's going to come over once a day on his way home and clean you up, like he does here."

"Really?"

"And we'll make sure when he does, you got the house to yourself. Will that be enough to get you to come home?"

Collins couldn't believe all the trouble Shawn had gone to for him. "I don't know what to say."

"Say you'll come home. I'm going to see Patrick tonight. Say I can tell him you're coming home."

"I guess you better tell him then."

⁂

Shawn paced back and forth in front of the big bronze Eagle at Wanamaker's, staring at the front doors by the Juniper Street entrance. He'd watched numerous couples come in, all dressed to the nines. They'd smile as they passed by then disappear up the elevators. The dinner was being held in a large ballroom on the ninth floor. Shawn had already been upstairs, confirming Lieutenant Winston had made room for his guests.

He had. The guy really was a wizard with details.

The celebrities had been arriving over the last twenty minutes from the Market Street entrance, to make room for their limousines. Unfortunately for Mrs. Fortini, Bing Crosby was not among them. But he knew she'd love this evening, from top to bottom. The Andrews Sisters were back. Comedian Jack Benny was supposed to make an appearance. He had been hilarious that afternoon. Hedy Lamarr and Bette Davis were still on the tour.

But Shawn just wanted to see Patrick. He looked up through the Grand Court atrium as the music from the band began to play, drifting down from the ninth floor. He looked again toward the Juniper Street entrance. There he was, coming in right behind a tall man in a black tuxedo and top hat.

"Daddy!" he yelled and ran hard until he jumped into Shawn's arms.

"Look at you," Shawn yelled as he spun him around. "All dressed up. Bow tie and everything."

"We gonna eat here?"

"Yes, upstairs." Shawn set Patrick down but still held his hand. He turned back toward the doors. Mrs. Fortini walked toward him, her eyes as bright as the chandeliers. She wore a shiny green dress and some kind of fur stole around her shoulders. "Look at you, Mrs. Fortini."

She smiled and looked away shyly. "I'm just glad this old thing fit," she said. She walked up and gave him a big hug.

"Where's Miss Townsend?"

"She's coming," said Patrick. "She's parking the car."

"But there's supposed to be valet parking," Shawn said. "Aren't they out there?"

"They are," said Mrs. Fortini. "But Katherine didn't know how much they charged."

"They're free," he said. "Everything tonight is covered."

"She'll be right up," said Mrs. Fortini. "She said not to wait for her."

"She know it's on the ninth floor?"

"Your message said the same floor as the Crystal Tea Room. She said that's her new favorite place. C'mon, she'll be fine. She's a very bright girl." They started walking toward the elevators.

Shawn put his hand on Mrs. Fortini's shoulder. "Before we go up, I've got something for you."

"For me?" she asked.

"You know Bing Crosby won't be here tonight, right?"

She nodded. "That's okay. I still can't believe I get to go to something so fancy."

"Well, here," Shawn said. He pulled out a manila envelope and handed it to her.

"What is it?"

"Open it."

She did and pulled out an eight-by-ten glossy photograph of Bing Crosby smoking a pipe. "Shawn, it's wonderful." She read aloud what he'd written:

> To Alessandra,
> So sorry I missed you.
> All the best, Bing Crosby

She giggled, or something similar, and pulled the picture close. "Shawn, thank you so much. I didn't know you knew my first name."

"I didn't. Miss Townsend found it for me."

Thirty-one

Shawn got Patrick and Mrs. Fortini situated at the table. The room looked fabulous. Big chandeliers, lush curtains, rich woodwork and trim, gorgeous mahogany pillars. Huge circular tables outlined the perimeter, clothed in fine linen and silverware actually made of silver. Each with a floral centerpiece dominated by roses and candles. Against the far wall a makeshift stage had been created, lined with American flags on flagpoles and, of course, the obligatory War Bond posters. The band was off to the right, playing soft tunes in the background. All about the room, men and women mingled, holding cocktails and exchanging compliments.

"Shawn, this is *so* beautiful," said Mrs. Fortini. "Guess somebody used up all their rationing coupons on this."

Shawn laughed. "The waiters are going to bring the salads first, I think. My aide said they'll be accompanied by a cold shrimp cocktail."

"I haven't had shrimp in ages," she said.

"Do I have to eat shrimp, Daddy?"

"No, Patrick. Tonight, you don't have to eat anything you don't want. Listen, I have to be gone a few minutes, just a few.

There's some people I have to meet. I'll try to get it all done now so I can spend the rest of the time with you. Okay?"

"Okay," he said.

Shawn looked toward the door. "I don't see Miss Townsend."

"She'll be here," said Mrs. Fortini. "You go do what you have to do."

Shawn spotted Lieutenant Winston across the room and headed that way. He was laughing at something an elderly man had just said. Shawn recognized Winston's fake laugh and decided he might appreciate the interruption. "Excuse me, Lieutenant," he whispered.

"Oh, Major Collins. Duty calls, Mr. Evans. So nice to meet you."

"Is this him, the major who's been making all the headlines lately?" asked the man.

"The very same," said Winston. He quickly introduced Shawn to Mr. and Mrs. Evans. Shawn spent a few moments making small talk, then Lieutenant Winston pulled him away. They had worked on this routine that afternoon. It was the lieutenant's job to make sure Shawn saw everyone he needed to that night without getting stuck in long conversations.

"Lieutenant, do you know everyone I'm supposed to meet tonight?"

"Most of them, sir."

"Could we get this out of the way upfront, instead of dragging it out all evening? I'd like to spend some time with my son if I could."

"I think we could—hold on. Who is that?" Winston was instantly distracted, looking over Shawn's shoulder. "My heavens, she is gorgeous."

Shawn turned to see a beautiful actress in a stunning red dress who'd just come through the front door. Must be someone new; Shawn didn't recognize her. He noticed several of the men in the room had turned to see her, some like Winston stopping conversations mid-sentence.

Wait a minute, he thought. It can't be. He looked at her face more closely.

But it was.

It was Katherine . . . it was Miss Townsend.

✑

The dinner for Shawn had been equal parts wonderful and unnerving.

It was wonderful to see Patrick, hear him go on the way kids do, jumping from one subject to the next, filling Shawn in on all he'd missed. The food had been wonderful. The entertainment, wonderful. Mrs. Fortini's warmth and sense of humor, wonderful.

Being around Katherine—Miss Townsend—on the other hand . . .

He found her transformation unnerving. The way numerous men in the room kept staring at her, unnerving. The way Lieutenant Winston had suddenly decided to eat at their table, unnerving. The way he dominated her time and conversation, turning his considerable charm loose on her, unnerving. And it was unnerving that she didn't seem to realize any of these things were even going on.

But perhaps the most unnerving thing of all was how much all this bothered him, to the point of distraction.

"Daddy?"

"Shawn," Mrs. Fortini said. "Do you hear Patrick?"

Shawn looked, first to Mrs. Fortini then Patrick. "I'm sorry, what is it? Would you like some more cake?"

"I'm full," said Patrick. "Miss Townsend keeps looking over here. I don't think she wants to keep dancing."

Mrs. Fortini chuckled. "Out of the mouth of babes."

Shawn looked out on the dance floor, scanning the various couples until he saw Miss Townsend dancing with Lieutenant Winston. This was the third dance they had shared since the show ended.

"She looks happy to me," Shawn said.

"Shawn, she does not," said Mrs. Fortini. "Your lieutenant is making her uncomfortable. Although he's quite a handsome young man, and a fabulous dancer, even I can see that."

Of course he is, thought Shawn. "She kept saying yes when he asked her," he said.

"Because he's your friend."

"He's not my friend."

"Well, she was saying yes because she thought he was and didn't want to offend him."

"She tell you that?"

"In a way."

"Are you sure, Mrs. Fortini?" Shawn looked again, caught Katherine looking their way.

"I'm sure. Shawn, go out and rescue her."

"I can't do that."

"Why?"

"I can't dance, Mrs. Fortini. Besides, it wouldn't be right."

"And why is that?"

"Because . . . she's Patrick's nanny."

"Daddy, why are you talking that way to Mrs. Fortini? Are you mad?"

Shawn shook his head. "No, Patrick, I'm not mad. I'm sorry, Mrs. Fortini, I didn't realize I was—"

"Apology accepted. Now go out and dance with Katherine. Do it because it's the right thing to do, and because you are a gentleman, and she needs a gentleman right now."

Shawn looked at Patrick, who smiled. He didn't need to look at Mrs. Fortini. He sighed and got out of his seat then weaved his way through the dancing couples. He came up to them and tapped on Lieutenant Winston's shoulder. "May I cut in?"

Winston looked stunned by the interruption but immediately said yes and backed away.

Shawn took her hands and tried to find the beat. "Mrs. Fortini said you needed rescuing."

"Thank you. The lieutenant is very nice but—"

"You don't need to explain. But I do. I am a terrible dancer. You may get hurt."

Katherine laughed. She looked back toward their table. Lieutenant Winston had taken his seat again.

"You don't have to dance with him," Shawn said, "or even be nice to him. Not on my account." In between words, Shawn counted off the dance steps in his head.

"Really?"

"Yes. In fact, my hunch is, if you're not crystal clear, he will keep pursuing you all night."

"But why?"

She really didn't get it. "You're wearing a very . . . attractive dress," was all he thought to say.

"It's the nicest dress I've ever owned. Thank you for buying it. I've got change, nine dollars. It's in my purse."

"Keep it, please."

"You sure?"

"Yes."

"The store I bought it from had a sale. Too many red dresses left over from Valentine's Day."

"It looks . . . very nice on you."

"Thank you, Major."

They continued to dance another few moments in silence,

Shawn counting the steps. It seemed like the song was ending. Yes, it was ending. Shawn was so relieved.

Relieved but still unnerved.

As he led Katherine back to the table, Shawn saw Patrick with Mrs. Fortini. As much as he'd miss him, Shawn decided it was a good thing the train was heading south for the next three months.

Thirty-two

May 15, 1944
The Pentagon
(Just over 3 months later)

Colonel Simmons dreaded this call, but he couldn't ignore it any longer. His secretary, Abby, had gotten the gist of what this Air Force general wanted from the last two times he'd called. Simmons had told Abby many times she was in the wrong branch of the military. They ought to ship her overseas, get her interrogating Krauts and Japs. She'd get them spilling the beans.

Essentially, this general wanted to take Simmons's cash cow away, the goose who'd been laying all his golden eggs. There was the buzzer again. He picked up the phone.

"Colonel, General Hardaway is on the line . . . *again*. Sir, he's calling from London. You don't take it this time, I can't be responsible for what he might do."

"All right, Abigail, put him through."

"Hello, Simmons?"

"Yes, sir. Am I speaking to General Hardaway?"

"You are. About time you took my call."

"Sorry, sir. It's been extremely busy around here."

"Sorry to hear it. Neck deep in a war over here."

Jab noted, thought Simmons. "What's on your mind, General?"

"Need you to send me a certain major you've got dancing in your little shows."

Simmons hated this. Little shows. "Who are we talking about, sir?" As if he didn't know.

"You know . . . Major Collins."

"Major Shawn Collins? He's not a dancer, General. He's the lynchpin of our War Bond rallies. Just finishing up his first four-month tour. Racked up the highest revenues we've seen since we started this. I don't think I can part with him, sir."

"You don't think? You don't have a choice, Colonel."

"I beg to differ, sir. You may outrank me, but you know the importance Washington places on these rallies. They won't want to mess with a good thing. I'm in the planning stages of a second tour for him on the West Coast."

"Well, I'm in the planning stages of a massive invasion of northern France. Maybe you heard about that. I got hundreds of fighters and bombers taking off every day laying the groundwork for it. And I just lost three of my best planners in a plane crash. I been asking around, and your major's name keeps coming up. They say he's a natural. I need him over here pronto. Talk to whoever you want, they're gonna back me on this."

"General, we don't keep the money flowing in, and you won't have any bombers to fly or fuel to fly 'em."

"Look," the general said, "I'm not trying to ruin your little operation. I know you need heroes to get the crowds going. I'm about to give you two for the price of one."

"What do you mean?"

"I got two fighter pilots who need a rest—both high-scoring aces, fly those new Mustang fighter planes. Real storytellers, both of 'em. One's from Texas, the other California. They'll fit right in with your plans out West."

Simmons liked the sound of this. "When would all this happen?"

"I could have them there by the end of the week. I've talked to both of 'em. They're all fired up about the assignment, especially when I told them about all those beautiful girls."

"Girls we've got plenty of," said Simmons.

"So we got a deal?"

"I think so, General. I'll get word to Major Collins today to start packing for England. Can I give him a couple of weeks leave before he heads out? Hasn't had any leave since he started."

"I don't have a couple of weeks. Give 'em one, then tell him to get over here. My aide will call you later today with all the details."

As he hung up the phone, Simmons's mind was already coming up with a plan. Two Mustang fighter aces. This had definite possibilities.

∽

Katherine walked slowly along a shady lane on her way to the playground next to Patrick's school. It was a fine Saturday afternoon. Patrick had already run on ahead, as soon as he saw the swing set and slide. Spring was in full bloom. The overcoats had taken their rightful place in the back of the closet, the boots were in the basement. Outside the leaves had returned to the trees. You could actually see a blue sky at midday, and the sun occasionally peeked out from behind the clouds.

Katherine walked slowly because Mrs. Fortini—the woman

who'd become her closest friend and the closest thing to a mother she had ever known—had asked to go with her today. It was nice they could finally leave Mr. Collins home unattended.

Since his cast had come off last month, he had become increasingly independent. He still slept downstairs in a bed tucked in a living room corner and only used the downstairs bathroom, *his* bathroom, it came to be called. Robert, his orderly, was almost a family member now. Katherine noticed how he scheduled his home visits increasingly near the dinner hour. He was obviously sweet on Katherine, which made things awkward at times. But he seemed harmless and was always respectful.

"How's that bench over there?" Katherine asked, pointing to one just off the sidewalk but still on the pavement. "We can see Patrick playing but we're far away enough not to hear all the noise."

"Looks fine, dear." She let out a groan as she sat down. "You seem a little sad. Is anything wrong?"

"Do I? I'm okay, just a little discouraged. I really shouldn't be."

"What about?" asked Mrs. Fortini. Katherine looked down. "The thing you're always discouraged about?"

Katherine nodded. "Let's don't talk about it." The last three months had been trying. The last time she had seen Shawn was the dance downtown. But he had danced with her. More than that . . . he had rescued her from Lieutenant Winston. And then he'd said she looked attractive in her dress. She knew she was reading way too much into it, but she couldn't seem to help it.

"He still hasn't written or called?" asked Mrs. Fortini.

"Just about Patrick or his father. And he's back to calling me Miss Townsend again. Meanwhile, his friend Captain Albert Baker writes me almost every week from England."

"Do you write him back?"

"Only occasionally, and I never include anything that might lead him on."

Mrs. Fortini shook her head in a gentle scold. "Are you interested in him?"

"He's very nice. He's got a good sense of humor. He's very persistent."

"But do you like him . . . *that* way?"

"He's not the one I think about when I'm thinking *that* way."

"Then Katherine, writing back at all might be too much encouragement for a man pursuing you like that."

"I know, but I just don't know how to be rude."

Mrs. Fortini looked at her and smiled. She knew exactly what Katherine was struggling with. "Katherine, I think you just have to be patient. Elizabeth died only five months ago."

"I know, I'm being ridiculous. I don't know what I'm expecting. I'm just afraid something will happen and Shawn and Patrick will be out of my life for good. His last War Bond rally was last night. My four months are up. What if he comes back and says, 'Thanks for watching Patrick while I've been gone, here's your final paycheck'?" She looked over at Patrick on the slide. He waved and she waved back.

Mrs. Fortini put her arm on Katherine's shoulder. "Katherine, I've been trying to help you see what it means to trust God for your life. Life is full of uncertainties and things we can't control. Worrying about things you can't change only changes you. It eats you up inside." She gently pointed to a spot on Katherine's forehead. "And it gives you wrinkles."

"I know," she said. "Pastor Harman has been talking about the same thing at church. I just can't seem to let go."

"Trusting God is a decision, not a feeling."

"I just wish I knew whether something will ever happen between us. I know it can't be soon, I just wish I knew if it could be. If I knew, I think I could trust God . . . while I wait."

"I think you might have it backwards," said Mrs. Fortini. "First you trust, then adjust."

"What? I don't know what that means."

"Put your trust in God's wisdom, in his love for you, then adjust yourself to whatever he decides is best. That's what I do, and for an old person, I sleep pretty well."

Katherine sighed. It was as if these wise words hung in the air momentarily, then drifted out of reach. They sat in silence a few moments. Katherine kept her eyes on Patrick. What would she do if he was suddenly taken from her? It could happen. In a matter of days.

"Katherine."

She looked up.

"Look down there, do you see that?"

Katherine looked where Mrs. Fortini was pointing, off to the left in front of them. "What am I looking for?"

"Do you see that flower, right there?"

Katherine looked down again and saw a little buttercup poking up through a crack in the sidewalk, surrounded by the smallest dab of green. It looked so fragile and out of place.

"Do you see?" Mrs. Fortini said. "God can make love grow through even the hardest places. Just give him time."

"You think there's even a chance?" Katherine asked.

Mrs. Fortini simply smiled and pointed back at the flower.

Thirty-three

Shawn couldn't believe it. London.

They were shipping him off just like that. A quick thanks, then off you go. After all he'd done. He knew the War Bond tour was ending. Lieutenant Winston had already talked about another one on the West Coast. Shawn had begun to think through a way to get out of it. One phone call later and everything had changed. Now he had a week, then he was flying back to England.

After getting the news, Shawn had made some calls overseas. Somehow he'd gotten reassigned to some top general's planning staff. They were suddenly critically short on personnel and needed help planning a new surge of bombing missions to support the big invasion of France. Very top secret. They were calling it D-Day. Sounded like it was just around the corner.

As Shawn drove home from the 30th Street train station in Philly, twilight was just giving way to complete darkness. He had called his father after the train got in and was glad to hear they'd be alone when Shawn arrived. The others were enjoying Saturday night dinner at Mrs. Fortini's next door. He pulled into the neighborhood on his father's end of the street, turned off his lights, and parked two houses down to avoid sounding any alarm bells. He quietly walked up to the house and let himself in.

"Shawn," his father yelled from his bed in the living room.

"Hi, Dad," he said, then put his finger to his lips, signaling him to lower his voice.

The elder Collins got up, grabbed his cane, and turned off the radio. "What's the secrecy about?"

"They'll find out everything in a little bit, but I wanted to talk to you first." Shawn was shocked at how thin his dad looked. His eyes were bright and he was smiling, but he looked so much older.

His dad hobbled over and gave him a big hug. "Where's your bags?"

"Still in the car. I'll get them in a few minutes." Shawn sat on the sofa, his dad in his favorite chair.

"You said you wanted to talk about your new assignment? Can I get you something to drink? Got some cold soda pops in the fridge."

"No, you stay put. I'll get one." Shawn did, then sat back down. He noticed a pile of wood shavings scattered on the floor between the chair and sofa, his dad's old leather pouch on the coffee table.

"Miss Townsend didn't get a chance to clean that up yet. Me and Patrick were carving up a storm just before he went next door for supper. He's doing real well with it, hasn't got a scratch."

Shawn smiled. "He's learning from the best." He was glad Patrick had gotten this kind of time in with his dad. "Look, Dad, I've got some big news. But not *good* big news like the last time. They're shipping me back to England in a week."

"What?"

"I know it's sudden. But I won't be in any danger this time. Not flying any more missions. For some reason they think they need my help on the planning staff. You probably heard rumblings on the news about an upcoming invasion of France." His dad nodded. "This has something to do with that."

"Isn't Hitler still bombing London?"

"Not for almost two months now," Shawn said. "The guys I talked to think they've pretty much crushed the Luftwaffe. So there really isn't any danger anymore. Which is why I want to ask your advice on something."

His father sat forward in his chair.

"I'd like to bring Patrick over there with me, just for the summer. I already talked with his teacher on the phone. She said he's only got one more week of school. His grades are top-notch, so she'd be willing to let him out early."

"He is doing real good at school," his father said.

"But if he came with me, I'd need to bring Miss Townsend along to look after him. I know she does a lot around here. I'd hire someone else to come in while we're gone."

"Shawn, I can look after myself."

"Dad, we have a bed in the living room. You haven't been upstairs in almost four months. You're walking with a cane. You need some help."

"Mrs. Fortini will look after me. She's the one trained Miss Townsend to do everything. You go on and do what you got to do. I'll be all right."

It was odd hearing his dad speak so highly of Mrs. Fortini, even willing to become dependent on her. "So you're okay with this?"

"I'm gonna miss Patrick something awful. But I can't imagine what it would do to him, you go back to England without him. You've got your duty. The country needs you. My place is here. I'll be okay."

"Are you sure?"

"I'm sure. But . . . what about the Medal of Honor? I thought FDR was gonna put that on you at the White House."

"They haven't even mentioned the medal, and I forgot all about it." Shawn got up and paced between the sofa and the front door. He had something else to say.

"What's the matter?" his father asked.

"There's one last thing I need to talk to you about. Something we've known about since you fell down the stairs. The doctor told us to keep it from you, thought if you knew it might make things worse. But I think it would be worse if I leave you here next week and you don't know."

"What are you talking about?"

"It's your heart, Dad. It's . . . not in good shape."

"That supposed to be a secret?"

"I'm being serious, Dad. The doctor said it's probably on its way out. He said if you didn't take it easy, really take it easy, your heart could snap. With your leg busted, you couldn't do very much, so we didn't tell you. But I'm concerned with you getting better, you're going to overdo it while I'm gone."

His dad stood up. He walked over and put one arm on Shawn's shoulder, the other steadying his cane. "Son, a man knows when his life's ebbing away. You feel it inside. Why do you think I fell off those stairs in the first place? I didn't trip. I could barely get halfway up. I'm not sure I can get back up there again if I wanted to."

"So you won't do anything crazy while I'm gone?" He was choking back his emotions. "I need you to be here, Dad. I want you waiting for me when I get back."

"I don't think I've got any crazy left in me. You just do what you gotta do, and don't worry about me." They exchanged hugs. "Now you go next door, get some dinner, say hey to everybody, then bring them all back here with whatever dessert Mrs. Fortini's fixed up. Then you can tell 'em all the news."

❧

When Katherine awoke the next morning, thoughts of what Shawn had shared last night pushed aside the fading images from her last dream. She welcomed them; they were better than a dream to her.

Mrs. Fortini had been right. She should have trusted God. Why was that so hard to do? She had feared the worst—that she would soon lose both Patrick and Shawn for good—and instead she'd been given a reprieve. Now she would spend the next three months with both of them in London.

She felt bad leaving Mr. Collins and Mrs. Fortini behind, but both had gone out of their way to assure her they'd be fine. She got up and began getting ready for church. When she came downstairs, Mrs. Fortini informed her that Shawn had just called. Patrick had a stomachache and Shawn was keeping him home from church. He said he'd take care of him and to feel free to go on without them.

She was saddened to hear Patrick was sick, but she really did want to go to church. She was running a little late. She skipped breakfast, hugged Mrs. Fortini good-bye, and headed out the door. The church building was just a few blocks away. She got there in a few minutes, found her favorite parking spot, and joined the rest of the congregation making their way through the front doors. Just before going in, she read the sermon title on the sign out front: "The Book God Has Written About Us."

She sat in her usual seat in the back row. After four months, she felt pretty familiar with the routines. During the hymns, she happily sang along with the rest, even recognized some of the songs. They took up the offering, read a few announcements, then Pastor Harman got up and greeted the congregation. She picked up her Bible and read along as he read his text. He said it was from Psalm 139:

"O Lord, you have searched me and known me! You know when I sit down and when I rise up; you discern my thoughts from afar. You search out my path and my lying down and are acquainted with all my ways. Even before a word is on my tongue, behold, O Lord, you know it altogether. You hem me in, behind and before, and lay your hand upon me. Such knowledge is too wonderful for me; it is too high; I cannot attain it."

Then he said, "Please skip down to verses 15 and 16." Katherine looked further down the page:

"My frame was not hidden from you, when I was being made in secret, intricately woven in the depths of the earth. Your eyes saw my unformed substance; in your book were written, every one of them, the days that were formed for me, when as yet there was none of them."

"Let's pray," he said.

She closed her eyes and listened. She didn't understand everything he said, but she knew one thing. She liked listening to him very much. She liked being in this place, being with these people. She liked the Bible passage she had just read. It had never dawned on her that God was intimately acquainted with all her ways, even knew what she was thinking. She'd always thought God was too busy for little people, that he only had time for presidents and generals.

After he prayed, Pastor Harman said, "We've just read from God's book. But did you see what David says here in this psalm? He said God has *another* book. A book he has written about *our* lives." As he normally did, the pastor spent the next thirty minutes going over each verse and explaining what each one meant, then how they applied to everyday life. Katherine was riveted by every word.

Then he said, "One of the most meaningful things the Lord has shown me these last few years is the value and importance of living for him one day at a time. To awaken each day aware of my complete dependence on him, then very quickly, before my mind begins to fret and try to take over, I begin to yield my heart and turn my thoughts toward him. If we don't, we wind up living like orphans fending for ourselves. Our lives become full of anxiety and fear, because deep inside, we know we're not really in control. Think about it . . . how much of your life—even this week—went just the way you planned?"

Katherine answered the question in her head . . . none of it. She realized that all she ever did was worry about tomorrow, what might go wrong. If not tomorrow then she worried about the rest of the week or the next month.

"Instead," he said, "we need to awaken each day as a disciple—as it says in Isaiah 50—to listen as one being taught. Our most important task is to begin each day drawing near to God. To surrender our will, our plans, our agenda for each day to the one who loved us and gave himself for us on the cross."

The cross; now she knew he was talking about Jesus.

"We know," said Pastor Harman, "that God's faithfulness toward us awakens with the sunrise. The Bible says his mercies are new every morning. And the psalm we've just read tells us that our future—all the days of our lives—though turning one page at a time for us, are already written in God's book. Have you ever thought of that? God has written a book for each one of us—the book of our lives. And each day is like a page. How many pages do you have, do I have left in my book? What things might happen in those pages?

I don't know. But this I do know . . . the one who made us, the one who died and gave his life for our sins . . . he knows how many pages we have left and what's written on each one. And we know Jesus has promised to be with us as each page unfolds, leading us and guiding us by his Spirit, as we take hold of his hand and follow."

Katherine knew at that moment that she desperately wanted to know God this way, the way the pastor and all these people did. The way Mrs. Fortini did. Pastor Harman asked a woman to come up and play the piano softly. As she did, he said he wanted to close his message explaining the gospel clearly, just in case there was anyone there who didn't understand it.

Normally, this was the time Katherine slipped out of the pew to head over to Patrick's classroom, so she could be there when he came out. She felt the impulse to go but realized this morning, she didn't have to.

She stayed put.

Pastor Harman said, "The God who made us demonstrated his love for us, not by connecting it to our fickle feelings, which shift rapidly like the wind. He demonstrated his love by sending his Son Jesus Christ to die in our place on the cross. Why did Jesus have to die? Why did his blood need to be shed?"

Katherine realized . . . she had never really understood the answer to that question. She sat forward.

"He shed his blood to pay the price for our sins. This shows how serious our sins are to God, but also his amazing grace and love. Left to ourselves, we would all just wander away. These sins, which we've been committing all our lives, separate us from God. They're the reason God can seem so far away. And they must be punished, because God is just and holy. But if we turn from them, if we ask God to forgive us, he will. Because Jesus paid the price in full. God is willing to completely wash our sins away and give us a gift of righteousness, the very righteousness of his beloved Son. And that's not all . . . God will become our heavenly Father and adopt us into his family."

Jesus died for my sins . . . God wants to adopt me?

As Katherine heard these words, tears rolled down her face. She had never been in a family before. At the orphanage where she grew up, she'd longed to be adopted by any of the dozens of couples who came by. But it never happened. By the time she was thirteen, she'd finally given up. She didn't even come downstairs anymore to see the parents who came.

But the pastor just said God wanted to adopt her, to be her Father. It was almost too wonderful to be true. But she decided right then . . . she did believe it; she believed everything she had heard. Pastor Harman asked if anyone wanted to pray with him to receive Christ as their Savior.

Katherine raised her hand. She didn't even notice she was the only one.

She closed her eyes and prayed along with him. She felt someone's warm hand on her shoulder. She looked up to see Sadie Robbins, the woman who first greeted her months ago. Tears flowed like rain; she couldn't stop them, didn't want to stop them.

She felt so light and peaceful inside. She had never known such intense joy.

She couldn't wait to go home and tell Mrs. Fortini.

Thirty-four

June 12, 1944
London

Katherine was sure she'd probably experienced more "firsts" in the past month than in the rest of her life combined. She had personally experienced God's love for the first time. She had traveled outside of Pennsylvania for the first time, to New York City, where they'd caught a plane to London, of all places.

Flying in a plane, that was a first.

It had been a fascinating experience, except for the times that terrified her, and there were too many of them. It was *so* noisy and bumpy. Several times she'd thought the plane would just pull apart and fall out of the sky. She kept looking at Shawn. He could not have been more at ease, like they were out for a Sunday drive to Valley Forge.

Patrick kept turning to her for comfort, burying his face in her coat. His father would gently pull him away. "Piece of cake, Patrick," he'd say. "Just some rough air, we'll be okay." Then he'd go back to reading his paper. He had flown much worse in England, he told her, almost every day . . . plus he was being shot at.

They had finally landed in London. Another first—she was in a different country.

Not just any country, but the fairytale land of her childhood stories and books. She might actually get to see the places she'd read about in Dickens and her Jane Austen novels. Perhaps they might take a drive out to Yorkshire, see the moors and mansions she'd read about in *Wuthering Heights*.

At the moment, Katherine felt far removed from the majesty and splendor of the English countryside. She stood in a long line at a bakery—a "queue," as the Brits called it—waiting for a single loaf of bread. In front and behind her, as best she could interpret, middle-aged women argued about how much rain was supposed to fall that day, the lousy service of the bloke at the counter, and something Churchill had said last night on the radio.

She paid for the bread using sixpence or shillings or some other coin of the realm, then stepped out into the crowded street.

The city streets and buildings had the charming old-timey look she'd expected, but her London fantasies had been marred by the stark reminders of war. On every block stood some of the loveliest row homes and businesses, many hundreds of years old. But like a smile with missing teeth, each street had horrible gaping holes. Homes and businesses no longer there, bombed-out shells, reduced to neat little piles of bricks and rubble. A neighbor had told her that every family she knew had lost someone in the Blitz. Entire families were routinely wiped out in a single night. And this had gone on for years.

She couldn't imagine living every day in such danger. At least they were safe now. There hadn't been a single bomb dropped on England since they'd arrived. Shawn said the skies had been clear for more than two months before that. She had stepped out into the street when a blaring horn surprised her. She fell back on the sidewalk. An army truck sped by; she barely escaped the muddy spray from its tires.

"Didn't you see the lorry, miss?"

She looked up at the kind face of an elderly man reaching out his hand. "I'm so stupid," she said. "Been here a month, and I still keep forgetting to look the opposite way."

"Figured as much," he said. "Seems we're killing more of you Yanks on the road than on the battlefield." He helped her up. "'Ere's your bag, miss. A bit banged up, it is."

"Thank you," she said and smiled as he walked away. The crowd on the sidewalk moved on, used to such things by now. She pulled the bread out, saw a wide crease right through the middle. It would have to do, she thought; she had no time to go through that line again. Shawn was coming home for dinner tonight from his base at High Wycombe, the first time she or Patrick had seen him since D-Day last week. She had four other stores to get to, then just enough time to get back to the apartment to cook.

That's right, she reminded herself . . . it's not an apartment; they call it a *flat* in London. But what sense did that make? Her flat was at the end of a long hill, then once through the doorway she had to climb a steep flight of steps. She came to the next intersection, stopped, and looked both ways several times.

It would be terrible for Patrick if she got run over.

After making her way through the stores, she headed home. She walked past the church she'd been attending since they arrived. It was smaller than her church in Allingdale, much more formal, and the pastor was not near the preacher Pastor Harman was. But she cherished her time there every Sunday.

Even here, the presence of war was evident. In the back corner of the sanctuary, light poured in, and sometimes rain from a large hole in the roof. She'd been told a German bomb made the hole and then, thankfully, failed to explode upon impact.

Katherine picked up the mail by the front door of their apartment. She noticed among the envelopes the now familiar handwriting of Albert Baker. He'd still written to her as often as when she was in the States. She had to admit, she did enjoy the idea of being pursued so eagerly but still wasn't ready to give in. He kept his letters safe and mostly non-romantic, other than always ending them the same way . . . *Love, Al.* She had mentioned in passing, in one of her rare letters back to him, the possibility of them coming to England.

She didn't know how he'd found out where they lived, but obviously he had. She put the letter in her purse for later. How she wished Major Collins would show even a fraction of the interest Captain Albert Baker lavished upon her.

∽

"That's it up on the left, Private," said Shawn.

"The brown one, sir?"

"You can just pull over anywhere, we're close enough."

"Right, sir."

As his ride drove away, Shawn caught a rare sunset descending between the row homes of Notting Hill. He'd picked this area because of its proximity to the two places he worked, the Eighth Air Force headquarters at High Wycombe and General Eisenhower's base in Bushy Park.

"Daddy!"

Shawn looked up as Patrick ran down the steps and jumped into his arms.

"You're finally home."

"I'm finally home," Shawn repeated. He moved Patrick to one arm and reached down for his things.

"You all done at your base?" Patrick asked as they walked up the steps.

"Not all done, but it looks like I can start spending more time with you and—"

"Miss Townsend is making us spaghetti."

"Really? Sounds delicious." They walked inside. Wonderful smells filled the hall. The door off the hall led into a tight living area. He walked in and saw Katherine still at work in the kitchen. She wore an apron splattered with sauce and a towel over her shoulder. She really had become quite a cook. "Where's Mrs. Cooper?" he asked.

"Major Collins, so glad you're home," she said, still stirring a pot. The kitchen was so small. "She's been visiting her sister near Watford for the last few days. It's given me a chance to cook some American meals for a change, at least something close."

"Patrick told me we're having spaghetti."

"And meatballs," she said. "Just don't ask me what's in them."

"Do I have time to get changed?"

"Sure."

"I'll just need a couple of minutes."

"Then I'll start putting the food on the table. Wanna help me, Patrick?"

Shawn walked back out into the hall. He shared a room with Patrick on the first floor past the stairs, but he'd barely been in it. He had rented both floors from Mrs. Cooper to give them at least some sense of home. She occupied the rest of the downstairs. She wasn't an adequate replacement for Mrs. Fortini or half the cook. But she was very kind in her own way, and Patrick really liked her. Katherine had a room—a locked room—at the top of the stairs.

He knew Mrs. Cooper would be upset to learn he'd come home when she wasn't there. "Run a respectable place 'round here," she'd reminded him several times. He put his things away and changed into casual clothes. Then joined Patrick and Miss Townsend for dinner.

"So what did you do today, Patrick?"

"Before lunch Miss Townsend took me to the park."

"Hyde Park," Katherine added. "We fed some ducks."

"And she threw the ball with me."

"Really?" Shawn asked. "Can she catch?"

"Pretty good," Patrick said. "But she throws like a girl."

"That's because I am a girl."

"Did you play with any boys?" Shawn asked.

"No, they were all playing that game, what do you call it?"

"Cricket," said Katherine. "I don't get it either, Patrick."

"The bat is flat," Patrick explained. "And they don't swing it right. And if they get a hit they just run back and forth. They only got two bases."

"When we get home," Shawn said, "we'll play baseball the right way."

"Would you like some bread, Patrick?" Katherine asked.

Patrick looked at it and said no thank you. Shawn looked at it too. It did look odd.

"I'm sorry. The bread here is so different. I toasted it to get rid of the gray tinge. The real problem happened when I fell on it."

"You fell?" Shawn asked. "Are you all right?"

"I'm fine, but, really, you don't have to eat the bread."

Shawn picked up a piece. "It looks fine. The spaghetti is delicious. You've really gotten Mrs. Fortini's sauce nailed down."

"It was quite a project finding tomatoes."

"Well, this beats anything I've had for weeks. I'm real sorry I haven't been home very much." Shawn couldn't tell them why. He'd thought things would ease up shortly after D-Day, but things were still going rough for the boys in Normandy. It put the planning staff on high alert, trying to find ways to give them proper support. "The radio work?" Shawn asked, noticing it perched on a table by the front window.

"It does," said Katherine.

"But they only got some of the shows like back home. They got a bunch I don't know," said Patrick. "And I can't understand how they talk."

"Well, after we eat, I'll help you get ready for bed," Shawn said, "and I'll see if I can find something fun to listen to. I've been here a lot longer than you guys. I can tell you what they're saying."

Patrick stood up. "Daddy, I have a surprise for you."

"You do? What is it?"

"It's not finished yet, but almost. I'll go get it." He ran back to his room. "Here," he said, holding out two sticks in the palm of his hand, one slightly longer than the other.

Shawn instantly knew they were some kind of carving project but couldn't imagine what it was. "What are they?" he asked.

"It's a cross I'm making for you."

"Really?"

"Grandpa taught me how before we left. First, he wanted to teach me something else. He thought I wanted to make it with Jesus still on it, but that would be too hard. I told him we could make it after Jesus got off, and so he showed me what to do."

Shawn smiled. "That's great, Patrick. How do you stick the pieces together?"

"Grandpa showed me how to make a special notch. That's the part I haven't finished yet."

"I'm sure he'd be real proud of you if he could see it. You still being very careful?"

"I am, 'cause I don't ever wanna get cut."

Shawn looked at Katherine; she was shaking her head and smiling. "Well, better put that away, Patrick," she said. "So you can eat the spaghetti before it gets cold."

Thirty minutes later, they were all sitting in the tiny living room, listening to a replay of a Bob Hope show. Katherine had the kitchen all cleaned up. Patrick was sitting on his lap.

They were almost like a regular . . .

Shawn sighed.

⸙

It felt like the middle of the night. Something was wrong. Shawn sat up in his bed. He heard the distinct sound of anti-aircraft fire off in the distance, sounded like it came from the southeast. Lots of it.

"What's wrong, Daddy?"

Then he heard an air-raid siren. It, too, was far away, on the other side of London.

"What is that?" Patrick asked. He jumped out of his little bed and into Shawn's. Shawn held him close. "It's okay, Patrick. It's far away."

"But what is it?"

He heard a thumping on the stairs. Katherine must be coming down. "It sounds like the British soldiers are shooting at something," he said. He picked Patrick up and turned on a light in the hall. Katherine rounded the stairway toward them.

"What's going on, Major?"

"I don't know. I don't hear any planes. And the racket is

way east of us." They walked outside and found many of the neighbors doing the same. They all looked to the sky in the direction of the sounds.

"What you make of that, Major?" asked an elderly man. Shawn had forgotten his name. "Thought we was through with all this."

"I don't know, sir."

Just then they all heard a loud boom, definitely a bomb of some kind.

"Not again," a woman said across the street. "Please, God, not again."

Patrick buried his face in Shawn's shoulder. Katherine moved very close; Shawn could tell she wanted him to hold her. Instead he offered words, said with far more assurance than he felt inside. "I don't know what's going on, but I don't hear any more explosions. I don't think it's another raid. Might just be a stray plane that got past our defenses."

They waited a while longer. Soon the guns went silent, then the air raid sirens.

"See, we're okay. Let's go back to bed," Shawn said. He led them back inside, totally puzzled by what they'd just experienced.

He and his neighbors in Notting Hill didn't realize they had just witnessed the beginning of a totally new campaign of terror Hitler had unleashed on London.

The boom they'd just heard . . . six Londoners had just died.

Thousands more would follow.

Thirty-five

Life in London soon became nightmarish and tense again.

For the first time in history, a pilot-less aircraft, actually a rocket, had flown across the English Channel and plummeted to earth. After the first rocket attack, there had been a four-day lull. The radio and newspapers had reported the incident as a lone German bomber quickly shot down by anti-aircraft gunners. But mysterious rumors began to spread from the locals nearby the crash site . . . no German bodies had been pulled from the wreckage.

Two weeks later, the truth was clear to all.

After that initial four-day pause, Hitler unleashed dozens of these unmanned rockets on London every day. Officially, they were being called V-1 rockets. Folks around London nicknamed them "doodlebugs" or "buzzbombs" because of their odd sound. Their introduction into the war created a massive increase in Shawn's workload. The mission-planning staff had turned all their attention toward hunting down and destroying the rocket bases, somewhere in northern France. So far they'd been unsuccessful.

Even with this added work, Shawn came home every night, trying to offset Patrick's and Katherine's fears. But it seemed with each passing day, his own increased. So far, all the attacks had taken place south and east of them. But you could hear each rocket and sometimes see them. This went on day after day, night after night, in good weather or bad. Shawn knew a few more gallons of fuel and these rockets could easily close the distance to Notting Hill. It had reached the point where he had no choice—he would have to send Patrick and Katherine home. He picked up the telephone to call Katherine.

"Hi, Katherine, it's Shawn."

"Major Collins, hello."

"They won't let me out of here right now," he said, "but I'm sending a car to get you both. You're leaving Notting Hill this afternoon."

"Really? I'm so glad. I just heard another one explode five minutes ago. It sounded closer than before. I actually heard the engine die. Thirty seconds later, a loud boom. Our windows actually rattled. That never happened before."

This wasn't good, Shawn thought. By now all of London was talking about these dreaded silent moments. As long as you heard the droning engine sound, you were fine. The danger came when the engine cut out. From that moment, you had maybe thirty to forty seconds before it crashed, setting off the one-ton warhead. *Hearing* the silence could mean only one thing—you were in the dead zone.

"Pack up everything," Shawn said. "I mean everything. You won't be coming back."

"Where are we going?"

"Back to the States in a couple of days. Until then, I found a place for you both in a little town nearby. We're far out of range up here." Shawn heard her sigh with relief.

"You'll get no complaints from me," she said. "How much time till the driver gets here?"

"How much time do you need?"

"Two hours tops."

"Two hours then."

∞

Three hours later, Katherine and Patrick pulled up to the guard gate at High Wycombe, the Eighth Air Force headquarters where Shawn worked. An army MP came up to the window of the cab and bent down.

"I ain't 'ere for meself," the cabbie said. "Got a missus and 'er little boy in the back."

Katherine leaned forward. "I'm Katherine Townsend, here with Major Collins's son, Patrick. He said he would leave word about us at the gate."

"Hi, Miss Townsend. Spoke with the major not ten minutes ago. Came to see if you'd arrived. Sir," he said to the cabbie, "you can drop her off right by that door over there, then pull back around. Miss Townsend, there's a receptionist and a waiting room just inside on the right. Just tell her who you are, and she'll call Major Collins."

"Right-o," the cabbie said, then drove through as the gate raised.

Katherine was so relieved to be out of London. She had never been more afraid in her life. She looked out the window as they pulled up to Wycombe Abbey; before the war it had been a girls' school. Like so many buildings she'd seen in England, it looked to be a place with a thousand tales, more like a castle than a school. They pulled up to the curb, and Katherine helped Patrick out.

"I'll get your bags from the boot, miss," the cabbie said.

"I'll help you," she said. "Patrick, you can stand just inside the door there. I'll be right in." They carried the bags up the steps. "How much do I owe you for the ride?"

"Not a bit, miss. The major paid me plenty 'fore he sent me after you."

"Oh no," Patrick said. "I forgot it." He ran back to the cab and looked in the back window. "It's not there." Instantly his eyes filled with tears.

"What's the matter? What did you forget?"

He walked to the first step and plopped down, then buried his head in his lap. "My grandfather's pouch and the cross I'm making for Daddy. I forgot them in my room. My grandpa will be so mad. He made me promise I wouldn't lose his bag. He's had it for his whole life."

Katherine knew Patrick wasn't exaggerating; she'd heard the conversation with Patrick and the elder Collins before they'd left. And Patrick had worked so hard on his father's cross. It was just a thirty-minute drive. She could hurry back, grab those two things, and turn right around. "Do you remember where you left them?"

"They're right under my bed. We were rushing around and I forgot all about it."

"Sir," she said to the cabbie, "could I pay you the same thing Major Collins did for a quick trip there and back?"

"Your money's as good as 'is," he said. "Got no other fares at the moment."

"Then let's go. Let me just get Patrick situated inside."

"Really?" Patrick asked. "You'll go back and get it?"

She walked him up the steps. "I have to. You were almost done carving that cross, right? We can't just leave it back there in London. Your dad said we weren't coming back."

She walked him inside and explained the situation to the receptionist and asked her to contact Shawn, let him know what had happened. "Is it okay if I leave him here with you until I get back? Shouldn't be more than an hour."

The receptionist looked at Patrick and smiled. "Take your time. We'll be fine."

Katherine gave Patrick a big hug. "Now don't go anywhere with anyone until I get back. Unless it's your dad."

"I won't," Patrick promised, then gave her another hug. "Thank you so much," he said.

She hurried out the door and got back in the cab. They drove back toward London after explaining things to the MP. Katherine said a quick prayer and tried to extinguish the frightening thoughts that kept finding their way to the surface. *I'll just be there a few minutes.*

Thirty-six

Katherine rode back to London mostly in silence. The cab driver seemed like the quiet type, and she was glad. She looked out the window, trying to take in the scenery along the way. While she was glad to be leaving all this danger, she was sad she'd never get to tour all the beautiful places she'd read about in her books. Then she had a thought. Maybe she should contact Captain Al. He'd probably jump at the chance of spending an afternoon with her touring the English countryside. And it would be the polite thing to let him know she was heading back to the States.

Quickly, an image of Mrs. Fortini extinguished Al's happy face. She could almost hear her. "Now, Katherine . . . is that really fair to Captain Al? Aren't you just using him? What message would that send, you calling him for something like this?"

Mrs. Fortini was right.

"Uh, looks like a bit 'a trouble up ahead, miss," the cabbie said. "Guess them Jerries are sending them doodlebugs further out these days."

Katherine looked through the windshield. They were coming to the outskirts of Notting Hill. The road up ahead was closed off with fire engines and emergency trucks. Dozens of people were crowding around. A section of row homes on the right had collapsed onto the street.

"I'll go the long way 'round, 'ave you 'ome in a jiff." He turned left, following the slow parade of cars being detoured around the rubble and smoke. "Guess our boys can't find them rocket bases. Sommut doesn't 'appen soon, all 'a London'll be a shambles. The Blitz all over again. Lost me best mate and two coozins then."

Katherine sighed, turning in her seat to watch the scene as they passed. Those poor people. She'd walked that very block a dozen times in the last month. She felt a little guilty. She would be getting away from all this horror, leave all this fear and danger behind. A few minutes later they came to her street. There was Mrs. Cooper's house up ahead.

"'Ere we are, miss. You need 'elp wiv anything?"

She opened the door. "No, I should just be a min—" She looked at the cabbie's face. He'd heard it too. Several people on the street all stopped in their tracks, heads looking up toward the southeast, toward the sound.

"Be quick, miss," the cabbie said, his face beginning to panic. He looked up through the windshield, searching.

Katherine ran up the steps to the door. It was locked. That's right, she'd already given her key back to Mrs. Cooper. She banged on the door. The deep, buzzing sound grew louder. "Mrs. Cooper, are you in there?" Now the anti-aircraft guns in Hyde Park began to fire. The V-1 was definitely heading this way.

The cabbie got out of his cab, staring in the same direction as everyone on the street. "Can still 'ere it," he said. "That's a good sign."

No one answered. "I'll just run around the back," said Katherine. "She usually leaves the back door unlocked."

The cabbie nodded, trying to look calm. He tapped his fingers on the fender. The droning sound grew louder.

It felt like the rocket was chasing Katherine down the narrow alley. She tried not to trip on a bucket and mop. Thankfully, the back door was unlocked. She raced through the dark hallway. Shawn and Patrick's room was the first one on the left. She ran around the bed and reached under. The pouch and cross were right where Patrick had said they'd be. As she came out the back door, she jumped down the steps, barely holding the rail. Then she froze.

The rocket engine cut out.

People out front began to scream. "Oh Lord, no," she cried.

Then silence.

She had what, maybe thirty seconds? Should she go back in the house? Should she hide in the alley? Seconds ticked away. She decided she'd never make it to the street; it promised no more safety than the alley. She looked back, remembering a small, makeshift shelter Mrs. Cooper had dug out in her tiny backyard during the Blitz. Nothing more than a shallow hole with a corrugated metal sheet for a roof. But it was something.

Katherine turned around and ran back toward it. The little door was blocked by some vegetable crates and old containers. Katherine frantically tossed them over her shoulder. She pulled hard at the door. She heard someone in the street yell, "God help us!"

A noise louder than anything she'd ever heard.

Someone or something tackling her from behind.

Her face in the wet mud and darkness.

Rock crunching metal.

She could hardly breathe.

Darkness.

"She did what?" Shawn asked.

"She went back to the apartment, just for a minute she said, to get something for your son." The receptionist sat up straight in her chair, obviously taken aback by Shawn's angry attitude.

"It's my fault," said Patrick, getting up from his chair. "I forgot Grandpa's tool pouch . . . and something else."

Shawn walked to the front door of the reception area, looked out toward the guard gate, then down at his watch.

"She should be back in thirty or forty minutes," the receptionist said, looking at the clock on the wall.

Just then another officer, a lieutenant, stepped into the room. He noticed Shawn's son standing by the front desk. "Is that Patrick, Major?"

Shawn nodded. "It is, Lieutenant."

"I'm so glad."

"Why?"

"Just heard a radio report. Two V-1s just detonated in the Notting Hill area, about an hour apart. That's where he was staying, isn't it?"

A look of horror flashed across the receptionist's face. Shawn walked over to Patrick and drew him near, covering his ears with the palms of his hands. *Oh God*, he prayed. *Please no, not Katherine.*

"What's the matter?" asked the lieutenant.

Thirty-seven

Shawn had the receptionist call Mrs. Cooper's number three times, letting it ring forever each time. But there was no answer.

He'd left Patrick with the receptionist, offering him some hasty excuse. He could tell Patrick was upset as he fled out the door of Wycombe Abbey, but there was no time to comfort him. He'd quickly grabbed a car from the car pool, refused the help of a driver, and took off. The MPs at the gate offered no resistance when he told them what had happened. He raced down the old London Road in the direction of Notting Hill.

He made the thirty-minute ride in twenty. The longest twenty minutes of his life. Twice he'd almost been run off the road, forgetting for a moment which side of the street he should be on.

Even from five blocks away, he could see the smoke rising from the area surrounding Mrs. Cooper's flat. As he came within two blocks, the scene was chaos and confusion. Fire trucks and Red Cross vehicles were parked at odd angles all over the street. The air was filled with voices, mostly orders being shouted and cries of grief or pain. Dozens of MPs and police tried to restrain the crowds. A fire raged through a collapsed pub, the apartment above it now in chunks and pieces on the street. Two old men carried the limp body of a small boy, no older than Patrick, toward an ambulance. A middle-aged woman, her hair and face covered with soot and dust, sat on the curb, staring into a puddle.

"Yer gonna 'afta keep movin', officer," a man with a pie-pan hat yelled to Shawn. "We need to keep the streets clear."

Shawn turned left with the traffic, which had slowed to a crawl. Forget this, he thought and pulled over. He grabbed the keys and hopped out of the car. He began to run and jump over the debris in the direction of Mrs. Cooper's street. There was so much damage, the area was almost unrecognizable. All the while, he kept repeating as he coughed, *Please let her be okay, please let her be alive.*

He carefully stepped over a small hill of bricks, stones, and broken furniture, then through a doorway, which somehow had been left untouched. As he came out onto a clear section of sidewalk, he looked left up a slight hill that led up the street and instantly got his bearings. There on the right were four familiar row homes completely intact, followed by three others completely demolished.

That could only mean one thing . . . directly across the street from the destroyed homes he saw an empty space where Mrs. Cooper's apartment had stood. The home next to it, across the small alley, was also gone. He ran as carefully as he could. There, parked just outside, he recognized the cabbie's car, completely buried under rubble and debris. Sticking out from a pile of stones on what used to be the sidewalk were the pants and shoes of a man's leg.

"Katherine!" he yelled, then rushed to the scene. The emergency workers hadn't made it this far back. A handful of neighbors who'd survived the attack—people he recognized but never got to know—were slowly removing rocks and stones and calling out loved ones' names. "Can somebody help me?" he yelled. "Katherine!"

A few people looked his way, but no one responded, their faces blank stares. He kept yelling out her name as he tossed stone after stone over his shoulder, but she didn't reply. He yanked a piece of torn upholstery out from under a large wooden beam. It was part of the chair he'd just sat in a few nights before, listening to the radio.

"Katherine!" he yelled. "Can you hear me?"

No answer. "Oh God, this can't be happening."

"I'll 'elp you, mister." Shawn looked down into the face of pre-teen boy. "My flat got spared, the least I can do."

Together they worked over the next two hours, rummaging through the tattered mess that had once been such a cozy little home. At some point, they had been joined by a middle-aged man. Shawn's heart sank lower with every new section they uncovered. No sign of Katherine. So far they had only been able to get down through the first few feet of debris. He hadn't seen a speck of floor or carpet.

Finally, they made their way to the back wall of the apartment, which had collapsed outward onto Mrs. Cooper's backyard. It was all twisted and torn. Shawn saw traces of wallpaper attached to pieces of plaster and stone. He felt so hopeless. Katherine had to be in here somewhere, but if she was, how could she have survived? What would he do now? How could he tell Patrick?

"So who's this Katherine, mate?" the middle-aged man asked. "The lady you keep callin'. She your wife?"

"No," Shawn said. But he immediately felt the same hollow ache inside that he'd felt for Elizabeth. A pain that had just recently begun to subside. Now it seemed he must start grieving all over again. *Why, God? What point could this possibly serve?* He picked up one half of a large beam lying across a big piece of corrugated metal. "She was my son's nanny."

"Hey, look there," the man said. "That a foot? There beside it, a lady's shoe, I think."

Shawn shoved the beam behind him and looked down. He instantly recognized the shoe. "Katherine!" he yelled. "Help me. That's her."

The man rushed over and helped him lift the biggest objects off the piece of scrap metal. In a few minutes they'd cleared most of it away. "Katherine!" he yelled again. "Can you hear me?" Shawn recognized the metal now. It was the little roof of that Anderson shelter Mrs. Cooper had put in her backyard. He reached down and felt Katherine's leg.

It was warm.

"She's alive!" Shawn shouted. "I think she's alive."

The man ducked down. "Looks like a little cave in there, just a foot or two, but it might 'ave been just enough."

The boy came over just as they got the last few bricks off the metal roof. "Let's lift it very carefully," said Shawn. "Don't want the sides to fall in on her."

"Don't cut yourself," the man said to the boy. "Use yer sleeve as a glove."

Together they lifted the roof.

There was Katherine, half-buried in a mixture of mud, brick, and dry goods. Shawn jumped down and pulled her up. He felt her pulse. It was weak, but it was there. He brushed the wet dirt that covered her face and cradled her in his arms. "Katherine," he said. "Katherine, it's me, Shawn."

He heard her moan. He stroked her hair and forehead. "Katherine, can you hear me?"

Her eyelids fluttered, then she opened her eyes halfway.

Tears formed in Shawn's eyes. "Thank you, God," he said

under his breath. "Katherine, it's me, Shawn. Don't worry, we'll get you out of here."

"Shawn?" she said faintly, almost seeing him. Then her eyes closed.

"Katherine?" Shawn shouted. He patted her face gently. She didn't respond. She seemed to be slipping away. He patted her face again, a little harder. "Katherine, we can't lose you now . . . I can't lose you." He felt her pulse then sighed with relief; it actually seemed a little stronger than before.

"It's that nasty bump on 'er 'ead," the man said. "Seen this before, call it a concussion. Medics said it's best to keep 'em awake if we can."

Shawn tried waking her again. Her eyes fluttered a few times but wouldn't open. He picked her up to carry her toward the street. "Katherine, I've got you, you're going to be okay. I've got to get her to an ambulance."

"Saw some round the block on my way 'ere," the boy said. "I'll show you."

"Thanks," Shawn said. He looked down and saw his father's leather pouch and the cross Patrick had carved for him lying in the mud. "Could you grab that pouch and cross for me, and put them in my pocket?" The boy nodded. Shawn turned to the older man. "I can never thank you enough for your help. I don't even know your name."

"Not important. You'd do the same fer me," he said. "Now go help yer lady there, lad." As Shawn hurried off, he heard the man mutter to himself, "Seems a bit more than a nanny to 'im, you ask me."

Thirty-eight

September 30, 1944
Philadelphia area
(9 weeks later)

Katherine sat up, glad once again to have slept through the night without any bad dreams. That made it three nights in a row. Yesterday the final bandages had come off her head. The hair around her stitches, with a little bit of work, was starting to blend in nicely. Mrs. Fortini had said they couldn't even be seen unless someone stared at them, and then added, "Why do we care about what people who stare think anyway."

Katherine got out of bed and put on her robe. The sun shone brightly through her windows. She looked down the street, happy just to see all the homes standing where they belonged. No rubble in the street. No anti-aircraft guns going off day and night. No explosions or the fear of when the next one might occur.

She couldn't remember all the details of the rocket attack that hit their street in Notting Hill. Shawn had said that was a blessing. She cherished a handful of memories, though; no more than flashes, really. A cloudy moment when she'd looked up into Shawn's face as he called out her name. Feeling the strength in his arms as he'd carried her to the ambulance. The expression on his face as he tucked her in the stretcher and promised to be right behind her.

Shawn had rescued her. He probably had saved her life.

Then there was the amount of time he'd spent with her in the hospital the first week after the attack. The flowers. The card. And perhaps the most significant thing . . . he'd stopped calling her Miss Townsend again. It really seemed he might care for her as more than just Patrick's nanny.

But even now, she wasn't sure.

She looked at her watch; she better get dressed. She took off her robe in front of the mirror and put on her shirt. Except for some large, unsightly bruises, the concussion had been her only serious injury. After the third week, the doctors had felt it was safe for her to fly, so Shawn sent her and Patrick home. He'd promised to join them as soon as the Air Force allowed.

Yesterday, a telegram had arrived. Shawn would be coming home this afternoon.

He'd written a letter a week ago, saying they had figured out how to shoot down almost 80 percent of the V-1 rockets now before they ever reached London. After she finished getting dressed, she put on a little face powder in the bathroom and all but glided down the stairs.

"Aren't you the happy one this morning?" Mrs. Fortini said. She wore her cleaning apron and was carrying some cups toward the kitchen.

"As if you didn't know why," she said.

Mrs. Fortini smiled through a half-scolding look. "Just be careful, my dear. That's all I'm gonna say."

"I'm being careful," she said. "Is there anything I can help you with?"

"I've got breakfast fixed for Patrick and Mr. Collins. It's all on a tray on the kitchen table. Could you take it over to them? There's plenty for you too."

"I'd be happy to," she said.

"Maybe after that we could do some shopping together."

"I'd love to," said Katherine.

"What time is Shawn supposed to arrive?"

"The telegram just said this afternoon, but I called the train station. The train's supposed to get in to Philly about 3:00 p.m. Then it will probably take him an hour or so to catch the train from there to here. So about 4:00, I guess."

"Patrick will be so excited to see him," Mrs. Fortini said.

"Yes . . . yes, he will."

∽

Shawn looked down at his watch, then out the window. The train should be pulling into the 30th Street station in about twenty minutes. That meant twenty more minutes of thinking. Then he'd get off, switch to the shorter line heading into Allingdale, and think some more.

He was tired of thinking.

He shouldn't be tired; he should be excited. He was coming home. Patrick sounded so happy when he'd called a few stops back. And Mrs. Fortini was undoubtedly planning a big dinner at his dad's house. Sounded like his dad was doing okay. His leg was healing up nicely, no new problems with his heart.

But Katherine would be there when he got home.

She was the source of his conflicting thoughts. Something had happened to him during those moments two months ago when he'd thought he'd lost her. The pain was unbearable,

∽ 261 ∽

almost equal to his heartache about Elizabeth. And then the joy at finding her alive. It was equal in intensity.

But he shouldn't be feeling things like this. So why was he? Something inside beckoned him to go there, to think it through, to let it go wherever it needed to. But he couldn't, wouldn't let it happen.

It was just too soon.

"Major . . . that you?"

Shawn looked up. A Pullman porter was looking down at him, smiling widely. Then he realized who it was. "Harry? Well, what do you know?" Shawn reached out his hand. "What are you doing here?"

"I was about to ask you the same thing. Last I heard, you was back in England."

"I was there this time yesterday. Just getting some leave to visit home. Not sure where they'll have me go next. So what, you give up on the Hollywood tour train? I just read in the newspaper it's still going on."

"Well, when they headed out West my bosses offered me a chance to go, but I got no business strayin' so far from home." Then he bent down and whispered, "Truth be told, them stars tip big, but only every now and then. I did some figurin' and turns out I was makin' more on my old train route. So I come back here."

"It's so good to see you," Shawn said. "Your family well?"

"Seems so. I'll be stopping in to see 'em tonight, once this train gets down south a-ways."

"I'll be seeing my family too. A few hours from now."

"Well, you take care, Major. Looks like the good Lord intends us to bump into each other pretty regular. I expect I'll be seeing you again soon."

They shook hands again, and Harry headed down the

aisle. Shawn smiled as he thought about Harry. He didn't recall ever seeing him when he wasn't smiling. He wanted to be that way again. He sat back down and looked out the window and sighed.

He didn't want to think anymore.

Thirty-nine

An hour later, Shawn stood outside the office door of Christ Redeemer Church. He could hardly believe what he was doing. Part of him wanted to flee, but he knew he had to talk to somebody. He'd already called Pastor Harman when he'd gotten off the train in Philadelphia, after recalling something his old pastor at Penn State had said: "Sometimes in life we need a pastor for more than a Sunday sermon." Shawn felt like this was one of those times.

He straightened up, pulled his shoulders back, and was just about to knock on the door when it opened.

"Oh, excuse me," said Pastor Harman, almost walking into Shawn. "Thought I heard a noise."

"Just me," Shawn said, forcing a smile. "Maybe my knees knocking."

The pastor laughed. "Come in, have a seat." He led Shawn back to his office, then sat behind his desk.

He had such kind eyes, Shawn thought. "This feels really strange for me."

"I get that a lot," the pastor said. "So . . . what's on your mind?"

Shawn shifted in his seat but couldn't get comfortable.

Over the next twenty minutes he managed to give the pastor a summary of the situation, highlighting the events that had unfolded from Elizabeth's death to the present.

Pastor Harman leaned back in his chair. "I know we don't know each other very well, Shawn, but mind if I ask you something? Are you mad at God?"

"What?"

"Do you think you might be angry with God . . . for taking Elizabeth?"

Shawn knew he was but didn't want to just say it.

"It's okay, Shawn. But see, if you are, I imagine you're feeling kind of stuck right now in your faith."

Shawn thought a moment. He'd come here to get help. He should just say it. "I can't see why God would put me through all this. Why he would take Elizabeth away." He realized he was raising his voice.

Pastor Harman didn't react. "Seems like you're struggling with the goodness of God."

"What?"

"Whether or not God is truly good."

Shawn thought that sounded about right.

"Did you *used* to believe God is good?" the pastor asked.

"I'm sure I did."

"How good?"

"Completely," Shawn said. "Loving and good. But what I'm going through now . . . this doesn't feel very good to me."

"I understand why you'd think that, Shawn." The pastor leaned forward, rubbed his brow. "Since the war began, I've had to deal with a lot of grief and grieving loved ones. One thing that's helped me is to redefine my concept of goodness, to measure it by what God does or allows, rather than by what I agree with or understand."

"I don't follow you."

"See, typically we measure goodness by whether we like something or not. I like this, so it's good. I don't like that, so it's not good. We can do this with God, pretty easily, in fact. If he does something we like or agree with, then he's good. If he does something or allows something we don't like, we're not so sure anymore. We won't usually say it out loud; that would be impolite. But we can go there in our hearts. And once we do, we start to pull away from the Lord. Do you think that could have happened here?"

Seemed like this was exactly what had happened to him, but Shawn still wasn't ready to admit it.

"Shawn, have you ever heard this verse before . . . Romans 8:28? 'And we know that God works *all things* together *for good* to those who love him and are called according to his purpose'?"

Shawn nodded. He'd even memorized it.

"God doesn't just do good, Shawn. He *is* good. His goodness flows from his very nature. Because we don't always understand what he's doing, some of it doesn't *seem* good to us. But that's where our faith comes into play. We must believe, as Paul says, that God is working all things together for our good. In time, his goodness and good purposes will become clearer to us. But it can take time. This making any sense?"

Shawn nodded, but he didn't exactly know how to say what he was thinking.

"What is it, Shawn?"

"Sounds like you're saying . . . Elizabeth's death was a good thing? I can't see how that's possible."

Pastor Harman's face was full of care and concern. He spoke softly. "Shawn, I don't want to sound like some Bible answer man. I know it doesn't seem like Elizabeth's death could ever be a good thing. But let's start with something simpler. Can you think of anything good God has done in your life?"

"Yeah."

"Like what?"

"He sent Jesus to die for my sins."

"Very good. The cross is the greatest display of God's goodness to us. What else?"

"My son, Patrick. I still have him."

"Patrick is a wonderful boy. I've really enjoyed getting to know him better. Can you think of anything good that has come into your life since Elizabeth died?"

Shawn thought a moment. "My father and I, our relationship has been restored. For years we didn't even speak."

"How did that happen?"

"God just changed his heart. Now it's better than it's ever been."

"Good. How about Katherine? I've seen the way she loves and cares for Patrick. Can you see any connection between her and God's goodness to you?"

Shawn had never thought about her like this. "I guess so . . . with all the time I've been away, she's been almost the perfect caretaker for Patrick. I never worry about him when I'm gone, because of how she treats him. And how he feels about her."

"See, Shawn. Although the gospel is the greatest proof of God's kindness, with just a little effort, we were able to come up with some pretty big things that demonstrate his love and goodness in your life. In time, you'll see a lot more. Because God has promised to work *all* things together for your good. I've got just one more question to ask. And this one might be a little tough to hear."

Shawn sat up straight, almost bracing himself.

"I'm sure you didn't know when you fell in love with Elizabeth how much time she had left on this earth, but if you did know, would you have walked away? Would you rather have never fallen in love and spent all the days you had with her, if you knew they'd come to an end when they did?"

Shawn shook his head, fighting back tears. "No," he said. "I'd do it again, every bit of it. I wouldn't trade the time I had with her for anything, or take back a single day."

"So," Pastor Harman said, "it was a good thing then that you met her, married her, and brought Patrick into this world."

A tear rolled down Shawn's cheek. He wiped it away. "A very good thing," he said. Shawn looked at his watch. He hadn't told anyone he was stopping off here, and if he didn't leave soon, he'd be late for that big dinner he was sure Mrs. Fortini had coming. "I've gotta be going, Pastor Harman." He stood up. "But I really appreciate you making time for me like this."

"Shawn, I'm here anytime you want to talk. I'll be praying for you."

They shook hands and Shawn headed out the door. As it closed behind him, he realized he'd forgotten to talk about the one thing he came in for. What was he supposed to do about Katherine? About all these conflicting feelings he had inside? He still didn't know.

The only thing he felt sure of was this—it was just too soon.

He and Elizabeth had talked about her remarrying if *he* died in the war . . . after a *respectable* time. He'd read an article about how wartime deaths were changing social mores. Some were saying now that six months or a year was plenty of time, because so many people were dying so young.

But this was Elizabeth. It was just too soon.

Forty

They were all together sitting around the table: Patrick, Shawn and his father, Mrs. Fortini and Katherine. "I haven't had chicken parmesan in I don't know how long," Shawn said to Mrs. Fortini. "And I don't remember it ever tasting that good."

"Don't thank me," Mrs. Fortini said. "It was my recipe, but Katherine made it."

"Really?" Shawn looked across the table at Katherine.

"Even I like it," said Patrick.

Katherine smiled and looked down.

"It is very good, Miss Townsend," said the elder Collins, stifling a cough. "Shawn, between the two of them I've been eating pretty good these last few months."

"You'd never have been able to make something like this back in England," Shawn said to Katherine.

"It's like we're not even rationing here compared to what they have over there," she said.

"Speaking of *over there*," Shawn's dad said. "Any idea when you're going back?"

"I'm hoping I won't have to," Shawn said. "We've pretty much shut down the V-1 attacks on London. Our boys have retaken Paris, and they're not far from pushing the Germans out of France and Belgium. Rumors are beginning to spread that we might have this thing wrapped up by Christmas. I'm hoping they're going to reassign me somewhere back here."

"Really?" Katherine asked. "Will they put you back on the War Bond tour?"

"Can I have some more bread?" Patrick asked. Mrs. Fortini passed him the basket.

"I think my celebrity days are over," said Shawn. "They've got plenty of heroes to pick from with far better stories to tell than mine."

"I don't believe that," his father said. "They ever say anything more about your medal?"

A startled look came over Shawn's face. "I forgot all about it." He stood up.

"Where you going, Daddy?"

"They already gave me the medal, three weeks ago. C'mon, Patrick, I'll show it to you."

"Can't we all see it?" Katherine asked.

"I'll bring it downstairs. I didn't get the Medal of Honor, though; they gave me the next one down, the Distinguished Service Cross."

"The next one down," Mrs. Fortini said. "What a thing to call it. You mean the second-highest medal of all the medals."

"Okay," Shawn said, "you could say that."

Shawn and Patrick went upstairs. Patrick came down holding the medal, a beautifully crafted cross of gold with an eagle in the center, suspended from a mostly blue ribbon, outlined in red and white stripes. It was set in a nice box like fine jewelry. "Look, Miss Townsend, it's kind of like the cross I made Daddy." He brought it to the table and sat down.

"I like your cross better," Shawn said.

"Really?"

"Really. And one day, when you're a little older, I'll give you mine."

Patrick passed the medal to Katherine. "It's beautiful," she said. "Congratulations."

"Thanks. And here's a picture a friend took when General Doolittle pinned it on me."

"Jimmy Doolittle?" his father asked. "The guy that flew that big mission to Tokyo two years ago?"

"That's him," said Shawn. "He's in charge of the whole Eighth Air Force in Europe now."

After Mrs. Fortini saw both the medal and the photo, she got up from the table. "I'm gonna put the coffee on and get dessert ready," she said.

Instantly Katherine got up. "Let me help you."

"You stay put and visit," said Mrs. Fortini.

So they did. Over the next few hours they caught up on each other's lives, moving to the living room after dessert. It was all very pleasant, and the time flew by. Shawn announced he was getting sleepy and noticed Patrick was barely awake. "And we should probably get out of Dad's bedroom here so he can turn in," Shawn said, looking at his father's bed still occupying the far corner.

As Katherine and Mrs. Fortini got up to leave, there was just one thing that bothered Katherine about the evening. And it bothered her a lot. Shawn never once called her by her first name, and twice referred to her as Miss Townsend.

So we're back to that, she thought.

Forty-one

May 2, 1945
(7 months later)

The war didn't end by Christmas, as so many people thought
it would. Instead, the Christmas season of 1944 ushered in perhaps the worst and bloodiest battle of the entire war. It came to
be known as the Battle of the Bulge. Over nineteen thousand
Americans died in six weeks of vicious fighting during one of
the coldest winters in Europe in the last fifty years.

But the Allies did win the Battle, and it really did seem like
the war in Europe was finally wrapping up. All of France,
Belgium, and the Netherlands had been liberated. The rug
under Hitler's feet was getting smaller and smaller; most
of Nazi Germany itself was now under Allied control. The
newspapers were reporting that Berlin was the only area still
in Nazi hands, but even now it was surrounded and under
attack by the Russians.

Shawn, thankfully, had missed out on all this action. He
did get reassigned in the States after his leave in September.
He'd become a test pilot for Grumman airplanes. Grumman
had a huge factory on Long Island, New York. For Shawn,

this was a dream assignment. Almost every day he got to fly fighter planes, putting them through their paces to make sure they were ready to be shipped overseas. And the best part . . . no one was shooting at him.

Shawn could come home every few weekends for a visit. Things on the home front seemed to be going smoothly. Patrick was doing well in school, had made a number of good friends in the neighborhood. Katherine, of course, was doing a wonderful job taking care of him and the house. His father's health seemed to be holding steady all this time. He never did move back upstairs. "No point in it now," he'd said. "Got a bathroom, the radio, my newspaper, and cigars . . . what do I care about going upstairs?"

Shawn smiled as he thought about his dad, how much he had changed over the last year and a half. He really looked forward to seeing him now on these trips home. Shawn picked up his duffel bag and briefcase; he was all packed and ready for the train ride from Long Island back home. He walked down the barracks hallway, noticing at the end the sad picture of FDR. Someone had taped black ribbon across the top.

He had just died a couple of weeks ago in Warm Springs, Georgia, stunning the entire nation. "Such a shame," Shawn's dad said the day after, when they'd talked about it on the telephone. "Leads us through the Depression, gets us all the way through the war, then up and dies before he can see the finish line."

Shawn had to admit, he'd never even heard of the man who'd taken his place. It felt odd speaking of President Harry Truman as the new commander-in-chief. Shawn was just about to head out the door to catch the bus to the train station when he bumped into a navy test pilot named George Ames heading into the building. His face was all lit up.

"Shawn, you see this?" Ames handed Shawn a newspaper.

"He's dead. It's official. Shot himself or took poison or something."

Shawn looked down at two huge black words, the biggest headline he ever saw: "Hitler Dead!"

"It says he's been dead for two days now," said Ames. "Can you believe it?"

"This mean the war's over?" Shawn asked.

"The article says no, but it's got to be ending soon. How they gonna fight with Hitler dead? You heading out somewhere?"

"Yeah, gonna see the family for the weekend again. You staying put?"

"My family's in Wisconsin. Maybe I'll head in to the city over the weekend, catch the Yanks playing. Oh here, I almost forgot. This is for you. That redhead in the front office said to get it to you." He handed Shawn a Western Union telegram.

"Thanks." Shawn dropped his bags just outside and quickly opened it. His heart began to race. Who would be sending him a telegram? As he started to read the words, he felt like he was going to be sick.

MAJOR COLLINS - PLEASE CALL HOME
IMMEDIATELY
YOUR FATHER'S HEART TROUBLE
DR MATTHEWS SAID TO CONTACT YOU
- MISS TOWNSEND -

✍

Katherine had just gotten Patrick situated at a friend's house around the corner from Mrs. Fortini's. Since the heart attack, they had been taking turns, one sitting with Mr. Collins and the other watching Patrick. Mrs. Fortini was with him now. Dr. Matthews said he would stop by the house again on his way home from the hospital. Collins had been insistent; he did not want to be put in the hospital. He was sure his time was up, and he wanted to die at home.

They had both asked him to please stop talking that way, but, when they were alone, they thought the same thing. It seemed only a matter of days. Dr. Matthews had all but said this when he'd asked her to contact Shawn. She looked at her watch. Mrs. Fortini would be coming back from next door in about ten minutes. Katherine realized she'd better call Al—Captain Al—and let him know what had happened, and that she couldn't meet him tonight as expected.

For the last four months Captain Albert Baker had been escorting her every other Friday night to dinner and a movie, unless it happened to be a weekend Shawn was coming home. Shawn's visits came at irregular intervals, and she hadn't told him yet about Al. Only Mrs. Fortini knew.

Katherine had never called her times with Al "dates." She knew Al did, and that was okay. She knew he probably even referred to her as his girlfriend when talking with his folks across the river in Jersey. That was where Al lived. Three weeks after she and Patrick had flown back to the States, Al got what soldiers referred to as a "million dollar wound," one bad enough to send you home but not bad enough to ruin your life. He'd taken some shrapnel in the leg flying a mission over Belgium. After a few months in a hospital in England, he had been medically discharged. Except for a slight limp, you'd never know.

Shortly after, he began pursuing Katherine again. Katherine had told him she wasn't interested in a serious relationship. "Okay," Al had said. "We won't get serious." But over the last month or so, it seemed like he was getting more serious about her. She had grown fonder of him and really did enjoy his company. But so far, not enough to make their relationship public knowledge.

"Hello?"

"Al, this is Katherine."

"Hey, Kath. You getting excited about tonight?"

"I'm sorry, Al, that's why I'm calling. I can't make it."

"What? I just went out and bought a new shirt."

"I'll have to see it next time."

"I won't be able to give you your present."

"I'm sorry."

"What happened?"

"It's actually pretty serious. Mr. Collins had a heart attack yesterday."

"The old man? That's too bad. Did he die?"

"No, he's holding on, but it doesn't look good. I'm really worried about him."

"Then let me come over and cheer you up."

"No, Al. It really would be better if we rescheduled. Me and Mrs. Fortini are taking turns staying with him. When it's not my turn, I need to take care of Patrick." She could hear him sighing through the phone. "What was playing, anyway?" she asked.

"*Eve Knew Her Apples*," he said. "A comedy starring Ann Miller. Supposed to be a riot."

"Why don't you go see it?" she asked.

"Aww, it won't be the same without you."

"I'm really sorry, Al, but duty calls."

"You would have really liked me in my new shirt."

Katherine laughed. "I'm sure I would. But I'll see it next time."

"Next time . . . I like the sound of that. Speaking of next time, have you given any thought to what I said?"

Katherine knew this would come up. Al had asked her about it the last three times they'd talked. "I have . . . some."

"I don't wanna push you, Kath. But if we're ever gonna get to know each other better, we need to spend a little more time than once every few weeks. I can't move over there 'cause of the family business, but I talked with my dad. One of the secretaries gave her two weeks' notice. I told him all about your last job, and he said he'd hire you just on my say-so. So what do you think?"

"I will definitely think about it and pray about it some more, Al. Well, I've gotta go. I'm really sorry for calling off tonight on such short notice."

"Don't sweat it. I'm a big boy. Just do what you gotta do and we'll pick it up next time."

"Thanks."

She could always count on Al, so easygoing. As she hung up, Mrs. Fortini walked in the front door. "Is that Al?" she asked.

Katherine looked at her.

"I can tell by that half-guilty look on your face. It was Al, wasn't it?"

"I just called to cancel our . . . *time*."

"Time?" Mrs. Fortini shook her head. She set her purse down on the chair. "He loves you, you know."

"What?"

"Al, he loves you."

"No, he doesn't. We're just good friends. How can you know that? You've never met him."

"Katherine."

"He's very nice," she said. "We're just . . . getting to know each other better."

"Did he ask you again about moving to New Jersey?"

"Yes, but I'm not sure I'm ready for something like that. How's Mr. Collins?" Katherine asked, changing the subject.

"He's sleeping, snoring like a buzz saw."

"I'll go sit with him," said Katherine.

"He can't be tired; I think he's just weak. Hasn't eaten a thing all day," Mrs. Fortini said. "I put some soup in the icebox. If he wakes, you could heat it up, try to get him to take a few sips. I'll fix something to eat and bring you over some. Is Patrick okay?"

"He's around the corner, eating with Kevin. His mom said I could pick him up anytime before 8:30." Katherine grabbed her purse.

"Shawn called," said Mrs. Fortini. "He should be here in about an hour. Said after he got your telegram, he borrowed a car to get here faster."

"I'm so glad," Katherine said. "Mr. Collins will be so glad to see him." She walked down the hall and gave Mrs. Fortini a hug. "See you in a little while."

As she walked out to the porch, she thought about Shawn, about seeing him again, about how she felt about seeing him again. She didn't know why he still made her so nervous. Months ago, she let herself think he might have some measure of affection for her. But it was time she faced the fact that it was all in her imagination.

He was kind to her, thoughtful and generous. He had always been very appreciative of the way she'd kept the house, the care she had given Patrick, and lately even her cooking. But really, he hadn't paid her a single compliment on a personal level. Except that one time, when she wore that red dress at that fancy dinner downtown. But what was that . . . February of last year?

No, she had no reason to be nervous about Shawn. He was—it was time she faced it—simply Patrick's father and a very nice man to work for. She looked at her watch. Shawn should be home in about fifty minutes.

And that thought made her nervous.

Forty-two

Before Shawn stopped in to see his dad, he went next door to get the lowdown from Mrs. Fortini and Katherine. He had missed seeing Dr. Matthews by ten minutes. They had filled him in, trying to sound encouraging and optimistic. They weren't very convincing. Since his dad refused to come in to the hospital, Dr. Matthews said he could only make educated guesses about what had happened and what they were facing. He said his father's already weakened heart was made much weaker by the attack, and it seemed like his body was starting to shut down. This attack came all on its own; his father hadn't been doing anything strenuous or difficult. Just reading the morning paper, still in bed.

Shawn opened the front door quietly, in case he was still asleep. The elder Collins awoke as the door shut.

"Shawn," he said through a cough. He didn't even try to sit up. "So glad you're home."

It was hard not to react at the sight. It was his father, but it was almost like seeing someone else, his body transformed by a losing battle with life itself. "I'm here, Dad."

Shawn set his things down and walked over to his bed. Instantly, fond memories of his childhood, moments spent with his father in this very room, began floating upward. Sitting on his father's lap in his favorite chair, as he read him the funnies on Sunday afternoons. The year they put together a Lionel train set before Christmas. His bed occupied the very corner where the family Christmas tree stood every year. "How are you feeling, Dad?" Shawn asked, taking his hand. His father squeezed his hand weakly in return.

"Not too good, son. Better now that you're here."

"You were doing so good for so long."

"Doctor said I've lasted much longer than he figured, back when I took that fall."

"Are you in any pain?"

"It's not too bad, tired mostly. No energy to do much."

"Can I get you anything?"

"Had some soup just before you got here, so I'm fine."

There was a stool beside the bed. Shawn pulled it over and sat down. "How about if I tell you some of my adventures flying fighter planes? Get your mind off this whole heart thing for a while."

"I'd like that. Imagine . . . my boy. A bomber pilot, a war hero, and now flying fighter planes. I'm glad you went off on your own, Shawn. Made much more of your life than you would've if . . . well, go on now, tell me a story."

Shawn choked back tears. They just sat together for the next hour or so and Shawn talked, trying to keep his dad's mind off the boredom of being stuck in bed and . . . other things. He had no shortage of exciting mishaps and near-misses with fellow pilots. His dad had a mechanical background, so Shawn included the finer points of the differing engines and performance specs for each plane he flew.

At one point, he could tell his dad was nodding off. "Say, Dad," he said loudly. His eyes snapped open. "Has Patrick been by to see you since, you know, your heart attack?"

"I don't think so."

"If you don't mind, I'd like to bring him by."

"I don't want to scare him, son. Seeing me like this."

"You and I both know, Dad, he's a pretty tough kid. He's seen things a lot scarier than his grandfather looking tired and weary."

His father smiled. "All right, I really do want to see him."

Shawn looked at his watch. "It's not far from his bedtime. Katherine said he's been sleeping over there since this happened. Okay if I bring him back, and we can sleep upstairs tonight?"

"Sure. She and Mrs. Fortini been treating this place like a funeral parlor."

"You be okay a few minutes till I get him?"

"I'll be right here."

∽

"Sit here beside me, Patrick. I want to talk with you a bit before we see Grandpa." Shawn sat on the top step of Mrs. Fortini's front porch. It had cooled a little in the last hour.

"Is Grandpa okay?"

Shawn put his arm around him. "Well, that's the thing. See . . . his heart is very old and it's not working too well right now."

"Is he gonna die?"

Shawn sighed. "He might . . . could be real soon."

"But he'll go to heaven, right?"

"I think so, Patrick. I'm praying for him so he'll be ready. That way he can meet Mom and Grandma when the time comes."

"And Jesus," Patrick said.

"And Jesus most of all. Does it make you sad to talk about this?"

"I don't feel too sad right now."

"That's good. You think you'd be okay if we walked over there for a visit? Maybe start sleeping back in your room tonight?"

"I miss Grandpa. And I made him this." He wrestled something out of his pocket. It was a wooden cross, similar to Shawn's.

"You make that all by yourself?"

"Yep, even the notch in the middle."

"He's going to be so proud. Let's head over, then." Shawn reached back and picked up Patrick's little suitcase. As they walked down the driveway, Shawn said, "He's going to look a little skinnier, you know. Because he's sick."

"He's been getting skinnier for a while now. I'm used to it."

Shawn had forgotten. He was the only one who hadn't seen his father for weeks. As they walked, he marveled at how well Patrick was handling this, how strong he was for a little boy. When they got to the vestibule, Patrick ran up the steps and burst through the front door like it was any other day. Shawn was just about to stop him, but he was already through the door. "Look what I made you, Grandpa!" he heard as the spring snapped the storm door shut. He walked in. Patrick was already leaning on the bed, holding up his gift. His dad was wide awake and smiling.

This was a good idea.

"You made that for me? All by yourself?" His dad held up the cross. "And look at that notch, just like I taught you." He put his hand gently around Patrick's neck. "Come here." Patrick leaned forward. His father raised himself up a few inches and kissed him on the forehead. Patrick looked back at Shawn; his face was beaming.

"You know what this means, don't you?" his father said. "It means my bag of tools belongs to you now."

"Really?"

"I think you're ready." He coughed hard a few times and looked away.

"Are you okay, Grandpa?"

"Well, Patrick, I'm not sure." The cough subsided. "But I'm happy, and that's better than okay." He looked up at Shawn, then back at Patrick. "I'm happy because you're here with me, and your dad's here." Tears welled up in his father's eyes. "We're all together like we should be."

"Maybe we should let Grandpa get some sleep," said Shawn, walking over to the bed. "I'll get him set up for the night, Dad, then come back and see how you're doing."

"That's good, Shawn. I am feeling sleepy. That's my full-time job now."

"You head upstairs, Patrick, and brush your teeth. I'll bring your bag up."

"Good night, Grandpa," Patrick said at the foot of the stairs.

His father held up the cross and smiled. Patrick ran up the stairs. Once he was safely out of sight, Shawn began to cry. He walked over to his dad and gently laid his head on his chest. "I love you, Dad." As the tears flowed, Shawn tried to cry quietly.

"I love you too, Shawn."

"I don't want you to go. I didn't get enough time with you."

"Shawn, don't be sad about that," his dad whispered. "You did your duty. I'm proud of you. Every spare moment you could be here, you were."

Shawn stood back up; he didn't want to hurt him. He wiped his tears on his sleeve.

"You know one of the things I'm most happy about?" his father asked.

Shawn shook his head no.

"Your mom, she would be so happy if she were here. That's what I was thinking about a moment ago. Seeing us all together."

"She really would," Shawn said. "But I really need to let you get some rest. You've had enough excitement for one night." They hugged again, and just before Shawn went upstairs, he thought about something his father just said.

And it gave him an idea.

Forty-three

By the time Shawn awoke the next morning, Patrick was already dressed and eating breakfast next door with Katherine. Mrs. Fortini was downstairs sitting with his father. They had conspired to let Shawn sleep in. He decided before he went downstairs to use the opportunity to execute his idea.

For the next forty minutes, he searched his dad's room, looking for a letter written to Elizabeth from his mom just before she died. He remembered reading it shortly after returning from England two Christmases ago. She told of how much she appreciated the things Elizabeth had taught her about the gospel, and how that understanding had taken away all her fears of facing God when she died. Shawn was sure that letter would help his father now. Shawn was partly convinced his father might already be in a good place from little things he'd said here and there, and especially the changes in his life. But he wasn't absolutely sure. Who better to explain the gospel to his father now than his own wife, in her own words?

But where was it? He couldn't find the letter anywhere. His dad would never throw out something like that. After searching through his room, he tiptoed up to the attic. He searched through a handful of places his father might have put it but didn't find it there either. Just as he came down from the attic, Mrs. Fortini called up to him.

"Shawn, you all right up there? I need to send up a rescue mission?"

Shawn laughed. "I'll be right down."

"That breakfast I made is getting cold."

"Say, Mrs. Fortini," he said, walking down the steps, "after I eat, let me take a turn with my dad. I'm sure you've got things you need to do."

"Sure, Shawn. Whenever you're ready, just come over."

He looked at his father, who was sound asleep. "Thanks," Shawn said and headed out the door. He said a quick prayer to release his frustration about the letter and tried not to think about how to approach his dad later on, without the letter's help.

✖

Shawn came back to the house just after 10:00 a.m. and relieved Mrs. Fortini. Just before leaving she'd asked him to try and get his father to sip on some fresh tomato soup she had made that morning. "He loves my tomato soup," she'd said. "And tell him I went to a good deal of trouble to get those tomatoes."

He sat in his father's favorite chair, reading the Bible, his thoughts regularly interrupted by imaginary conversations with his dad. He was rehearsing various opening lines, ways to transition from small talk into perhaps the most serious conversation they would ever have. His tension was not unfounded. The last time he tried to share the gospel with him went horribly. It ended with his dad throwing him out of the house and began a bitter feud that lasted for years.

"Is that you, Shawn?" he heard his father say in a voice just barely above a whisper.

Shawn stood up and walked to the bed. "I'm right here, Dad. You hungry? You slept right through breakfast."

"Maybe in a little while."

"Mrs. Fortini made fresh tomato soup. She said to tell you she had to kill someone to get those tomatoes."

He smiled. "Now I know I'm dying."

"What?"

"Turning down Mrs. Fortini's tomato soup."

"Well, it's in the icebox. I can heat it up when you're ready." Shawn dragged the stool next to his father's bed. What should he say? How could he shift the conversation?

"Shawn, there's something I've been wanting to say to you for some time now."

The question caught Shawn off guard. "What is it?"

"It's about Katherine."

"Katherine?" This was totally unexpected. Shawn wondered if he'd ever heard him call her by her first name before.

"I don't have much time left, I can feel it. Lately, when I'm awake enough to think straight, I keep thinking about you and Patrick after I'm gone. Do you ever think about Katherine?"

"In what way?" Shawn asked, but he knew what way.

"I can hardly believe I'm saying this, considering the way we started, but I think she's a pretty special lady."

Shawn was stunned. "Dad . . . at best, I'd have thought you just tolerated her."

"That's 'cause I'm a stubborn old stinker, as Mrs. Fortini likes to say. But I'd hate to see you and Patrick all alone. I've seen how they are together. She's really taken the sting out of his sorrow, the way she loves him. And Patrick . . ." Tears started to fill his eyes. "He deserves the very best."

Shawn could hardly reply. He took a deep breath, trying to suppress his emotions. "I think I know what you're saying, Dad. I'm just having a hard time getting past Elizabeth. I can't imagine replacing her with anyone else."

"Then don't."

"What do you mean?"

"I mean don't replace her. I'm no expert on these things, but I've watched my heart go places this last year I didn't think possible. Elizabeth will always be in the same place in your heart, probably all your life. It's a room you should always cherish. I've got a room just like it for your mom. But you're young. So build a new room, one for you and Katherine. That's what I'm saying."

Shawn didn't know what to say. All his life he wanted to have conversations like this with his dad. "Dad . . . I hear what you're saying. And I will think long and hard about it. I'm not just saying that."

"That's all I ask. Guess talking serious for a few minutes is all I can handle. I'm feeling sleepy again."

"Dad, before you nod off, there's something I want to talk to you about. It's another serious thing, so you'll probably sleep the rest of the day when we're done."

His dad opened his eyes.

"I really don't know how to say this, it's just . . . like you said, this could be *the time*. I've been putting off talking about this. The last time we did, it didn't go so well." His father turned, looking straight at him, but there was no anger in his eyes. "I just need to know that you really are ready . . . if it is time."

"Do you think I might not be?" his father asked weakly.

"I don't think so. It's so obvious that you've changed so much, but I just want to be sure about a few things, and we've never been able to talk about them before. I tried to find that letter Mom wrote to Elizabeth just before she died. She said what I wanted to say so well. I thought it would help you hearing it from Mom. But I looked for over an hour, can't find it anywhere."

His dad smiled widely, almost as if he was about to laugh. Was he hearing anything Shawn was saying? It didn't seem like it was sinking in.

"Could you lift my head a little bit?" his father asked.

"What? Sure."

As he did, his father reached his hand beneath his pillow and pulled. Pinched between his fingers were two sheets of wrinkled paper. "You looking for this?" he asked, handing it to Shawn.

It was his mom's letter.

"I've had it under my pillow for over a month, read it every night."

Now Shawn smiled. He couldn't believe it.

"And I know exactly what she was talking about now, about the gospel, I mean, what Jesus did for us on the cross. I don't think I ever understood it before. I thought the most important thing was me doing things for God. But the most important thing was what Jesus did for me, and me putting all my hope there. I don't know when the lights came on, but when they did . . . I'm actually looking forward to heading out of here now."

Tears rolled down Shawn's face. Tears of joy, of relief. "I'm so glad, Dad."

"You going to be okay now?" his father asked.

"More than okay, Dad. You get some sleep now. I'll be fine."

Forty-four

The next day, it was clear . . . the war in Europe was very near its end. At 8:00 p.m., British commander Field Marshall Montgomery reported to the supreme allied command that all enemy forces in Holland, northwest Germany, and Denmark had surrendered. The Russians were on the verge of capturing Berlin.

Across the Atlantic, it was early afternoon in the Philadelphia area. Shawn had taken another turn watching his dad for Katherine and Mrs. Fortini. He was sitting in his father's favorite chair looking at some photo albums he'd brought down from the attic. He'd grown used to the rhythm of his father's gentle snoring over his shoulder. Today was supposed to be Shawn's last day before heading back to Long Island to resume his flight duties at Grumman.

He carefully turned a page in the photo album when the snoring simply stopped. At first, Shawn thought nothing of it. He listened closely a few moments and didn't hear him breathing at all. Shawn got up. "Dad, you okay?" He shook him gently, but he didn't respond. Shawn checked his pulse, but he could already tell.

He was gone.

Ian Collins had received a great mercy, dying peacefully in his sleep in his bed at home.

Shawn stayed with him a few moments more, then walked next door. Katherine and Mrs. Fortini instantly knew what happened the moment Shawn walked through the door. Shawn didn't cry until he saw them. Then Mrs. Fortini hugged Shawn, and she began to cry too. Shawn looked up and saw Katherine sitting at the dining room table, her head down, also crying. He comforted them with the news about how peacefully he died, then asked, "Where is Patrick?"

He was playing at Kevin's around the corner. So Shawn walked over there, regaining his composure along the way. Patrick and Kevin were playing in the front yard. As soon as Patrick saw his dad, he ran over and wrapped his arms around him. "Daddy!" he yelled.

Shawn bent down and said quietly, "Patrick . . . Grandpa's with Mommy and Grandma now." It took a moment for the news to sink in. Patrick looked into his father's eyes, saw the tears beginning to form, and understood. He collapsed in his father's arms, sobbing. Shawn held him for a moment, then picked him up. "Sorry, Kevin, Patrick's grandfather just passed away. I've got to take him home." Kevin nodded, a look of confusion on his face.

Halfway home, Patrick stopped crying. As they turned into Mrs. Fortini's driveway, he said, "I think I can walk now." They walked inside holding hands.

Mrs. Fortini had put on a pot of coffee and had a plate of cookies and a glass of milk for Patrick. Shawn excused himself, saying he needed to go next door and call Dr. Matthews, then start making the necessary arrangements.

∽

Respecting his father's wishes, Shawn arranged for a wake and funeral mass three days later, conducted by Father O'Malley down at St. Joseph's. It was followed by a short graveside service. Shawn, Katherine, and Mrs. Fortini put all their rationing coupons together and hosted a nice lunch in Mrs. Fortini's home for Father O'Malley and the handful of neighbors who came by. Patrick held up quite well through it all.

After the crowd had left, Shawn said, "I've got to report back this afternoon. The colonel said he could only give me a couple of extra days when I called him after Dad passed. But I'm going to pull some strings when I get there, see if I can't get a week or two off real soon. I hate leaving you guys."

"We understand, Shawn," said Mrs. Fortini. "We'll make do until you come back."

Shawn looked at Katherine. "Thanks for all the help these past few days. It's meant a lot having you here."

He bent down and gave Patrick a big hug. "I'll get back here just as soon as I can. This war should be over any day now. If that happens, I think they may let me come home for good."

"Really?" Patrick asked.

"I think so. You be good for Miss Townsend and Mrs. Fortini till I get back."

"I will."

⟡

Shawn went upstairs to use the bathroom and get his duffel bag. Katherine quietly walked over to her purse in the living room, pulled out an envelope, and stuck it in the back sleeve of Shawn's brief bag by the front door. Shawn came back down, grabbed his brief bag and hat, and, after a final wave, headed out the door.

⟡

Shawn arrived back at Grumman just after 8:00 p.m. He was surprised to find the factory closed; all the evening shift workers had been given the night off and the next day. The employees still at the plant and the test pilots were all laughing and celebrating the news.

Earlier that day, the German leaders who'd replaced Adolph Hitler had signed documents signaling Germany's unconditional surrender. Tomorrow, May 8, the whole world would find out.

The war in Europe was over.

Shawn could hardly believe it. It had been coming for weeks, but now that it was here, it felt almost unreal. He didn't even know how to respond. The sadness of his father's death was still so vivid, but this news was so fantastic, he couldn't help but laugh. He set his bags down on his bunk and decided to join a makeshift party already underway downstairs.

Someone had gotten hold of a bottle of champagne and passed it around. Shawn drank two glasses, even though he couldn't stand the stuff. His fellow test pilots all began to reminisce and tell stories of their exploits over the past four years; occasionally someone offered a toast for their buddies who'd paid the ultimate price. Shawn thought about his crew from *Mama's Kitchen* and wondered where they were tonight, how they were celebrating the news.

An hour later, Shawn slipped out the door and headed back up to his room, totally exhausted. He shifted his bags from the bed to a chair. As he did, his brief bag fell on the floor. A white envelope fell out. Written across the front it said: "Major Collins."

He recognized Katherine's handwriting. This couldn't be good. He sat down on the bunk and opened the envelope:

May 7th, 1945

Major Collins,

   This has to be the hardest letter I've ever
written. I'm writing this because I can't see
myself ever finding the courage to say these things
to you in person. Mrs. Fortini is the only person
I've talked to about any of this (just so you
know, she understands the reasons for my decision
but thinks I should have talked to you in person).

   I'll just say it. I've decided to move to New
Jersey to pursue a relationship with Al Baker (you
remember Al). I've been seeing him every other
week or so for the last few months. I'm sorry I
haven't told you, but we don't ever talk about my
life on a personal level, and I couldn't think of a
way to bring it up.

   He's been discharged from the service and works
in his father's business. They've offered me a
job and a place to stay. Al has been asking me to
consider this for a while, using his words, to
"move things to the next level." Hard to do that
when we live so far apart.

   I have loved working for you and love Patrick as
if he were my own. I'm sorry for not being able
to give you two weeks' notice, but I can't imagine
being around you or him even a few days after
deciding to leave (as I said, I am a terrible coward,
the pain would be unbearable). Mrs. Fortini said
she'd be more than willing to care for him until
you find another nanny.

   I wish you all the best, and will pray for
you both every day. You are a wonderful man.

Sincerely,
Katherine (Miss Townsend)

"No, no, no," Shawn said aloud. "Lord, she can't do this. She can't leave." He looked at his watch. It was too late to call. He stood up. Should he drive over there? No, the car pool would be closed for the night. He could call a taxi, catch a late train, be there by midnight. But then he'd wake everybody up, scare them half to death at this hour.

Wait a minute, he couldn't just leave. He was still in the military; he needed permission. The war is over, he thought, it'll be all over the news tomorrow. His CO would have to let him go, he was sure of it.

He set his alarm to wake him at sunrise. He didn't care if it meant going AWOL. One way or another, he had to stop Katherine from leaving.

Forty-five

May 8, 1945, was a day for the ages.

Millions of people throughout America, England, France, Russia, and so many other nations awoke to a world without Hitler, without Nazis, without bombs and battles and bloodshed. People alive on this day would remember it for the rest of their lives. The powers that be decided to call it V-E Day—Victory in Europe.

Shawn Collins would remember this day also, but for a different reason.

He did get up at sunrise and, after locating his commanding officer, was released to do whatever he pleased. "No missions today," he'd said. "In fact, I don't care what you do today, Major Collins. As for me, I plan to get plastered and stay plastered pretty much the entire day."

Shawn got showered and dressed in his finest uniform then ate some breakfast at the mess hall. He decided that was long enough. They should be awake by now. He walked out to the phone booth he always used to call home, within eyesight of the main gate. As he dialed Mrs. Fortini's number, he watched as one Grumman worker after another arrived, those who hadn't yet heard the news. They were too far away for him to hear, but he saw the jubilant reaction as each one was told they had the day off and why.

Mrs. Fortini's phone rang only twice.

"Hello?"

"Mrs. Fortini?"

"Shawn, isn't it wonderful? I just saw the morning headlines. My Dominic will be coming home soon."

"I know," Shawn said. "It's almost too hard to believe." There was a pause. Shawn didn't know what to say.

"But I suppose that's not the reason you're calling. Is it about Katherine's letter?"

"Mrs. Fortini . . . I don't know what to do. I can't let her walk out of my life. Is she there?"

"No, she's not."

"I'm too late?"

"Not exactly. Her bags are packed and by the door. She wanted to slip out before Patrick woke up. She's next door, gathering a few things she left over there. You could call back in ten minutes or so."

"No, I need to see her, to talk to her in person. Would you do me a favor? I'm going to send a telegram to her. I don't know if it will do any good, but please ask her to stay long enough to read it. I'm going to hang up right now and get it sent. Would you do that?"

"I'll ask her, Shawn. But she seemed pretty set in her plans."

"Please try."

He hung up and literally ran to the Western Union office nearest the Grumman factory. There was such a long line. He seemed to be the only one in line not jumping with excitement. As he neared the counter, he could hear the messages of those just in front of him, all about the war ending, and wasn't it great, and how they'd be catching the next train home.

"Next."

What should he say? What words could he say that might get her to at least give him a chance?

"Sir, we're sort of in a hurry here."

"I'm sorry," Shawn said. "I want to get this sent right away. I'll pay double or triple if I have to. But it's got to be sent right away."

"We can do that. So what's the message?"

Shawn thought just a moment. "Okay, here it is . . ."

KATHERINE,
PLEASE DON'T LEAVE ME. PATRICK NEEDS YOU.
I THINK I NEED YOU EVEN MORE.
WE NEED TO TALK IN PERSON—TODAY.
MEET ME AT THE EAGLE.
I CAN BE THERE BY NOON. PLEASE.
SHAWN

"Did you say *eagle*?" the man asked.

"She'll know what I mean," Shawn said.

"Whatever you say."

❧

Shawn walked out to the first busy street and hailed a taxi. "I need to get to the train station right away."

"Why so glum, pal? Didn't you hear? The war's over."

"I'm not glum, just in a hurry. I need to catch a train in twenty minutes."

"Hop in."

Shawn made it to the station just in time to catch the 9:00 a.m. train to Philadelphia.

The train was mobbed; he had to stand for most of the

two-and-a-half-hour ride. Everyone was in high spirits. News of the war's end dominated every conversation. Shawn could only think about one thing.

Losing Katherine.

How had he been so foolish not to at least give her some hint about his feelings? He'd taken her totally for granted. It was Katherine. She was Patrick's nanny. She would never leave. He remembered what she'd said in her letter. *We don't ever talk about my life on a personal level.* He realized it was true. They never did. Obviously, she had wanted to, but he'd been afraid of where any such conversation would lead. Well, here's where his great idea had led them. She was about to walk out of his life forever.

Lord, he prayed, *please let her get my telegram in time. Please don't let her leave.*

When the train pulled into the 30th Street Station, it took forever for Shawn to make his way through the mob out to Market Street. As he stepped onto the sidewalk, the city had been transformed, like New Year's Eve at midday. Buses and trolleys were barely moving. The streets were packed with people hugging and kissing. Confetti was falling from the sky above. There was no chance of finding a taxi to take him a mile down the road to the Wanamaker's Building.

He looked at his watch. Only twenty minutes till noon. He began to trot east on Market, snaking his way through the crowd, trying not to knock anyone over. Crossing the 22nd Street intersection, he had to run around a dozen young women holding hands, dancing like little girls in a circle in the middle of the street. At 17th Street, he was almost run over by a car with at least ten college kids piled on top and standing on the running boards.

He made it to Penn Square with five minutes to spare. Wanamaker's was right around the corner. But the entire square was filled with people celebrating. He literally had to push his way through, foot by foot. Finally, he made it through the glass doors on the Juniper Street entrance, the one closest to the Wanamaker's Eagle.

Once inside, he noticed the store was nearly empty. Everyone was outside.

But there was the Eagle. No one standing around it.

No one.

He walked around it, but he knew she wasn't there. He glanced at a clock. Two minutes after. Okay, she could still be coming. She would run into the same crowd he had. Nearby, he saw a saleswoman at the jewelry counter.

"Have you seen a young woman standing around the Eagle by any chance? Brown hair, very attractive."

"Sorry, sir. People have been walking by, but no one looked like they were waiting for anyone. I can't believe I'm stuck back here. No one's in the mood to shop."

Shawn walked back toward the big bronze Eagle. He paced around it, looking toward both sets of doors every few moments. Fifteen minutes went by. Then thirty. He decided to call Patrick.

"Is there a phone booth nearby?" he asked the jewelry counter lady.

"Just head out those doors and look to the left."

"If you see a brunette come by while I'm gone, please tell her not to leave."

"You got it."

Shawn walked outside and quickly found the phone booth. Closing the doors only minimally reduced the noise. Mrs. Fortini answered.

"Hi, it's Shawn. Is Patrick there?"

"He is, Shawn. He's listening to the radio. It's so exciting."

"Has Katherine left?"

"Yes. She left before Patrick woke up, so he doesn't know anything yet."

"Did my telegram arrive?"

"It did."

"Did she read it?"

"She did."

"When she left, did she leave her bags there?"

"No, she still brought them with her."

Shawn's heart fell.

"Can I speak with Patrick?"

"Sure, I'll get him."

Shawn wondered . . . did it even matter now, what he was about to ask Patrick?

"Hi, Daddy."

"Hey, buddy, isn't it great about the war?"

"Does this mean they'll let you come home for good?"

"I think it does. But listen, I have something very important to ask you."

"What is it?"

"It's about Katherine. What would you think if I asked her to marry me? Would that make you happy or sad?"

"Really? You're going to ask her that? I would love it if she never ever left. I've been worrying about that sometimes."

Shawn sighed. Even Patrick picked up on the struggle in Katherine's heart, but not him. "Well, I'm glad. I don't know what she'll say, but I'm hoping to meet her soon. And when I do, I'll ask her. And you'll be the first person I call if she says yes."

"Okay, I'll say a prayer."

Yes, thought Shawn, pray.

Forty-six

Shawn walked back into Wanamaker's. His eyes went straight to the Eagle. Still no Katherine. He looked at his watch. It was just after one o'clock.

Was he too late? She had taken her bags with her, Mrs. Fortini said, even after reading his telegram. Was she even coming? He walked back and resumed his silent pace around the bronze statue. Another ten minutes went by, then fifteen.

"Shawn?"

He looked toward the sound, the beautiful sound of her voice. "You came."

She walked slowly toward him. Her face looked tense, almost afraid. "Can you help me? My taxi is outside, but I can't get my bags by myself. I'm so sorry I'm late."

"Your bags?"

"I brought them, just in case. But I didn't plan on this crowd. It took forever to find a taxi, then the traffic barely moved from the station to here. I would have walked, but my bags are too heavy."

He met her halfway. "Stay right here. I'll get your bags."

He walked through the glass doors, paid the taxi, and grabbed her bags in both arms. He came back into the store.

As he passed her, he said politely: "Follow me, we need to talk." He set the bags leaning up against the Eagle. When he turned, she was standing right there. He looked into her eyes. Why hadn't he seen how beautiful she was?

"I'm sorry for writing that letter. I'm such a chicken. You didn't deserve that. I'm just—"

"Katherine," Shawn said in a serious tone. "I love you."

"What?" Tears began to form in her eyes.

"I love you," he said. "I have been such a fool. I have loved you for a long time."

"You have?" A tear escaped down her cheek.

He put his hands gently on her shoulders. "Please don't leave me, leave us, Patrick and me."

"You love me?"

"I want to marry you."

She started to cry. He reached his arms around her and pulled her close. He let her rest there a few moments till she seemed to calm down.

She pulled back and looked up into his eyes. "I don't want to leave. I've never wanted to leave," she said. "But you didn't seem to care for me . . . that way. And I didn't think I could ever measure up to your love for Elizabeth. She was such an amazing woman. Who am I?"

"You're the woman I love," said Shawn. "I don't understand all the reasons why God took Elizabeth. I may never understand this side of heaven. But I do know, God brought you into my life. You don't have to measure up to Elizabeth or anyone else. I love you just the way you are."

She started crying again, so he held her some more. As she rested her head on his shoulders, he said, "My dad taught me that."

"Your dad?"

"Before he died, it was one of the last things he said to

me. He said you didn't have to replace Elizabeth, I could just start a new place in my heart for you. Then I realized, you were already there. I was just too afraid to see it."

"And you see it now?"

"Katherine, I don't want to live my life without you. I want to marry you. Patrick wants me to marry you. I called him just a little while ago. He said he would love it if you never left."

"He said that?"

Before she lost it completely, Shawn leaned over and kissed her, and she responded, removing any lingering doubts he had about her feelings for him. Then, right there at the Wanamaker's Eagle, Shawn got down on one knee to make it official. "Katherine Townsend, will you marry me?"

"Shawn, I think I've loved you since that first Christmas dinner. And I have loved you every day since. Of course, I will marry you."

He stood up and they kissed again. "I wasn't sure how you'd react," he said. "I don't even have a ring. But we'll come back here tomorrow to that jewelry counter right over there. Then we'll have lunch at the Crystal Tea Room upstairs."

"I'd like that," she said.

He picked up her bags. "Let's get these back home where they belong." He led her by the hand toward the Juniper Street doors. Just outside, he looked to the left, saw the telephone booth, and remembered something.

"Hey, Katherine, let's call Patrick."

∽

When Katherine awoke the next morning, not in some strange place but in her bed at Mrs. Fortini's house, she could hardly believe how dramatically her life had changed since waking up in this same bed the day before.

All day yesterday, she'd kept waiting for Shawn to slip and call her Miss Townsend again. She kept looking at him, expecting him to regret the things he'd said by the Eagle at Wanamaker's. But every time he'd return her glance with love in his eyes and a big smile.

As they'd walked up the driveway to Mrs. Fortini's house, he'd even left her bags by the sidewalk so he could hold her hand to the front door. Before they'd even reached her porch, Mrs. Fortini and Patrick came running out the door and almost knocked them over with hugs and congratulations.

Then just before they'd parted last night, Shawn had walked her back out to that same porch, kissed her gently good night, and said, "Don't forget, tomorrow we have a date back at Wanamaker's. While I waited for you today, I saw the most beautiful diamond ring. I want to put that ring on your finger tomorrow and see it sparkling under the chandelier at the Crystal Tea Room."

She got out of bed, walked over to the dresser, and picked up her Bible. Something fell out and landed softly on the floor. She looked down and smiled. It was the little buttercup she'd kept from a visit to Patrick's playground almost a year ago, the one that had grown up through a crack in the sidewalk.

And she remembered what Mrs. Fortini had said: "God can make love grow through even the hardest places. Just give him time."

Epilogue

September 8, 1945
(4 months later)

As Shawn, Katherine, and Patrick walked up the stone steps of the cemetery leading toward Elizabeth's grave, Katherine reflected back on the whirlwind of changes that had taken place in their lives over the past few months.

They were married by Pastor Harman at Christ Redeemer Church six weeks after Shawn had proposed. Like Shawn, Mrs. Fortini's son Dominic had earned enough points to be discharged shortly after V-E Day. He and Shawn had been boyhood friends. Dominic was Shawn's best man. Shirley O'Donnell, Katherine's old friend from Child Services, served as her maid of honor.

Patrick sat on the front row beside Mrs. Fortini, happy as he could be. On Mrs. Fortini's other side was her son Dominic's big surprise. His war bride from England—Jane. Jane was not Italian. Her skin was white as snow. She called tomatoes *to-MAH-toes*. And Mrs. Fortini loved her from the first moment they'd met. But she'd admitted, saying "Jane Fortini" would take some getting used to.

Shawn had some surprises of his own to unveil.

When his father's estate had been settled, Shawn learned he was just a few thousand dollars short of being a millionaire. And the income was still coming in. Carlyle Manufacturing—the business his father owned a small percentage of—had just signed a deal with Chrysler to stop making tank parts and start making engine parts for the millions of cars they planned to manufacture after the war.

Shawn had decided to spend a little of that money. First, he took Katherine on a honeymoon back to England. They spent ten days touring the English countryside, and she finally got to see all the enchanted places she'd read about in her books.

When they got home, Shawn took Katherine and Patrick out for a leisurely drive about fifteen miles outside of Allingdale. They drove past some lovely estate homes in an area called Radnor. Then Shawn turned into the driveway of one of these beautiful homes, got out, and said, "Welcome home, Collins family." Katherine was overwhelmed. It felt like something out of the pages of *Pride and Prejudice*, like she was staring at Mr. Darcy's mansion.

That evening, when they got back to Shawn's childhood home on Chestnut Street, they ate dinner next door at Mrs. Fortini's. Dominic and Jane joined them. After dessert, Shawn handed Mrs. Fortini one envelope and Dominic another. Inside were two mortgages marked "Paid in Full."

He had paid off Mrs. Fortini's home and gave his father's house to Dominic free and clear. "God has been good to me," he'd said. After the tears and hugs, he told them they could have these homes on one condition. Mrs. Fortini must serve as Patrick's grandmother and Dominic and Jane as his aunt and uncle. "You're the only family we've got," he'd said.

Mrs. Fortini had said she'd do it for nothing.

When they reached the last step of the cemetery walkway, Shawn said, "It's just another fifty yards or so over there."

Katherine looked out at a gently rolling field of tombstones and monuments that seemed to stretch for miles. She knew this was going to be a difficult moment, but she prayed God would help her be strong for Shawn. She'd insisted that Shawn not feel the need to hide or diminish Elizabeth's memory in their conversations or in their new home. She'd made a collage of the few family pictures they'd had of her and framed it in a special corner of their huge living room.

"I haven't seen it yet," Shawn said, "but the caretaker said it came out perfectly."

In a few moments, they stood there in front of the new gravestone Shawn had made for Elizabeth. It stood chest high, made of solid marble. Below her name, date of birth and death, Katherine read the words:

Beloved Wife and Mother

Having with firm Christian zeal
and true feminine affection
filled to the full measure her many duties of life,
she was called home to be with the Lord,
leaving in the hearts of her loving family and friends
a shining record of surpassing worth;
which neither time can efface nor changes of life obscure.
"Now we see through a glass darkly,
but then we shall see face to face." (1 Cor. 13:12)

Katherine took Shawn's hand. "It's beautiful. Did you write it?"

"No. Elizabeth found these words on a gravestone in an old cemetery from the 1800s. We used to love to walk through old cemeteries together. It so affected her, she wrote it down.

I found it when I was going through her things. As soon as I saw it, I thought . . ."

Katherine squeezed his hand. "It *is* perfect." The words were so eloquent and, from all she'd known of Elizabeth, all true. She looked down at Patrick. He was wiping a tear from his face. She bent down and gave him a big hug.

He looked up and said, "I'm so glad you're here."

After a few minutes standing there together in silence, Shawn led them back toward the steps, Patrick in the middle, holding on to both of their hands. "What's for dinner?" he said.

Katherine smiled.

Dan Walsh is the author of *The Unfinished Gift* and a member of American Christian Fiction Writers (ACFW). He is also a pastor and lives with his family in the Daytona Beach area, where he's busy researching and writing his next novel.

"Make sure you have a tissue nearby, because you are going to need it!"
—TERRI BLACKSTOCK, bestselling author

A YOUNG BOY'S PRAYERS, a shoebox full of love letters, and an old wooden soldier make a memory that will not be forgotten. Can a gift from the past mend a broken heart?

Revell
a division of Baker Publishing Group
www.RevellBooks.com

Available Wherever Books Are Sold

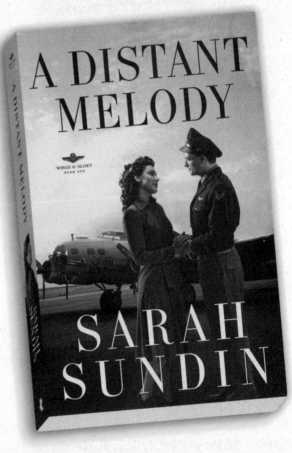

You will laugh, cry, and fall
in love with this stunning
southern novel!

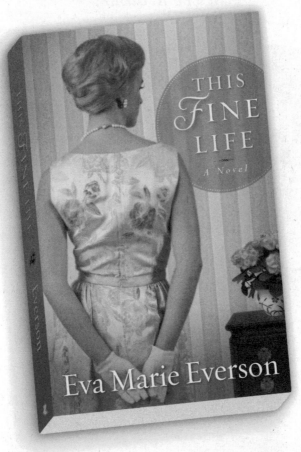

THIS
FINE
LIFE
A Novel

Eva Marie Everson

"*This Fine Life* proves that growing into love can rip one apart
and quitting might be the easiest thing, but walking away is out
of the question. I bled with these characters as they struggled to
become who they were meant to be."—**Lauraine Snelling**, author
of the Red River of the North and Daughters of Blessing series

ℛ Revell
a division of Baker Publishing Group
www.RevellBooks.com

"A lovely and deeply moving story.
I didn't just read this story, I lived it!"
—ANN TATLOCK, award-winning author
of *The Returning*

Jo-Lynn isn't sure she wants to know the truth—but sometimes
the truth has a way of making itself known.

Revell
a division of Baker Publishing Group
www.RevellBooks.com